P9-DMT-629

# *the Maiden* OF ALL OUR *Desires*

Also by Peter Manseau

Fiction

*Songs for the Butcher's Daughter: A Novel*

Nonfiction

*Vows: The Story of a Priest, a Nun, and Their Son*

*Rag and Bone: A Journey Among the World's Holy Dead*

*One Nation Under Gods: A New American History*

*Melancholy Accidents: Three Centuries of Stray Bullets and Bad Luck*

*Objects of Devotion: Religion in Early America*

*The Apparitionists: A Tale of Phantoms, Fraud, Photography, and the Man Who Captured Lincoln's Ghost*

*The Jefferson Bible: A Biography*

Collections

*Killing the Buddha: A Heretic's Bible* (with Jeff Sharlet)

*Believer, Beware: First-Person Dispatches from the Margins of Faith* (with Jeff Sharlet)

# the Maiden OF ALL OUR Desires

A NOVEL

PETER MANSEAU

ARCADE PUBLISHING • NEW YORK

Copyright © 2022 by Peter Manseau

All rights reserved. No part of this book may be reproduced in any manner without the express written consent of the publisher, except in the case of brief excerpts in critical reviews or articles. All inquiries should be addressed to Arcade Publishing, 307 West 36th Street, 11th Floor, New York, NY 10018.

First Edition

This is a work of fiction. Names, places, characters, and incidents are either the products of the author's imagination or are used fictitiously.

Arcade Publishing books may be purchased in bulk at special discounts for sales promotion, corporate gifts, fund-raising, or educational purposes. Special editions can also be created to specifications. For details, contact the Special Sales Department, Arcade Publishing, 307 West 36th Street, 11th Floor, New York, NY 10018 or arcade@skyhorsepublishing.com.

Arcade Publishing® is a registered trademark of Skyhorse Publishing, Inc.®, a Delaware corporation.

Visit our website at www.arcadepub.com.
Visit the author's site at petermanseau.com.

Grateful acknowledgement is made to reprint an excerpt from "Vignettes of the Wind" in *Collected Poems* by Federico García Lorca, translated by Christopher Maurer. Translation copyright © 1991 by Christopher Maurer. Reprinted by permission of Farrar, Straus and Giroux. All Rights Reserved.

10 9 8 7 6 5 4 3 2 1

Library of Congress Cataloging-in-Publication Data is available on file.
Library of Congress Control Number: 2021945518

Cover design by Erin Seaward-Hiatt
Cover illustration: © Julio Romero de Torres, *Nun* (1911), courtesy of Wikimedia Commons; Dove illustration © Getty Images

ISBN: 978-1-950994-21-2
Ebook ISBN: 978-1-950994-41-0

Printed in the United States of America

What maiden will marry the wind? . . .
The maiden of all our desires.

Federico García Lorca

# PROLOGUE

IN THE DAYS before, a storm had touched half the known world.

The snow fell gently at first, in the shadow of distant southern mountains, where clusters of flakes dusted the stones of cobbled roads and a fresh chill in the air reminded villagers that Advent had come and winter was at hand.

It blew north, over the ragged countryside, covering forgotten grave fields filled by the plague, weighing down twenty years of overgrowth before moving on, to beaches and port towns, where the storm warped the tides and flooded the streets, leaving beggars and drunkards sodden in its wake, and on, across the sea, where the gale mingled stinging salt water with the tears of families cowering in their hovels and wailed as it cracked to splinters both the homes of the living and the abandoned shelters of the dead.

Even as it raged, some who witnessed it believed this storm to be the Devil himself, come to beguile with a new vision of every mortal's end. For the wind, they said, would steal the soul away and leave the body, the blood slowed in its veins, to be devoured by the icy teeth of the squall. It was a more perfect death than the world had seen, for death before had been an ugly creation, a carnival mask of decay. But this death, this storm, was beautiful—beautiful as the snow floated free from the clouds; beautiful, shimmering, as the flakes flew earthward and freckled the sky; fragile and beautiful as they played in the treetops, powdered hair and lashes like particles of skin. It was beautiful even as it changed, as the flakes grew mean and whipping; impossibly beautiful as they quickened, as they pelted cheeks raw, as they stung eyes blind, as they tore like knives through flesh to bone. This storm was death perfected, for now it was so magnificent none could help but watch in wonder as it approached.

Others claimed the blizzard was younger brother to the pestilence that had engulfed the world like the fires of hell a generation before: a White Death to follow the Black. It would become the stuff of bards' tales and poetry, recalled in German-speaking lands with the name it was given when the storm shook the Rhineland, where stone churches were said to have vanished in the wind: *der Gottverlassen*, a phrase that for years would be spoken only in frightened whispers and later would be shouted as promise and threat at children too young to remember what the words once meant. In time, the tales of the storm would become laughable, innocuous—superstitions belonging to the past. To the great grandchildren of those who had seen it, those whose ancestors had survived by miracle alone, the storm was only a story.

In truth, it was many stories. Near Paris it was said that the bell ringers at Notre Dame had seen angels falling to earth, their wings iced flightless by demons that rode the wind. Visitors to the city of Clermont swore that the grand church then under construction succumbed to frostbite and turned black as pitch, though locals insisted its somber hue was merely a consequence of the region's volcanic rock. The only spot spared in Bruges was thought to be the private chapel of the Count of Flanders, where a crystal vial containing blood collected at Golgotha had been placed following the sack of Constantinople a century before. Turkish sorcerers, some believed, had concocted the storm to retrieve this treasure, but the Saracen spell battered the holy stones to no avail.

In the southeast of England, as one version of the legend goes, pilgrims witnessed Saint Peter draw his sword and make his stand high on the rooftop of the Canterbury Cathedral, slicing through the air at the dark heart of the churning clouds until the snow fell black with evil's own blood. This alone, it was declared, had saved the seat of the new archbishop from the fate suffered by so many of Christ's churches and chased the blizzard north, where the storm then rushed as if this had been its destination all along.

The stories told in the upland forests most often concerned a woman who was taken by the wind.

# PART 1
# MATINS

# Chapter 1

ADVENT WIND AT midnight pulled her from the mud of sleep. Windowless and thick-walled, fire-glow in the corner, the abbess's cell was yet safe from the night's new chill. The song of it, though, low tones fluted through the cloister's arches, called all through the convent, and she was at its heart.

Lying veilless in her narrow room, Mother John looked not a nun but a crazy woman, a hag, locked away for the crimes of losing mind and youth. Locked away or worse—with her body hidden under the shearling blanket that was the privilege of her office, she appeared just then only a head, the skull of a martyr on a lambskin pillow. Still breathing, and already she was the perfect relic: A withered globe of skull-white flesh. Eight brown teeth like rats in a hole. Close-cropped hair on a grandmother's face. Grandmotherly, yes, though the last of any children who might have been bled quietly onto a wad of wool a dozen years before.

When the wind called again, Mother John's eyes blinked open to air thick and black as dung-fed dirt. She thanked Jesus for the grace of waking and rose from her bed plank, then took two short steps toward the corner of the cell to warm herself in the firelight. By instinct, faith, and the sheer sameness of her days, she knew that though night was far from over, it was nearly time for morning.

Morning, Matins, was the name given the night office, their first hour of prayer, held in this season as near as they could figure to two hours past midnight. It was the first of eight times through the day when the nuns of Gaerdegen would gather for plainchant and psalmody. The other offices of prayer charted light's transit through the day: Lauds, when they offered praise for the coming of the light to the world; Prime, the first hour of daylight; Terce, the third hour; Sext, the sixth; None, the ninth; Vespers, the decline of light as evening descended; and Compline, the acceptance of the inevitability that all light must fade. But it was Matins that was Mother John's favorite. Morning, they called it, though neither at its beginning nor its end could any sign be seen of the dawn. Morning, because it was then, when night was at its darkest, that they prayed for light to return to the world.

What little light she saw now warmed her only as much as it illuminated the room. Of the fire she had built before sleep, a struggling feather of flame remained. It flickered in the cell's constant draft, shining in flashes on the rough stone walls, on the dark wood of the bed plank's frame and the lighter Scots pine of her writing table. Nothing else here but soot dust and a bucket under the bed.

Such meager lodgings for the mother of a house. In fact this was not even a room meant for sleeping. It had been an anteroom to the sacristy, intended for the preparations of priests before Mass. But the previous abbess's cottage burned in the plague twenty years before, and its repair never seemed practical with so few men left living and wages so high. Nor did it ever prove necessary. Mother John had soon found she welcomed the proximity of her cell to the chapel. Now she would not trade the damp stones of this tiny room for five such fine cottages as she saw burn.

Others in the Order did not find these accommodations at all appropriate for the abbess of Gaerdegen. On a visit earlier that year, John's counterparts from two sister houses seven and ten days' travel distant, Abbess Albreda of Thrisk and Abbess Matilda of Osmotherley, scolded her for the conditions in which she lived, conditions beneath the dignity of her office. And far worse than where she slept were the ways she acted on waking.

"Is it true, good Mother," Abbess Albreda had asked, "that you continue to rise first to prepare the abbey church for the night office?"

"By His grace," John answered.

"In civilized houses lay sisters are called to make these preparations."

"At Gaerdegen those without dowries are not called such. Nor are they made to wash below our backs. As I have heard of civilized houses."

"Please, Mother John," Abbess Matilda said. "Do you mean to tell us you think it proper for the mother of a house to be burning her fingers on the drippings of sheep fat candles, tearing her palms on the rope of the church bell?"

"Oh no," John said. "Those things would not be proper at all. But I have not torn my palms since I was a girl." She held out her hands for her sister abbesses to see. Yellow with calluses, tough as the soles of a poor man's feet. Her fingers found a candle on the table between them and moved through its flame, lingering at the tip of it, where the heat was most intense. "And my flesh, thanks be to God, seems unable to burn."

"Your antics do not impress," Albreda said. "We are here as colleagues, not postulants nor possible benefactors. There is no need for you to play the saint."

"Holy fool is more like," Matilda interjected. "You are an embarrassment, with your filthy habit and unwashed face. And the additions you have made to the liturgy are enough to boil the blood. You act so not only to the detriment of the Order and the Church, but at your peril."

"What have I done against the Church?" John asked. "I labor each day as Our Lord and his disciples labored, with their hands and not with ledgers. And what against the Order? Does not our Rule call for the abbess of the house to lead those in her care in work as well as in prayer?"

"Indeed it does," Albreda said. "But the Rule was written in times far different than these."

"Simpler, nobler, holier times," John said.

"Sadly, yes."

"When the head of a house could be about the business of work and prayer the same as any nun."

"Good Mother, you are filled with nostalgia for a time that never was. Today, as always, an abbess had better first be about the business of business or her house will fall to ruin. As surely you must know."

"The poorest house of the Order mine may be, good Mothers," John said, "but it is your own that have fallen to ruin. Souls, not convents, are the houses of the Lord."

Matilda shook her head impatiently; she'd heard this speech before. "Are all Gaerdegen's sisters so embittered? Has the wilderness hardened all your hearts?"

"The wilderness has blessed us with humility."

"Such humility has only made you proud," Albreda said.

"Our house is a holy one, Mothers. If we are proud of our holiness it is as a bird is pleased with its flight. If the birds conceal God's greatest gift to them, how will the lizards know what they lack?"

The two visitors stood at once. They had arrived only the day before, but the reptilian squint of their eyes and serpentine pinch of their lips said they'd had enough of her insults and would not be staying another night.

"Your flesh will burn yet, John," Matilda assured her. "If not in a candle flame, then bound to a stake in a pyre."

"By His grace," John had said.

Standing alone in her cell, Mother John wondered if she had scoffed too openly at their threats. How often she herself had prayed for such an end. Daily she was visited by visions, in sleep as often as not: Visions of women with eyes pulled from their heads. Of arrows tipped with iron piercing pale white flesh. Of heathen blades tearing at the curve of a breast. These were the stories of saints she had heard throughout the novitiate and her girlhood. Poor souls whose once-real deaths became fantasies to be told and dreamed again and again. Souls for whom Christ's passion was at last a crying and unquestionable reality. To know his pain, to feel the fire of his wounds, who would not pray to be so consumed?

But tonight John had little time for such thoughts. There was work to be done, and if it was done quickly there would remain for her an hour or more alone in the church before Matins.

Each night for twenty years it had been so, her days beginning always in the darkness of this cell. And always, each night, from here she would move into the cloister and, starting at the end closest to the dormitory, clear the floor of any debris that had blown in during the night: leaves and branches from the trees in the courtyard; birds from the same, having miscalculated, apparently, and broken their necks on the smooth stone arches. Depending on the season, there were also occasional dustings of snow, scatterings of hailstones, the droppings of vagrant sheep. On a night like this, when the cold had come without warning, she would not be surprised to find a rock-hard rodent huddled in on itself in a futile wreath, out for a quick scavenge then frozen to the ground.

When the floor was clear, she would again move through the length of the cloister, lighting the thick candles that stood on each side of the walk. If the candles needed replacing she would do so, lugging them like logs from the dry cellar beneath the refectory, then setting them head-high on iron stanchions, ten paces from light to light. On the darkest nights these candles seemed to John an apostolic procession, the original saints passing through the cloister to the church with only the glow of the *Spiritus Sanctus* visible to her old sinner's eyes.

She was pleased to make light where there was none, to be present and part of this daily reflection of creation. For work too could be prayer. Whatever was not was missed opportunity.

"A light shines in the darkness," she would say from Saint John's gospel as she went about her task. Then, rather than continue his bleak phrase—"and the darkness knew it not"—she would jump back to the preceding verse and make of it her own simple interpretation, "And the light was life." This sentiment she voiced with every candle lit, blazing a trail of scripture and flame for her sisters to follow. Inevitably, as many as half the lights would struggle and die in the night wind before the time for rising had come.

With all in the cloister prepared, John would pass each night into the lavabo, to rinse sleep from her eyes and kindle a fire for the warming of the room and its large stone basins. Each night also she would relieve herself in the adjoining chamber, the necessarium, glad to do so before the pit beneath thawed and became foul with the morning's use, and setting a good example, she thought, lest the necessarium become necessary in the midst of their prayers.

From there it was on to the church, where she would light a single candle and kneel silently by the altar until the time came to ring the abbey's one bell and summon her sisters to choir.

Such was the labor some found objectionable. But to John it was a blessing. In this lonely place one was rarely alone. When any sister had volunteered to replace her in this duty, often on pretext of penance but always truly to give an old woman an extra two hours' sleep, the abbess had answered without elaboration, "One day, perhaps."

Many thought her a great saint because of this, but there was a less divinely inspired reason for her obstinacy. By now Mother John could remember no other way.

She threw a block of turf onto the fire and dropped her sleeping clothes as the peat buried and then fed the flame. As the light grew, her full body became visible, and she beheld what so many identical mornings had made of her. Though her wrists were almost thin as candles, folds on her upper arms were loose and hanging. Each breast was a change purse, dangling with the weight of a single coin. Her belly, too, she saw as being somewhat bag-like: dry as burlap, bulged, and bumpy as if filled with the thumb-sized tubers grown beside the abbey barn. Yet ascetic austerity had ensured she looked malnourished despite all this extra flesh.

A sack on sticks, she judged herself in the half-light. Naked, alone, and surely fading, Mother John could only offer up what she had become as an ongoing martyrdom. Offer up this comic body, made by forty years of fasting and the impious droop of age. Offer up to Jesus this mule of human will and God's strange design. Offer up her life and pray for the acceptability of so small a sacrifice.

From the cloister, Advent wind called again, deep and low, like the slow knelling of bells. For the first time its true cold found the doorway of this former warming room, found the darkness inside, found the old skin exposed in the light. At its touch, Mother John crossed to the far wall, where her robe and veil hung from a single wooden peg. These were the garments she donned each night: Simple robe of scratching wool, once white, now gone a dozen shades of gray. Black sackcloth veil that covered ears, cheeks, and temples, falling behind to the small of her back. Two sturdy lengths of fabric, made, shaped, and stitched within the abbey's walls, they had been patched and mended countless times but fully replaced not once in the four decades since her vows. And they would cover her that much longer at least, through whatever days she had left and even beyond. She would wear them until they rotted and sunk into her skin, for they were the very garments that would one day serve as her shroud, robe tied at the bottom, veil wrapped tight over her face. Simple pieces of coarse cloth and wool but also constant reminders that each waking hour is a word spoken in the long liturgy that prepares the body for the grave.

Mother John lifted the robe from its place on the wall, then stretched her arms into the night air and let it fall around her.

# Chapter 2

THE ABBEY OF Gaerdegen was quite young, as convents go: sixty-seven years since its founding, just ten years older than its second and current abbess. First peopled with nuns in the first decade of the century, its main buildings were built atop the ruins of a monastery that had been sacked some five hundred years before.

Though no written record remained, the few monks who had survived the attack were believed to have fled the uplands for good, leaving behind all they could not carry. Objects taken included the usual church ware: chalice, monstrance, altar stone, a cross they had brought with them from their motherhouse. The precious remains of Saints Oswald and Cuthbert, a thumbnail and an earlobe, were also rescued, but not the bones of the murdered brethren, which now lay deep under the remains of more recently deceased nuns.

In the years following the monks' exodus, the larger, stronger, longer-lived bones of the Viking raiders were also buried nearby, in a clearing a long journey to the south, where their descendants built a town and lived ever after as if their grandfathers' grandfathers had never seen the open sea.

Five centuries later, it was from the more prominent families of this town that several of the abbey's first nuns were drawn. Ursula of Gaerdegen, as she would later become known, was then a young widow. Her husband had been a glutton and a drunkard who died of these sins before she had produced a living heir, leaving her the sole beneficiary of his considerable fortune. Suddenly solvent and having no wish to remarry, she sought the permission of the local bishop and the abbot of a nearby monastery to establish a convent cleaving to the Rule of Saint Benedict as closely as the limitations of their sex would allow.

"A fine aspiration. But tell me," the bishop had wondered when she made her appeal in the grand receiving room of the episcopal palace, "why not simply join an existing house of the Order? Why all the fuss and danger of starting anew so far from Christian comfort?"

"Because the existing houses reek of excess and sin," Ursula told him. "The nuns keep puppies in their cells, letting them run in the cloister and even the church, urging them to defecate in a hated sister's choir stall."

The bishop nodded and puffed out his cheeks.

"So I have heard," he said. "But should one incident discredit the whole Order?"

"There are worse sins yet. With or without such distractions they rush through the Divine Office," she went on, "defiling the Hours of the Liturgy, mocking the work Our Lord through

Saint Benedict set before us. I would sooner sprout flesh and seek Holy Orders than join such a house."

Ursula stood more than a dozen paces away, an expanse of polished floor between them, but still she could hear the two churchmen whispering to each other as they considered her request.

"God protect us," the bishop muttered behind his hand. "She's a holy woman or a whore."

"Either way she's sure to be a problem," the abbot said in his ear. "Send her to the wilderness. She'll be dead in ten days."

So it was that blessings were given, land was acquired, and Ursula—along with her younger sister Anna, her cousin Philomena, and their widowed aunt Elizabeth—settled in a wooden shack beside the monastic ruins. The new abbey would sit halfway up a mountainside, above a vast forested valley through which flowed a river containing an unending supply of stone. The ready availability of building materials did not lessen the sense that whatever the abbey came to be, it would be impossibly distant from the lives these aspiring recluses had known. Daughters of wealth who had lacked for nothing, they sat up praying through their first night as the noises of the mountain seemed to claw at their shelter's bark roof.

"Here Christ will ravage us," Ursula told her sister.

"More likely we'll be eaten by wolves."

Yet in ten days they were living still, and within ten years these four women numbered twenty and then twenty-five, who together oversaw the construction of the abbey as it stood at its best. They lived by the motto of Saint Benedict, author of the Rule that now would guide their days. *Laborare est orare.*

To work is to pray. These earliest sisters raised sheep, spun wool, brewed beer, and copied manuscripts, gaining a reputation for fine illumination that often featured Ursula's favored avian motif.

"Birds see all but say nothing we can understand," she was known to say, "which make them a perfect symbol of the divine."

At its height, Gaerdegen was nine structures of stone and wood, all sturdily built but relatively unadorned, the austerity of each a rebuke to the ostentation of the religious houses to the south. Five of the buildings—dormitory, chapterhouse, refectory, lavabo, and church—were joined by a stone-arched cloister. The rest—gatehouse, barn, bakehouse, and the cottage belonging to the abbess—were scattered on the south side.

At Ursula's instruction, no wall surrounded them in those early days. The abbey buildings were open to anyone willing to make the long journey from the cities to the south, through the forest, and up the slope of the valley to the edge of the mountains. The sisters were available for counsel and the giving of alms to all who asked. Too many convents, she insisted, had been founded on fear and continued to make it their Gospel.

"Raids on convents and monasteries are things of the distant past," the abbey's foundress said, "and the walls constructed to protect against them belong to another time. We live open to all God's possibilities, for good or ill. We need no wall choking us to grow in virtue and number."

And grow they did: The combined professed and postulant population soon reached three dozen, which not only guaranteed the continued patronage of a score of affluent families but solidified the abbey's reputation for holiness. That a group of women should prosper where men had struggled and failed suggested to many that the nuns of Gaerdegen were clearly part of the divine plan.

Then the plague came, however, and this belief became less widely held.

# Chapter 3

TWENTY YEARS AFTER the pestilence, Gaerdegen's roll and morale were again on the rise, bolstered by the daughters of parents somewhat baffled to be alive. Contrary to expectations, not all in the world had died, leading those who survived to retake to procreating—zealously, piously, in barebacked abandon. It was said that the fervor was such in the nearest village that a dozen infants were born before weeds covered the grave fields. Deals had been struck with heaven during the plague years, patron saints promised prayers beyond counting, children offered in quantity to the service of the Church. Gaerdegen was the beneficiary of all those debts coming due.

The convent tonight numbered nineteen women: Mother John with her candles, muttering about light in the darkness of the cloister; old Sister Simon, asleep in the gatehouse, stretched out near the door lest anyone sneak past; the refectoress, Sister Thomas, who was said to guard the dry cellar more fiercely than her chastity; Sister James the embroideress, whose ornate altar cloths accounted for a fair percentage of the abbey's income; Sister Matthew, who oversaw the scriptorium; Sister Lazarus, the baker; the shepherds Sister Stephen and Sister Zosimus; Sister Gaius, still known as the new infirmarian though she had served since the plague years; the sacrist, Sister Silvanus; the herbalist, Sister Caspar; the brewer, Sister Priscilla; Sister Rufus, the almoner, though since the plague Gaerdegen had received very few of the poor; Sister Phillip, the magistra noviciarum, teacher of Gaerdegen's novices, and the novices themselves, Sister Andrew, Sister Bartholomew, the actual sisters Sister Jude and Sister Thaddeus, and Sister Magdalene, who had been born in the abbey. It had been the practice since the days of Mother Ursula for the sisters of Gaerdegen to take a consecrated name drawn from the New Testament or the communion of saints, the better for the sisters to draw closer to Christ.

In the dormitory, each nun had her own bed plank: a narrow pine board scattered with straw, neither manger nor cross but something in between. Among these planks another nun sat heaped on the floor by the firepit, legs tucked beneath her, chin on her chest. She had fallen asleep late in the night and let the fire die, leaving barely glowing embers where before had been a roaring blaze.

The youngest sisters were arranged closest to the room's one window, an equal share of night draft for each. They squeezed their fists and shivered, curling up inside their robes. Sister Andrew called softly, "The fire, Sister, the fire."

But Sister Phillip remained in her heap, either deaf to the girls' pleas, or else, as teacher of the convent's novices, ignoring them for their failure to address her with proper pomp.

Perhaps sensing as much, Sister Jude called her sister with two Latin words she'd made a point to remember for just such an occasion: "*Sorore Bove*, Sister Cow, wake up, you're on night watch!"

Harsh or idle talk was forbidden by the Rule, especially to one's superiors, especially after Compline, the last prayers of the day. But just as dire, in the novices' opinion, was letting the fire die on the first bitter night of the season—especially if one was a rotund old nun who did nothing between lessons but chastise her students and tug at the hem of Mother John's robe.

"Hush," Sister Magdalene said from her bed plank. "Let her be."

At twenty, Magdalene was not much older than Gaerdegen's four novices, but she had lived in the convent all her life, and so spoke with authority.

"Hush yourself," Sister Bartholomew hissed, then sat up straight and dropped her feet to the floor. "We'll freeze to death without a fire."

She padded barefoot across the floor and threw two handfuls of sticks and bark on the smoldering coals. After a moment they flared up before her, casting orange-red light on the wood-beam ceiling and the dark stones of the chimney and the chamber walls.

Sent to the convent to rid herself of pride and petulance unbefitting a nobleman's bride, Bartholomew now owned more of each. She stood with clipped brown hair and an egg-shaped face, tall in the flickering light. Though her lips were pressed tight just above her chin, poking between them could be seen two yellow teeth, growing like spider's fangs at odd angles from her gums.

No doubt mistaking Bartholomew's act for self-sacrifice or concern for her sisters, the other novices gave her a quiet cheer at the sight of the fire. As if in response, Sister Phillip let out a long, scratching snore that dragged through the room like a log on stone. Her whole kneeling body shook as it left her, the heft of the sound was so great.

"You hush too," Bartholomew said then raised her foot from the floor and pressed dirty toes against the old nun's shoulder.

"Sister, please," Magdalene whispered.

Bartholomew showed a crooked smile in the firelight.

"Please," her sister said again.

*Gladly.* With a good kicking push, Bartholomew sent Sister Phillip tumbling over, a neat black footprint on her white wool robe. The magistra landed heavily, flat on her back, dust rising around her like a flour sack dropped to the floor. Her head clopped hard onto the dirt and her veil pushed forward, covering her face to the chin. From within this tent came another long snore, thick and wet, more like a ram's-horn trumpet than a human noise in the night.

Across the chamber the novices buried their faces in their sleeves, sure such a bleat would wake their older sisters. Yet around the room, not one stirred. In the moment that followed they again heard only the convent's deep silence. Kindling cracking in the firepit. A cold southern wind whistling in from outside.

Sister Bartholomew placed a log on the fire, then started back across the room as quietly as anyone would move past nine sleeping nuns. She had nearly reached her place when another drowsy groan rose from the flames. It was louder and sharper than before, like thunder rumbling and crashing in the clouds above the convent. The novices could feel it in their bed planks. It crawled along the floor and shook the wood beneath them.

"Bartholomew, do something," one of them whispered.

"She's done quite enough," Magdalene moaned.

But Sister Bartholomew already was rushing back to the center of the chamber. She knelt down by the magistra's side, grabbed her habit with both hands, and with one great grunting motion lifted, pushed, and rolled Sister Phillip first to her side and then fully over. The back of the old nun's habit was black with dirt and soot, her body round and rising like a boil on the floor, but otherwise she seemed peaceful—belly down and undisturbed. Her lips pressed into the charred ground beside the firepot, muffling to an acceptable volume her labored breaths, which droned like bellows from a distant pasture.

"It must be Advent," Bartholomew whispered as she returned to her sisters. "Look, already there's a heifer for the crèche."

From the next bed plank Magdalene spat, "You deserve a beating for this."

But Bartholomew stretched out on her yellow straw and closed her eyes without a care. "Magdalene, you are two years my senior, but I am a lifetime your better. Mind yourself, or when a new abbess rules the house you lay sisters will sleep in the barn."

"Mind your tongue. It's an awful sin to speak of Mother's successor, even in jest," Magdalene said. Succession generally followed death or scandal, two fates she could not imagine for the only abbess she had ever known.

"Pureheart, I could put out your eye and you would call it a jest. But this is nothing of the kind. My cousin at our sister house tells me what the rest of the Order thinks of our Mother John."

"They must think her holy, as she surely is."

Bartholomew sighed. "What must it be to have known no family, Magdalene? No souls in paradise to pray for you, no souls living who care enough to explain to you the ways of the world. You'll be forever in the dark."

"The prayers of our sisters living and dead are offered for each of us, Bartholomew. Mother says we must pray for you most of all, or the Devil may take you completely."

"The Devil take you, orphan. What will you do without dear Mother to hen over?"

"You might take more care with her. She is your Mother as well as mine."

"Yes, but not for long. Some say she has lost her mind."

"The world's ways are not hers."

"Then perhaps she will kindly leave it. Already she is rotting in her shoes. Even the bishop must notice the stink."

Magdalene rolled from her bed plank and needed only one step to stand beside Bartholomew's prone robed form. She stared down at lips moving, though the eyes above them were serenely closed.

"And if the bishop has neglected to notice," she said, "someone who cares for the future of the house will certainly point it out to him. Then maybe he will do something about the smell."

Magdalene uncurled the fist she had considered using and slapped her open hand on her sister's smiling mouth, more to close it like a lid than to cause it to bleed. But bleed it did, in a hot gush from the inside of her nose. Blood pooled around Bartholomew's tongue, painting her teeth. And so too did Magdalene bleed. Palm punctured by Bartholomew's misdirected grin, she dropped rose petals to the white wool of her robe.

In the center of the room Sister Phillip sat up with a start, eyes wide, cheeks soot-smudged. She coughed and wheezed with the dirt in her mouth, like a corpse returning to life.

"The fire," she said, as the two younger nuns fell back to their planks. "Goodness, the fire."

In the instant that followed the slap of flesh on flesh, the flame had gone out again, killed by a puff of Advent wind.

# Chapter 4

Cold wind crept through the shutters then crept back out again to stir the shrubs and grasses of the courtyard. Already new debris had blown into the freshly swept cloister, and now the stanchion candles danced with too much air to breathe. Every scattered stick and leaf seemed alive and doubled, each reflected by a jumping shadow on the gray slate floor.

As if not content to blow where no damage would be done, the wind slid over and around the rooftops and walls of the convent's connected buildings, pulling at wood, pushing at stone. And soon it penetrated, moving through entryways, filling like lungs the tucked-away chambers, then exiting as it had come, exhaled to the night.

Only in its attempt on the church did the wind find resistance. There alone the abbey's portals were plugged not with pieced-together slats of wood but with actual glass, carried at great distance and expense not for its value as ornament but solely for its ritual significance. Set high above the altar in the stacked stone walls, each day these windows first showed the nuns of Gaerdegen that morning had come, showed them that the sun had risen just as they raised their heads to receive communion on their tongues. Christ in mouth and eyes to heaven, church walls suddenly filled with his bright and golden light, could there be any doubt who brought the dawn?

There were six such windows above the altar, three to a side, each holding a clouded framework of lead-lined glass squares, tall as an arm, wide as a body, thick as a board. Amber-toned and bubble-filled, later in the day, after the second gathering for prayer, Lauds, they would serve their higher purpose. Just now they stood guard against the wind.

Not all from without was kept there, however. In the southern wall the windows let in the light of the moon, shining like day as it only can on a clear cold night. On the floor by the altar, Mother John's robe was yellow with its rays. Yellow too was the man who stared down at her from the cross above. Along with this dull tint, her face and his wore the glow of a single candle. Its flame flickered, lighting alternately on the nun's withered features and on the wide-eyed agony of God's eternal youth. They stared at each other as if rapt in conversation.

With the day's first work done, Mother John had taken what precious time remained until Matins to kneel by the altar and indulge in private prayer. While outside the wind called as it had since it woke her, here in the church not a sound could be heard save the soft popping and hissing of her lips. Breathlessly came words well memorized but half understood, syllables running in on each other like sheep through the pasture gate.

*"Pater noster qui es in caelis,"* she said and followed with forty-four more Latin words, ending with Amen. Her study of the language had ended while she was a child, and yet she knew these words as well as she knew anything. Better perhaps, for like language itself, she could not remember precisely when they had been learned. Nor could she recall ever using any of them in a context other than this. But it was not all dumb repetition. Strange as they would be in her own tongue, she recalled, more or less, what the words meant.

*Father of us who is in heaven,*
*Blessed be your name,*
*Come your kingdom,*
*Let it be done your will in heaven and in earth.*
*Bread of us daily give to us today.*
*Dismiss from us debts of us and we will dismiss debts to us.*
*And not us lead into temptation.*
*But free us from evil.*

In truth, to Mother John the meaning of the words mattered little. This was not like other prayers, not like her spontaneous petitions, Lord grant, Lord forgive, Lord protect, which were best spoken when needed, with no call for official incantations or theological correctness. No, this was a tried and sure tool shared by all Christendom. It was a stool to stand on to reach high overhead, a familiar place to rest when you grew weary with the day, often simply something to say to the one who knows your words before you make them, your needs before you need them.

Paternoster, paternoster, paternoster, she prayed, on and on and on. She prayed so for nearly an hour, becoming only these sounds. Prayed until there was no distance between the cross she saw above her and the eyes that did the seeing—no distance from Jesus to the nun who prayed to him. She prayed until this resting-place prayer became their bridal bed. Prayed until he came to her there and let her touch his wounds. Prayed until the moonlight dimmed and then was all but gone, until she was alone again, separate again from her love.

Crossing herself slowly as she finished a final prayer, Mother John clasped her hands at her chest and looked to the arched windows, looked up wondering at the loss of light.

The clouded panes were colorless, gray as the stone walls. John could not see the cause of the change, but she could hear it, hear things only as one listening for God can hear, hear things and put images to them, images that explain the things we sense but cannot see.

Outside she heard deep darkness spread like spilled wine, smothering the moon. She heard clouds roll in to blind the stars. She heard a hush of wind move through the hollow of the abbey barn, heard it crawl across the frost-hardened mud in the barnyard. She heard it slip, in the distance, through the trees that kept Gaerdegen hidden from the world. Soon she heard this same wind find the bell tower high above and felt it as it blew down around her, rustling her robe and veil.

Usually, the air here hung in stagnant pockets; now now it came alive. The church smelled as always of sheep fat candles and stale incense, but a draft moved in and out of every corner, sweeping across the floor and up the walls, cold swallowing everything it touched.

As best she could, Mother John ignored the church's new chill. She knelt still by the altar and looked away from the windows, refocusing on the face and the pain of her sweet Jesus. His cheeks were sunken, his eyes rolled back, his mouth frozen in an agony John thought must be close to the pain of childbirth. She had seen it once before.

The cold dug through the abbess's habit, creeping up her ankles to her calves through the open-bottomed gown; bending upward with the backs of her knees; caressing the pale of her thighs. The wind caused her to shudder, her whole body to tremble with surprise. And it continued to climb: tracing through the folds of her stomach, rounding her breasts, crawling up her neck, tickling beneath the collar of her veil. It touched softly her old, unkissed lips and dried her teeth when she smiled at the unfamiliar feeling of being held.

The candlelight began to flicker as the breeze fed its fire. Sheep wax formed a yellow puddle beneath the finger-tall flame and soon spilled over, sliding down the candle in exaggerated drops, fat and slow, while the light shone brighter, in flashes, on the cross of the Lord. He stared off mournfully, hopelessly, searching the darkness for the one who had ignored his call. His carved limbs went limp, and his lips seemed to tremble in the flickering light.

Then the flame grew larger still, burning bright but uncertain, vulnerable to the wind. Beads of wax sulked down the candle shaft like drool on an infant's chin. It puddled again in the black iron of the candle dish, then dropped heavily to the floor, falling and splashing like water in a cave, the wet tap of each drop's impact somehow echoed before it occurred, calling: *oot . . . oot . . . oot . . . oot . . .*

Mother John's eyes widened at the sound, then narrowed, searching for its source. Searching frantically, for this calling seemed to come from none but Christ. She bit hard on her lower lip, and listened again, squinting to see through the single candle darkness.

*Root . . . root . . . root . . . root . . .* she heard. His lips moved with the light.

"Lord?" she gasped, hands flying to her mouth, her whole body shaking as pain crept upward from the floor. Through her knees, through her hips, piercing her sides, finding the palms of her hands, she felt the pain and fright she usually could only imagine. Each tap knocked against her like a stone. Her thoughts began to flicker with the flame.

John saw Christ's chest rise and fall with each forced syllable. His fingers, blistered and bent, tightened to fists and gripped the nail heads as men hold coins. His wooden wounds seemed to open and bleed. The wax kept tapping, even as the wind whistled and snuffed the flame, tapping steadily in the darkness a long moment more, speaking slowly, clearly, calling:

*Ruth.*

*Ruth.*

Mother John covered her face, hiding from the darkness in the palms of her hands. She had not heard the name since her first years as abbess. It had been her name, but that was so long ago that the name of her childhood had become little more than a vaguely familiar syllable. It was a Bible story she didn't care for. It was a name she had been glad to forget.

She had been Ruth once, but no longer. She was now Mother, as she had been for nearly half her life. Before this, since her adolescence, she had been John, Sister Saint John the Baptist, a name given her as a reminder of the day she joined the nuns of Gaerdegen and as proof of the purity and strength of her desire to overcome the sinfulness of her sex. Each call echoed behind her eyes; the silence between them stopped her breath.

*"Ruth . . . Ruth . . ."*

Why Jesus should at last call her with this name she could not fathom. When she was Ruth, she scarcely knew him. Knew him as girls do: Thanked him for his birth, for the gifts it sometimes brought. Said his name on her knees when the priest came calling or the nurse was in earshot. But kneeling was no place for a girl. Her place then had been on her feet, in the fields.

She remembered feeling the ground wet beneath her, puddling in her footsteps. When she was young and small but did not know it. When she was a child, naked and running from a bath. There was a voice crying out to her, she recalled. Tired and troubled, jerking from high to low, falling away then struggling back. Her mother's voice, "Ruth! Ruth!"

When the wind warmed her body and seemed even to lift her from the ground, when her hair blew long and red about her face, into her eyes, and swung across her back, from shoulder to shoulder, as later would her veil, her mother was chasing her, calling, "Ruth, please, Ruth!"

With the nurse busy at another task, it had fallen to her mother to wash her—but the girl would not have it. From a field's length away, Ruth watched her mother rushing out from the bathhouse, dress lifted to her knees, legs thin and shaking. Watched her shuffling carefully along until she slipped in the wet and landed face and dress in the brown manure mud.

"Ruth, you devil, come back!"

John remembered pausing in her flight just long enough to turn and laugh, thinking, *Mother needs a bath more than me.*

"Ruth!"

Hearing this name again, she thought of how she ran on and on that day, a little girl naked up and down the hills. Ran on and on with no destination, changing direction with the wind and forgetting her mother and her home, though a voice called until after the sun had set.

Christ's calling continued like a slow heartbeat, like the pulse of a dying man. But if life was draining from one of them, Mother John was sure it was herself. She knelt motionless and mortified, unable to answer. The church had never seemed so dark.

"Ruth," she heard. "Ruth?"

She heard it and kept quiet just as she had in her father's house, though then the voice calling was of a man who was a man alone, a man for whom there would be no resurrection.

"Ruth?"

Calling through the manor, Ruth's father finally found her in her bedchamber, at her reading table. Lately she had been reviewing her French, preparing for a trip she hoped to make with her mother come spring. At the sound of his approach she hid the book she had been reading, *Roman de la Rose*, for as a merchant often abroad Ruth's father knew the tongue and might catch her lingering at the description of the Lover gently peeling back his Rose's petals, inspecting her depths.

"Ah, Ruth. Here you are."

Though he wore the curled beard that was common in portrayals of the Lord, with his red cheeks and round head, Ruth's father looked more like the jolly host at Cana than the holy vintner guest. Plump and noble, he had wide, kind eyes that shone always with tears that would not fall. His lips were wet with spittle that jumped to his beard when his words came quickly.

"It is finished," he said triumphantly upon entering. "We have reached an agreement on your dowry, and now all has been arranged."

"We, Father?" she asked coyly, for she knew the answer well.

"We, Ruth. Jerome, the Lord of Wergild, and myself. His messenger has just left here. We've planned for the wedding to follow Christmastide."

She had met the man just once. He had looked her up and down then claw-grabbed what he could of her stomach through her dress. "Skinny," he said to her father. He had placed what first seemed an admiring hand on her cheek, and it took her a moment to realize he wanted her to open her mouth to show her teeth. He had peered inside like a man buying a barrel.

"Forgive me Father, but that seems more a *vous* than a *nous*, the two of you deciding who I am to marry."

He shook his head impatiently, *tut tut tut*. "Daughter, Wergild is a man of rank, reputation, land, and means. A birth noble—unlike your father, whose family had to purchase respect. *Tu comprends*?"

She understood. Her spring trip would be not to France, but to dastardly Wergild. Such a waste; she had nearly mastered the tongue.

"*Oui*," she said. "*Mais je ne trouve pas bien*."

He smiled at her accent, her grammar, her child-chosen words. "If you mean to say you are not pleased, I am sorry but all is arranged. The dowry has been set. We have decided for our best interests."

"Had truly it been a *we*, Father, *we* would not have reached agreement on my selling price. And we would not have deemed it in our best interest to share a stranger's bed."

"Then I am glad we were not there."

Ruth rose from her reading table and crossed to the chamber's wide double window. Then too it was December, Advent wind blowing outside. In the fading daylight the hills and fields of her youth were white as eyes, pinkened with the last efforts of the sun. Suddenly winter; she had known it was coming, why was she surprised?

"I'll not have him," she insisted, then turned and followed with a thought that had not occurred to her until that very moment. "I'd sooner become a nun."

Her father let out a quick, ecstatic hoot. She had always been such a curious girl. Whatever she wished he had allowed her to study, because, yes, he spoiled her and also because he had hoped to prepare her for a life among the nobility. French, Latin, the ancients, she reveled in such high and useful things. Yet pious subjects had always left her yawning. He liked to believe it was his influence. He had seen so much of the world.

"Ruth, were the idea not wholly laughable, I would ask you not to threaten me."

"And why is it laughable? Laughable that your daughter should have some choice in her life?"

"I will tell you come Sunday, when again the nurse must wrestle you into your church clothes."

"I would don church clothes every morning for the remainder of my days before I would wear the skin of a man of your choosing."

Her father's wide eyes narrowed and his hand moved into the air. The discussion had taken a turn he had not foreseen. "You will lie beneath whomever I please," he found himself shouting, spittle leaping to his beard. "And when you've borne his children, we will be part of this Lord's esteemed family."

"You, Father, not I. You will be part of his family," Ruth shot back. "I will be his breeding sow."

He reached out and slapped Ruth with the meaty palm of his hand. "Did I pay for your education to make you fit for a brothel? Know your station. And know too there is a greater we than you and I. This match has been made for your namesake, my mother, as well as for your children, one of whom you shall give my name. You will have this man, and God willing, all will benefit."

Ruth reached to her face and fingered the warm patch that would later be a bruise. "And if I won't you will have me beaten, I suppose?"

He looked to the floor, shocked by his anger, shocked by his beloved daughter's sudden lack of gratitude.

"No," he said. "There'll be no need. We will be joined to Wergild. For you, Ruth, on this matter there can be no I."

When her father turned and started from the room, she saw he was fully twice her size, walking heavily across the floor. Had he hit her as he might a man, it would have snapped her neck. Watching him then, she realized with both anger and relief that even in violence he did not treat her as one fit for the world.

"May I ask, Father," Ruth said. "You mention my dowry. What sum shall we contribute to this union?"

He spun back to her and showed a grin in his round face. His wet eyes shined. "There is the practical girl I know! Never let it be said that your father chased down a bargain for his Ruth. You will have a pension of twenty-five pounds each year. With this you will live well, have no fear of that."

"Thank you, Father."

"Back to your studies while I find your mother and share our good fortune."

"Yes, Father," Ruth said.

He was not three steps through the door when Ruth retrieved her *Roman de la Rose* and tore a thick blank page from inside its cover. Hand-copied, hidebound, a book such as this was a great extravagance, but this matter could not wait for the nurse to be sent for parchment. Sitting again at her reading table, she poured a few drops of water into a bowl and then ladled in a measure of pigment. She mixed this compound with her smallest finger, then dipped a cock feather in the ink and addressed the top of the page.

*To the most holy Bishop of the Cathedral City, on the Feast of Saint Ambrose.*

She blew on the page to dry it, and then reflected for a moment before moving to the body of the epistle. Because she suspected, indeed hoped, the letter would one day find her father's eyes, she began with a large calligraphic flourish, a single letter challenge he alone would understand. I, she wrote.

*I, Ruth, only daughter of the merchant Thomas Murray, write to inform you of the great longing in my heart for Christ, to be his virgin and lifelong bride. By His Grace our Lord has called me to be among his poorest and truest of maidens. He has bidden me to take the veil in the far corner of your bishopric, under the obeisance of the Abbess Ursula, at the holy Abbey of Gaerdegen.*

The location she decided upon only as the words found the page. She had heard impressive tales of these women in the wilderness. And besides, if one is to be away from home, better to be far from it. She dipped her pen again and continued the letter, for a girl's longing would not itself move a bishop to act.

*Certain as I am that this calling comes from heaven alone, my good father Thomas would see the dowry he has prepared for me awarded to the Lord of Wergild and not, through your grace, to the one true Lord and his most holy Church. That a yearly pension of twenty-five pounds be so misdirected I cannot bear. In the name of Christ Jesus, I beg your intervention, that the funds in my name be placed in your charge, in accordance with God's own will.*

Though quill, ink, and the book from which she had torn this page had been purchased for her by him, though she had learned to compose such a message from tutors her father had provided, she did not feel a pang of guilt as she summoned her nurse and handed her the letter. Nor did she hesitate even a moment in adding to the delivery three coins from Thomas Murray's coffer.

"Take these to the priest and ask him see the letter to its destination," Ruth said softly. "Advise him there will be more when I receive a response, the sooner the reply the greater the sum."

Then the nurse left to continue what a girl who had not yet seen sixteen winters had set in motion.

Within the week she had her answer. It came in the guise of her father, shouting through the manor again, storming into her bedchamber, finding her in candlelight, late at her books. He stood barefoot and in bedclothes, a fat man in a gown.

"These have just arrived," he said, "to trouble my sleep."

Slapping one yellow sheet onto the reading table, he held another in his hand, crushing its upper corners.

Before her Ruth recognized immediately her own tidy words, her own overlarge *I.* On the other sheet she saw what she believed to be the red wax of the bishop's seal. Or else a drop of blood. Difficult to tell in her father's angry fist.

"You've written your own death warrant, Ruth," he said.

"No. I believe it is my reprieve. You will support my decision?"

"I've little choice. The bishop's faith is in the One True Lucre. It would be marked heresy now if my payment stray from the teachings of his purse. What have I done that you would make such an enemy for me? Would you see me on a spit?"

His daughter nodded slowly. Thoughtfully, she thought. Practicing her piety. "God's will must be done, Father."

"Stubborn, stupid girl. You think you've won freedom, but you'll be walled up and dead all your days."

"So long as the days are mine," Ruth said.

Six months later on a bright June morning she stood just south of the church at Gaerdegen, in the yard by the gatehouse. The warmth of the sun made her usually pale face as red as her father's beard.

It was the Feast of Saint John the Baptist: The day she promised herself to a life of poverty, chastity, obedience, and stability. The day she was born anew as a member of the community, formally accepting her new life and formally accepted by the nuns of Gaerdegen. Today she learned that both she and her father had been correct about her letter, to what it would amount, for that morning she heard Abbess Ursula welcome her with the words, "The girl called Ruth is dead. Sister Saint John the Baptist has risen from her grave."

Now she was standing in sandals, scratching at the cool earth with the tips of her toes. Her father and mother stood there with her, nodding and brooding, saying goodbye. The courtyard was empty but for a family of chickens, pecking about in the dirt by the abbey barn, and the fine two-horse carriage her parents had arrived in the previous night. A coachman sat there, John remembered, waiting.

In the distance, she saw white habits moving over the hills like doves, three of her new sisters chasing sheep that refused to graze with the flock.

"Ruth," her father said bitterly, sighing. "Ah, Ruth . . ."

She did not know it then, but this was the last she would see of him. He would never offer to visit, she would never ask, and then he would be dead. His well-fed flesh would blister and bruise purple before splitting open at the joints. Blood and pus would leak through his bedclothes and stain his featherbed. Thomas Murray would die alone and weeping. But on this day his cheeks were full and red, burning as he spoke.

"You have proven your point, Ruth. Come home with us and you will have a man of your choosing."

He took his daughter's hands in his own and squeezed her fingers as if they were twigs to be broken and thrown on a fire. Then he spread her arms wide to see what she had become. On this day for the first time she felt the weight of her habit, thicker and whiter than it would ever be again. Her face was framed in the white veil of the novitiate. Her cheeks carried a drum-tight tension, as if the skin there was pulled taut and the slack tied behind her headdress like a bun. Her eyes were pretty and bright, wrinkling at the corners when she smiled.

He looked his daughter up and down, his tight-lipped smile showing his thoughts. My daughter, he seemed to say, my only daughter, who had grown up so quickly, my daughter, who was the only real beauty in an opulent life, my daughter, she has grown sexless and holy.

His hands squeezed tighter; he would not let go. She has taken all he offered and thrown it back at him. She has given her dowry, his gold, to the Church to buy herself salvation. She has robbed him of his grandchildren. She has cast off the name of his mother. His lips curled, fighting a frown, and his eyes shone sadly, saying finally only this: *My daughter is a cold and rigid thing.*

"I'll have no man, Father," Ruth said. "I am here now, here I will remain." Then she added happily, "God willing, of course."

But that day, she remembered, her joy had little to do with God. Vows aside, she gave him rarely a thought. She thought instead of the marriage bed she had avoided and the life she had chosen for herself. The life she had *chosen*. She thought of her sisters beyond the wall, their veils flapping in the warm wind, habits blowing smooth against their stomachs.

Her mother stood five or six feet off, approaching only when her husband had moved away. Her face was swollen and round, as Ruth's own would never be; her hair bound and tied beneath a traveling hat; her lips gray and lifeless. She too would be taken by the plague. She would awaken one night to find her husband painted with blood, marked by the sickness that came though the windows were guarded and the doors shut tight. She would run from his bed, leaving his side even before he woke, packing their valuables in silence and haste then riding off under cover of night in the same fine carriage they rode today, running from the sickness she could not escape, to be found later in a puddle of roadside mud.

She touched her daughter's cheek and chin with the soft tips of her fingers and steered her daughter's eyes to meet her own. She spoke softly, staring. "Pray for us, Ruth." Struggling with her words, taking deep, painful breaths. Her chest and stomach fought to swell beneath the elegance of her dress, where tight undergarments brought order to the chaos of her flesh. "You mustn't forget those you leave in the world," she said, but her eyes flashed blamefully; they glowed with accusation, asking: So, you will leave me to my fate?

Ruth looked away and nodded slowly, biting hard on her lower lip. "I will never forget," she said, and her words became a solemn promise, if just for the instant they occupied the air.

"Now, now," her father jumped in, spittle leaping to his beard, "we'll return soon enough. It's not such a long journey that we can't visit once a year!" He smiled at his daughter, then pulled his wife to his side, tugging at her arm. "And if I know my daughter, Ruth will rule the house in a year's time! Then she can have all the guests she likes."

"You shouldn't say such things, Father," Ruth said.

But if he heard, he made no show of it. Instead, Thomas took Ruth again in his thick-fingered hands and kissed her on the cheek, scratched her with the only whiskers that ever would scratch her lips.

"You will do well by us. I know you will."

"I will try, Father." She answered mechanically, almost ignoring him to study her mother, who was looking away, taking a last glance at the grounds of Gaerdegen. Ruth wondered if she one day would wear her wrinkles. "Mother?"

The older woman's face grew pale and stricken, as if frightened by premonitions of all that was to come. Her gray lips opened slightly, and her eyes found her daughter's then turned back to the walls of the abbey church.

"Pray, Ruth." She barely spoke, but her whispers sounded like warnings. "Pray for us in this holy place. And I will pray that you find what you need here." Her voice shook, falling away then struggling back.

"Thank you, Mother," Ruth said, looking to the ground, to the holes she had made with her toes. "I will try."

They left without another word. Her mother stepped first into the carriage, looking back gravely, hopelessly. Her father put one foot on the step, kissed his hand and raised it into the air as if to block the sun. The coachman stared down from atop the carriage and smiled crookedly, tipping his hat before snapping the reins, setting the horses to a trot.

Ruth watched the carriage pull off through the abbey gate and along the southern road. A cloud of dust rose behind as the horses kicked dirt and stones into the air and the carriage wheels stirred the packed earth of the roadway. They would not return to Gaerdegen. She would pray rarely for them and would hear details of their deaths months after they were in the ground. By then so many had been taken that she never bothered to wonder if more prayers could have saved them, if more prayers could have saved any of the souls she remembered tonight, the souls who without will or knowledge had brought her to this very moment, as though she had walked on corpses to the church. Her parents, her nurse, the priest who delivered her letter, even Jerome, Lord of Wergild, the betrothed whom

Christ had made a cuckold. All who had known her as Ruth, all who had conspired to make her John, all were long dead, all dead in the plague. Only she who had written her death warrant remained.

In her dreams she had seen them bleeding, seen them reach for her from the varied venues of the end. Her father in bedclothes, her mother in mud. Long after they rode off on that June morning of her youth, she still heard them calling, calling to her as Jesus seemed to now:

*Ruth.*

*Ruth.*

*Ruth.*

A whistle of wind snuffed the candlelight, cooling solid the molten wax where it had pooled, sending a final drop splashing quietly to the floor.

Mother John lifted her eyes to search for the one who had spoken her name and crossed herself slowly, then clasped her hands over her heart. The calling had stopped and now awaited an answer.

And answer she would, answer because she had been called; because if the call was genuine, it needed to be answered; because if the call was genuine, then all it brought with it had meaning. Meaning and reason for her pain and regret, meaning and reason for her guilt and her fear. If the call was genuine, it brought meaning to her memories, her life. A hidden meaning, but certain, one she could not now know, but one day by his grace would somehow understand. If the call was not genuine, if the voice she heard was illusion, fantasy, then her answers were unnecessary, then her penances went unnoticed, her ceaseless prayers unheard. Then her life had been wasted, her sisters' lives wasted. Then she was a fool and God was a lie, but what then? What then?

She opened her lips lightly, as if again to utter a prayer, and whispered to her Lord. Her voice was calm, resigned, forgetting the wonder and fear the first taps had caused, answering because she had been called. Answering because when God calls us it is not to what we believe we are but to what we have been from the beginning and what will be until the end.

"Here, Lord," Mother John said. "Here I am."

The words clouded about her face in the cold of the church. They echoed in the emptiness, ringing off the walls, amplified by the wood of the ceiling, but went otherwise unanswered. Unanswered as loudly as only words in a church can be.

# Chapter 5

MOTHER JOHN KEPT to her knees a long moment more, searching for the cross though it was just a few feet away. She waited for a reply until the waiting seemed foolish, then struggled to her feet and relit the candle, clicking together the flint and steel kept there for that purpose.

As light returned to the church, it flickered in John's eyes once more and glinted off her cheeks and chin. It shone on the gray slate tiles and shone on the crude hewn stone of the altar, on rocks remade to glorify their maker.

When the abbess's eyes grew accustomed to the half-light, again the cross loomed before her. She drew nearer—cautiously, reverently—to examine it, her eyes just below the statue's feet.

Candlelight flashed on the nail wounds and on the smooth curving lines of the statue's legs. It lit the ripple of its loincloth and the sunken arch of its belly. It lit the lines of the chest, the rounding of the ribs, the deep gouges where the neck began, the thin strain of its lips and jaw. The eyes were in darkness, shadowed, their light stolen by the rise of the cheeks and the sharp angle of the nose. She wondered at her Lord.

*A light shines in the darkness*, Mother John thought, forming again the candle-lighting phrase in her mind, forming it slowly, considering separately the first word, then the second, then the third. Her eyes scanned upward and down, following the light of the candle as it rose and fell on the carved body. She considered the words again, then added her simple interpretation that had been an undeniable truth: And the light was life. But what she saw now was not life. It was the same man who had called her just moments before, the same man she had given her life to in the mischief of her youth, the same she had later come to love as she learned to love her life. It was the same man, but somehow different, transformed by the light. The man on the cross was not flesh at all. His lips could not move, his wounds could not bleed.

She reached out timidly to touch the crucifix, to be certain of what she saw. With two cracked, scratching fingers, her hands shaking like a bride's, she moved down the leg from knee to ankle. The wood was cold and smooth, carved perfectly. She traced her fingers along the rounded line that joined the legs, and felt the angles that made its curve: numberless angles, like a tiny and perfect mountain range; peaks formed meticulously by a skilled hand and the finest of edges, undetectable by sight, but so apparent to the touch. She felt too the grain of the wood and the remnants of rings, the signature of the tree this once had been.

She cradled Christ's feet in her palms, smoothing her thumbs over the nails that joined the body to the cross. She felt no flesh, no blood. She knew that human hands had formed these feet; that a man's knife had carved these legs, these hands, these wounds; that the hands of a sinner had shaped these lips, and that these lips could never move, would never speak.

Her eyes shifted to the candle flame, to the pool of wax collected at its base. She watched clear yellow beads spill over and trace down the sides of the candle, saw them fill the small curve of the candle dish. Her gaze then dropped to the floor, following the wax as it fell, finding there the viscous puddle each drop joined with a distinct wet tap. The echoes of the falling wax resumed and continued as if they had never ceased. Mother John heard her name again. She saw its source and felt her age.

The abbess turned her back on the altar and the cross and hurried to the darkest corner of the church. There she found the bell rope, stretching upward from a coil of slack on the floor, and took it in her hands. It hung mysteriously, disappearing into the darkness of the bell tower as if unattached, or else strung to the darkness itself; as if when she pulled, it would either fall limply to her feet or else bring down the sky. She held it tight, gripping with two strong fists, and tugged downward, pulling her hands to her chest.

High above, the heavy bell began to rock. John heard the high creak of metal on wood, the squeak of iron set in motion, stirred from sleep. The rope pulled suddenly away, tugged by the top of the bell as its lower half swung like a pendulum and jerked her arms up over her head.

Light as she was, Mother John answered with a good strong tug, giving all her weight to the rope. Then she let it pull away again, this time lifting her to her toes. Another slow pull and a quick, jerking rise, and the bell rang out, a thick, low tone that lit the night. It rang once, then again, again, again, heavy, persistent, relentless, and Mother John rose and fell with each ear-splitting toll.

The full force of the sound flooded the church, drowning the nun with its waves. It rose away from her, up from the tower, stretching up to the clouds, ringing through the convent and echoing through all the surrounding wilderness. It rang out as it would seven times more through the coming day, as it had through all the days before, searching for and summoning all the nuns of Gaerdegen and the spirit of their God. The bell's sound reminded them of prayer, and, they hoped, reminded him to listen. If it was a word, it was one that called together all who heard it. A word cracking then hollow then humming into the night:

*Come . . .* it said. *Come . . . Come . . . Come . . .*

The bell tolled on and on. Below it, Mother John worked the rope hard and waited for her sisters to answer the call.

*Come.*

*Come.*

*Come.*

In minutes they appeared: one after another, emerging from the darkened entryway to the church like crumbs dropped to a tabletop. Their footsteps echoed, and light found their habits as they approached the altar, one by one, to bow before the cross.

Mother John released the rope and watched from the corner, surprised by the silence after being lost in sound. She could not see faces but easily distinguished the sisters by the care of their movements and the speed of their steps.

First to enter were the youngest, slim and tall in their white robes and white veils, moving with all the grace granted by their years, bumping in the dark. Then came the recently professed, six sisters who bowed low and slowly, one lower than the next, all as if involved in a competition of holiness.

The older nuns came next; other than Mother John, only four had been cloistered at Gaerdegen since before the plague. Among these were Phillip, still dark with floor grime, and Sister Simon, similarly so, fresh from her nightly vigil in the gatehouse. Sister Magdalene was the last to enter. She paused before the altar then hurried away as if frightened.

When everyone had arrived and gathered together in the choir stalls, their abbess took her place among them. As one, they bowed once more to the cross, veils falling over their faces, then rose to face Jesus and offer him prayers. The time for the first Hour had come. Nine to one side, ten to the opposite, the sisters turned to face each other across the church.

Magdalene sang first, breaking the silence. She had done so almost as long as she had lived, but tonight her voice shook nervously, like a lost child's cry.

"*Domine, labia mea aperies . . .*" she sang. *O Lord, open my lips.*

Her voice hung alone, and then was answered with the song of her sisters. Her lonely call answered by a wall of sound. Eighteen voices in the night:

"And my mouth shall declare your praise."

Magdalene called out again, her voice to John's ear the loveliest of all the nuns of Gaerdegen. A voice that found Mother John and touched her with a sweetness that told her only God could make such music.

"O Lord, open my lips . . ."

Mother John and all the sisters sang out strong in reply, because one voice was not enough.

"And my mouth shall declare your praise."

They sang together to their Lord, filling the church air with their prayers. Their voices rang with a tone that told the abbess to rest again in the Hours, to put her doubts away for the next dark night. A tone that brought comfort and said that God indeed had called her and was calling even now. Sister Magdalene sang alone and was answered one last time.

"O Lord, open my lips . . ."

"And my mouth shall declare your praise."

For the second time today Mother John thanked Jesus for the grace of waking. She thanked him for his birth and gifts it sometimes brought. Thanked him for the death that had given her this life.

As was their custom, she then offered a short reading from the Book of Ursula: "Remember my sisters, do not trust the works of men, which seek to mimic the glories of creation but indeed are their undoing. There are those who would destroy and call it building; there are those who will divide and call it joining; there are those who would draw a blade and insist it is to make some greater mend. But do not fail to see cutting for what it is: an act that removes and discards those things deemed unneeded. Never will it lift up the world as needs to be done. So much better is the work that keeps all and shows it how to become at once what it was and something more."

An hour more they sang into the night, as their brothers and sisters did at just this time all over Christendom. Psalms, hymns, readings, and then silence as their voices floated high above the convent, shaking the clouds until snow began to fall.

# PART 2

# LAUDS

# Chapter 6

THE FIRST SNOW of winter. Clouds gathered and settled as low as fog upon the uplands, robbing the hills of their height, filling the valley below with flurries. Clusters of flakes fell slowly through the wind like coins dropped in water. Fat and pretty in the night sky, shining silver at the hint of moonlight. A Christmas snow come early.

Flurries dusted the smooth stones of the gatehouse, spreading in patches in the courtyard beyond, powdering down on chill-hardened footprints in black convent mud. It whitened the tarred wood crosses in the nuns' cemetery and around them clung to the grave grass. Bowed with hoarfrost since the Feast of Saint Cecilia, the blades now arced fully to the ground.

Snow drifted across the slate roofs of the dormitory, the refectory, and the church. It hissed on the twin chimneys of the bakehouse, still hot to the touch with the previous evening's fire, and it fell on the dark, squat shack between the bakehouse and the cloister.

From outside, the chaplain's residence appeared half-sized. Its walls stood shoulder high and tilted inward, leaning in on themselves. With shifting soils, rotting wood, and the accumulated force of winter upon winter winds, the walls seemed kept from meeting by the thin support of a thatched roof.

Of course, the cottage's smaller features had also warped with years, those problems more easily fixed having gone as untended as the larger dilemma of apparently imminent collapse. In the center of the church-facing wall, the doorway had strayed from square, requiring a sound kick to its lower corner to gain entry or exit. Waist-high in the same wall, the shack's one window had been similarly skewed. A plank wood shutter swung forward and back with each breath of the storm, opening and closing like a floodgate, letting flurries spill inside.

Father Francis stood barefoot on a thick carpet of wood chips, startled from his prayers. Rusted with years, the hook-latch had come loose, and now the shutter clapped in its frame so violently that it shook the cottage like tremors of the earth. Tufts of thatch floated down from ceiling to floor, spinning with the draft. When he looked up toward the disturbance, the cold air stung his eye. A phantom pain throbbed in the empty socket beside it, which was covered with thick, scarred skin. The top left side of his face was a blank slate, features rubbed away like words carved in stone eroded by time.

The priest's one room served as his workshop, home, and chapel, though at a glance it seemed just the first of these, cluttered as it was with the implements and media of his craft. Heavy woodwork table, round chopping block at its side. Wide logs and piles of scrap wood, large and small. Hatchets, mallets, and carving knives—tools of all kinds lay strewn on the table and on the frozen floor among the shavings. Only in the corner, where a narrow sleeping plank lay across three shin-high stumps, was evidence that the cottage was home to any activity other than the shaping of wood.

He had built this cottage himself when he had felt strong enough for such labor, and he believed he had built it well. True, the walls leaned in a bit, but he had dug them deep into the earth for insulation, and they had surprised even the builder with their resilience, having served far longer than intended. Despite its appearance from without, the roof had not dropped an inch. Still, when the chaplain stood in prayer or woodwork, he did so stooped in his robe. Gradually, the floor had risen, his back had curved, his chin had tucked down into his shoulders, and he came to carry himself as a man much smaller and older than his true size or age.

What to blame but so many years of carving? Spoons, bowls, saint statues for the church, statuettes for convent guests, crosses, crosses, and more crosses for the plague dead—he had carved a forest by now, he was sure. He had brought order and use to the chaos of the wilderness surrounding them, one tree at a time. He had worked so quickly, so constantly that as wood chips collected and layered upon the dirt floor, he had paid no mind to the loss of height inside the cottage with each year's layer of wood. Shaving by shaving, such an enterprise had raised the floor toward the ceiling, and the once tall friar had bent in the process. Little surprise that, to Francis, life had come to seem a series of choices with always the same options: Shrink or bump your head.

The cold wood chips pushed between his toes while he prayed. He moved from Matins to Lauds without a moment between, singing both sides of a call and response. "Oh Lord come to my assistance," he said. "Oh God make haste to help me." Then he slid his hands to his knees and bowed slowly toward his bed plank, toward the dark wood cross that hung above it.

Normally between the first and second offices Francis would break long enough to sink into the pages of his *lectio divina*—sacred reading, reading as prayer, which, with its word-by-word consideration of a Greek or Latin text, became something more than Bible study, something less than trance. On most nights, even as he finished the final hymn of Matins, he would reach for the single hand-copied volume he had managed to carry with him when he was exiled to this outpost half a lifetime ago. He had personally filled it with passages from the texts that had been most meaningful to him during his study for the priesthood. The night before, he had turned to Augustine, taking great solace that a saint could be made of so lust-filled a youth. *What is man*, the saint had written, *but a particle of creation?*

In such words Francis would immerse himself and hope to come up clean of the filth of vanity. He reminded himself that nothing else should matter when contemplating the greatness of God. If all his life was but a speck in the sweep of the divine, what were his many sins?

Most nights he would seek solace in the remembrance of this knowledge. And yet, in this early morning darkness, his woodwork seemed more pressing, so pressing in fact that he had forsaken his sacred reading, moving without delay through the first and second Hours of prayer to make time for the work ahead of him, for a recent confession had troubled him from his routine.

The nun's name, if ever he had known it, now escaped him. She had come to his cottage from her chores in the kitchen, on the pretense of delivering a snack of spiced wine and hard bread. A tall girl, spider-fanged but not uncomely. Light and awkward in her walk as an ass freed from the yoke.

When she had set the tray on his workbench, she asked his leave to make her confession. This he granted, if grudgingly, not merely because it was his role in the community but because, yes, she was not uncomely, and because absolution tended to be a simple matter with the younger nuns, usually requiring little more than a moment or two.

But this particular young nun had a catalog of sins to report. Minor faults, but many: She had tarried in her work, nearly missing Vespers. On another occasion, to avoid shoveling out the sheep stalls, she had put on enthrallment in prayer, fainting and claiming to have had a vision of Christ. And later, she had feigned receiving the grace of great sickness to remain under thick blankets for days in her bed. Typical sins for the unmarriageable daughters of nobility. Yet she was not without peculiar offense. While in the lavabo, she confessed, she had fallen into the habit of looking too long on the oldest of her sisters, standing lock-eyed in fascination at the gray slump of their bodies. Sister Phillip, the magistra, had a shape she found especially compelling.

"Truly, she has udders, Father," the novice had swooned. "They hang from her collar long as my arms! We novices have been tempted to grab hold and swing around the maypole!"

Francis sighed. "You increase your sin in the pleasure of the telling, Sister."

The girl's mouth tightened and crooked to one side as if in thoughtful consideration. Then she asked, "May I add the increase of my sin to this confession, or shall I wait for the next?"

*By the next I could be dead*, Francis supposed, *and the duty to hear her would leave me.*

"Better you wait," he said, "Have you need to confess any faults in excess of these?"

"Oh, yes."

She gladly told of other sins: Desiring what seemed to her the ease of work in the scriptorium but lacking both the patience and the talent for illumination, she had spilled ink across a sister's psalter in a jealous rage. Another sister she had stuck in the thigh with her stylus. On several occasions in the refectory she had made lewd gestures toward Sister Phillip, though only twice had she been caught.

"And once," the novice continued. "I spat in my sister's soup."

"Spat?" Francis said.

"Spat, Father," she repeated, then made a pucker of her lips and allowed a drop of saliva to squeeze through in explanation.

"I know of spitting, Sister. Did Magistra Phillip find you in this action?"

"Oh no, Father. It was not the magistra's soup. For that I think I would have been beaten. It was the soup of a junior sister—and surely she deserved it."

"Did she then."

"Oh yes. I found her failing to pay proper attention to the mealtime reading."

"And to her soup," Francis said. "So you did this for piety's sake? Sinning for benefit of your sister's soul?"

The novice's eyes shone at the suggestion. "Why, yes! I surely did exactly that."

"And did your sister see you in this sacrifice, to better profit from it?"

"Not she—but others," the girl said hopefully.

"These others called attention to your charity, I suppose? For the benefit of your sister's mindfulness?"

"No, Father," the girl replied. "Not before she sipped."

Petty jokes and insults, like so much he heard from the youngsters crowding Gaerdegen's cloister. Such trivial days. Just twenty years later and already children knew nothing of the Death.

When it seemed the girl had told all she might, Francis gave his *absolve te* and was about to proffer penance when he noticed the intensity of her gaze. Most of the nuns were used to his appearance, but she was new and apparently shameless. She gawked openly at his damaged face.

"Father, may I pose a question?" she asked.

He had no wish to explain his scars to this girl, and she had no doubt heard some half-true version of the events surrounding his injury. But just as he prepared to deflect her prying, she asked something unexpected.

"Is it your duty to report to the Lord Bishop even those faults you hear within the holy walls of this sacrament?"

Such questions were uncommon from novices. While many were naive enough to imagine a worldly tally of their sins was kept somewhere, few were sufficiently astute to know sins absolved are not always forgiven. This novice, however, seemed to Francis to possess each of these traits in equal measure. Wise in her perceptions, if not in her sins. What should a bishop care of her offenses? And could the girl believe her chaplain took sufficient interest in her soul to think ever again of her faults? Truth be told, in confession, Father Francis had honed the skill of hearing sins without considering them, the better to forget.

"You flatter me in assuming I have the bishop's ear," he said by way of answer. "When would a humble convent priest have opportunity to make such a report?"

"Why just next week, of course," the novice had said. "When we are blessed with visitation by His Grace."

Francis's pinched eye went wide. Every fifth year the bishop or his representative made an inspection tour of all the women's houses in the bishopric, testing the soundness of their leadership, their trueness to the faith. Francis had endured several visitations. Had it been so long since the last? No, he recalled, it had not.

"You are mistaken, Sister. Gaerdegen is not yet due for inspection."

"It must concern a grave matter, then," she said.

"Would not the chaplain be told? His ignorance on the matter would embarrass the house."

"Forgive me, Father. If so junior a sister as myself knew of the visitation, I was assured you did as well. Even in chapter we have spoken of it."

These nuns keep their secrets as they keep their crotches, was the only sense Francis could make of the surprising news. Perhaps the chaplain would not be told, to embarrass not the house but himself.

"You say it is the bishop who is coming so far into the wilderness?" he asked. "And not a clerk from his court?"

"My cousin is abbess of our sister house to the south," the novice said proudly. "She tells me the bishop will make an inspection in advance of schedule at her urging." The novice then dropped her voice to a conspiratorial whisper. "For many in our sister house have heard that Gaerdegen has strayed from the spirit of the Rule."

"I see," Francis said.

"And so to my question?"

"Of reporting your sins?"

The girl went tight-lipped, her cheeks puffing indignantly. "My sins?" she scoffed. "What would the bishop care of my sins? I ask only because the magistra has dealt with such questions in our lessons."

A strange issue for the education of nuns in the novitiate, Francis thought, but who knows? "If it is a canon question, Sister, ask it as such."

"Very well: Does a priest's obedience to the bishop govern his service as chaplain to an abbey?"

"A priest serves a convent until he is bidden otherwise, but the oath I have sworn is to Mother Church, not to Mother Abbess."

"So you will report faults to the bishop, faults that might do harm to the Church, no matter whose faults they may be?"

"What the bishop asks I will tell."

The novice nodded with satisfaction, as if finally having prompted an appropriate response. Suddenly, she seemed impatient to leave the chaplain's side.

"May I now have my penance, Father?"

"Of course."

Francis took up the pitcher of spiced wine the girl had brought and poured a measure of it into a wooden bowl. Her faced brightened at the sight: a warm drink on a December day was not a bad penance at all. But then the priest began to hack and cough, as though attempting to free the root of his tongue from the back of his throat. When he had regained himself, he held his head over the bowl and puckered his lips. Then he dropped a yellow-green glob into the center of the purple wine.

"Your penance, Sister," Francis told her. "Drink. Then go and sin no more."

He had little patience for the machinations of this place. They seemed small-scale enactments of the dramas of the world, dramas he had imagined well quit. For drama he had seen, and he had come to have scarce interest in it. Nor had he interest in whatever conspiracy this brash novice had in mind. But a visit from the bishop—from the bishop himself and not some underling—struck the chaplain as not entirely without possibility.

The bishop was well known to have transported craftsmen from the far corners of Christendom, and even beyond, to brighten the episcopal palace with works of pious and aesthetic beauty. It had been some time since Francis had carved anything closer to art than a replacement spoke for the abbey oxcart, twenty years since he'd made his masterwork, the crucifix that hung above the altar in the abbey church. But such things, he told himself, never fully leave a man. The memory of grace is often grace enough.

It was memory then that sent Francis slowly through his room now, five days after the nun's confession, though even this slight movement was made difficult by the morning's fierce cold, barely remediated by the cabin's meager fire. Difficult too was his selection of the tools he would need to complete the project he hoped would be his last within the abbey walls. As he went, he said as loudly as he had prayed, "And when I've finished it, he'll take me from this place."

He could imagine the scene to the last detail; he had carved it with his mind's eye like a relief. The bishop, having suffered to hear the nuns curse each other from Sext through Vespers, would give hale greeting to the chaplain, glad to lay eyes upon a brother priest after so much nunnish quibbling. He would then call two of the bishop's men to bring into view the priest's gift, the statue of the Virgin he would finish carving this very morning.

On his workbench, Francis lit a sheep-fat candle; its glow fell on parchment sketches of ink and coal, on unpolished blades of chisels, glinting off their sharpened tips.

"What an artisan you are, Father Francis," the priest muttered in the candlelight. "To think you have been wandering in this wilderness these long years when you might have been peopling my cathedral with saints."

Even as he spoke the words, he knew their absurdity. Carving saints had sent him into this exile in the first place.

# Chapter 7

HOW HAD THE years fallen away like so many shavings? If his life now was what remained after the raw material of time had been carved away, Father Francis felt he could remember what it was like to be uncut wood.

When he was a boy, he had often traveled on an oxcart with his father, brother, and a pair of village woodsmen, thick-handed fellows who rarely spoke but swung their axes with the authority of preachers in the pulpit. And if they were the evangelists, Francis's father was scripture itself, the authority behind their every movement. Master carver Hugh Budge was lead craftsman of the cathedral that was to be the gem of the province, as his father had been before him. The grand church had cast its shadow over every life and death in the vicinity for approaching sixty years. Everyone hoped they would see it completed, but the math of measuring such hopes against the length of a human life was merciless. "We build not for you but for your children," the bishop told an impatient flock. That the same had been said to their grandparents they did not need to reply, and nor did they mind much. Construction kept half the town employed.

They rolled to the edge of the wood and then continued on foot, one of the woodsmen leading the mare that would drag the fallen timber back to the cart. At the time it was a mystery to Francis what his father looked for on these excursions. Sometimes he wanted only the straightest of trees, other times the thickest. Occasionally his eye was drawn to a slight bend in the trunk, or the curve of a branch where it had strained toward a patch of light for years on end. Just like men, his father often told him, trees were formed by resources and desire.

Standing in a clearing, he pointed to the trees at its edge, on the border between open field and dense forest. Even their upmost branches extended horizontally, their leaves fanning out to catch the sun's every ray. Francis stared intently at the spot to which his father's hand directed; his older brother Robert glanced upward but continued sharpening his ax.

"Look," he told his sons. "See how they contort themselves? They need the light to grow, and so they stretch toward wherever it may be found. But too much wanting will do them in. If too many branches grow in the same direction, what will happen?"

Francis had two good eyes then. Just an upward tilt of his chin and without turning his head he could take in the treetops and half the surrounding sky.

"The whole tree topples?" he said.

In his memory his father nodded with such significance that he seemed to say: *Such is the price of longing, my son.* But really, he only said, "This one."

The woodsmen looked at the tree, then at each other. It was bent, useless for lumber. They might chop it and dry it for firewood if it fell in a storm, but to take it down with axes was hardly worth the effort of resharpening when the work was done. Only a crooked house could be built of such deformity.

Their hesitation was not new to Francis, nor were his father's unusual choices surprising to them.

"Yes," Hugh Budge said as if in answer to an unspoken question. "I am quite sure."

The oak's knots did not make it easy. The woodsmen worked the better part of the morning, alternating blows like the arms of a windmill, first this ax upright in the air, poised to strike, then that, with a steady thwack between them, keeping time.

When it finally came down, Francis inspected its rings. The grain had a deep rich red, which would run beneath the flesh of the saint his father would carve like a network of veins, old life hidden behind the new.

"Let's get it to the shop," his father said.

A man-high length of tree trunk is far more difficult to move than even the stoutest of fellows or their most stubbornly held opinions. It will not be wrestled or cajoled but must be hoisted by a horse, a winch, and a web of leather straps. The woodsmen hauled it from the forest and through the winding streets of the artisans' district. After they had lowered it into place on a platform in the Budge workroom, Francis's father directed them to remove its bark while he sharpened his carving implements, and then the real effort began.

Full-sized standing figures like those for which the Budge shop was known were made from sections of tree trunk split down the middle and then hollowed out at the center, leaving a sturdy arc of hardwood to be clamped securely to a moving workbench, allowing the massive slab of lumber to turn as easily as a well-greased wheel on its axis. Hatchets did the rough work of finding the outlines of a human form, followed by curved and straight adzes and chisels of varying blade widths. As Francis watched his father's helpers work, it had been this crude hacking that had been most astonishing to him. That there seemed to be a saint hidden in every block of wood was an unending miracle to the boy. When he walked through the woods, he put his ear to the bark to see if he could hear them speaking, asking to be found and shown to the world.

Only after the rough work had been done did Francis's father step forward to ease his chisel into the hardwood. The tip slid into the grain like butter, a curl of almond-colored shaving rolling in on itself. The miracle that this act of reducing raw material, decreasing its volume, narrowing its profile, shedding weight with every incision—that this act of destruction could somehow also be an act of creation—how was this possible? And yet after an hour spent in such reduction, the master could step backward and see the wood block had not become less than it had been, but more. Even a glance would register no longer the tree it was but the figure it was becoming.

"Do not suppose God would have us make use only of perfection," Master Budge said. As he lowered his knife, Francis saw the oak's twists and knots had been fashioned into the whorl and sweep of an angel's wings, its natural lines directed in such a way it seemed the wood had always been intended only for this purpose.

In his more blasphemous moments—rare in those days and kept resolutely to himself—Francis wondered if this was not the true transubstantiation. It did not go quickly, of course. Unlike Communion, carving was not accomplished with just holy words and a tinkling of bells. It began always in the forest. When his father was feeling mystical about it, he would trace every carved figure in the Budge workshop back to the acorn it once had been, a world of detail in a drab little shell.

His own work lacked such grace. While his brother clearly inherited their father's skill, Francis's figures were static. No matter how many hours he spent perfecting lines and curves, then polishing his carving until it was as smooth as soap, he always came up short.

After their return from the forest one winter evening, he had sat with his father, brother, and the two woodsmen as his mother and his brother's wife, Helena, served them a hearty stew.

Hesitantly, he took a small figure he had been working on from his pocket. A female saint, which one he wasn't yet certain, but he hoped it might be the Virgin, for his father had told him that along with Christ on his cross, she was the greatest achievement to which a carver might aspire. "But you'll never do her justice until you have found a model worthy of the subject," Hugh Budge had said. "She is the maiden upon whom all the world depends. And you must first be ready to know what that means."

Studying his work, Francis wanted desperately to believe he was ready. He was particularly proud of his statue's eyes, which he managed to make round rather than boxy, as in his previous efforts, and more or less the same size.

"Let's see what you've got here," Robert said, smirking at the younger boy's handiwork. He turned it over, ran a thumb across the figure's face, then held it out at arm's length to take in its full effect. "Sorry to tell you this, Brother, but it looks carved of wood."

"Of course it does! It *is* carved of wood!"

"Yes, but should it look as if it was?"

To illustrate his point, Robert rummaged a moment in a waist pouch, and then presented his hand with a flourish. At the center of his palm was a carved depiction of the stray cat that haunted the woodshop. It sat in precisely the manner it was most often: its paw held aloft, a tongue lolled out of its mouth to clean itself. Even unpolished and unpainted it had a startling effect. It was nearly alive. In its uncanny facsimile of life, his brother's dirty rat catcher seemed more holy than his own meager effort to depict the Mother of God. Francis ran his finger over its back, half-expecting it to purr, or to scratch.

"Maybe with more practice, I—" Francis began.

"Not everything is effort, Brother. Your carving has no life in it because you have not yet lived life, and when will you start? You always prefer only to watch, to observe. And then when you carve you make endless markings on the wood to avoid making any mistakes or nicking yourself with the blade. If you fear the chisel, there can be no blood in the flesh you bring to life. You must allow yourself joy and pain. You're very smart, but what do you feel?"

"The boy needs a woman," one of the woodsmen said, "then he'll get a good feel."

"Not if he tries to feel them first," the other woodsmen answered, "then he won't be able to catch them when they run away."

"Leave Francis alone," Helena cut in. "When you lot learn your letters as well as he has, then you can lecture him on life."

She had always been kind to him. The barrel maker's daughter, his playmate in the courtyard of the artisans' district since childhood, she knew well his skill with letters. They had learned together from the cathedral architect's draftsman, who in idle moments traced words for them in the abundant construction dust. They had practiced writing messages to each other in the dirt, delighting in the open secret of it when so few adults around them could read. How like magic it had seemed then, the notion that meaning could be conveyed through patterns of shapes upon the ground. And it became all the more so when her ability outstripped his own. He still kept several of the rhyming missives she had written for him on strips of birch bark, comic descriptions of their neighbors that made him blush.

Then as now, Helena looked upon him with the protective fondness of an older sister. Though she was scarcely a year his senior, her look told him she still saw him as a child, as did they all.

"Don't worry, my boy," his father said in a whisper. "God has more sense than to make everyone a master craftsman." He had meant his words to encourage, but it was as though the tip of a shoulder knife had been thrust into Francis's heart. Surely his father had never offered such encouragement to his brother, who God had indeed made a craftsman with a talent on course to surpass even Hugh Budge himself.

Talent aside, Francis might have lived and died a member of the guild no different than generations of his family had been. There was plenty of work to be done by carvers who were merely capable. "Adequate is better than most," his father would say at other moments of ill-conceived reassurance. But one day in the shop the bishop's clerk had noticed the boy poring over his father's account ledger.

"A child like that ought to serve the Church," the clerk had told his father. "I'll see to it the bishop makes necessary arrangements."

His family had long had the favor of the bishop; ultimately it was the carving that would give the cathedral its most notable detail and so it was upon their skill that his legacy rested. For two generations, the family had kept the cathedral on schedule, such as it was. Still they had been astonished by the offer. That a craftsman's boy would become a priest was not unprecedented—"Our Lord himself was a carpenter's son," his father liked to say—but it usually required extravagant patronage, which they soon learned the bishop would provide.

The remainder of his adolescence was spent in a friary several days' travel from the city, where he passed his days mastering Latin, oratory, theology, and logic—a year of each. None of it offered the immediate satisfaction of his family's craft, but he was relieved to be free of the burden of inadequacy. As he learned the gestures a priest must make during Mass, he hoped no one noticed that his hands moved as a carver's might, as if he always held a mallet or a blade.

# Chapter 8

FRANCIS HAD ONLY just begun his final year of study when he received word of the accident. His father and brother both, while installing the Holy Spirit in the form of a dove high above the cathedral's main altar, had fallen from their scaffold. Witnesses said the brother had lost his footing and the father had slipped when he tried to steady him. Both men had landed on the altar thirty feet below.

"Thanks be to God," the bishop's clerk's letter to Francis had said, "the dove remains in place."

He made his way quickly home for the funeral and found the guild had made it a fine affair, held in the unfinished cathedral with special permission, with a Mass offered by the bishop himself. He assisted as an altar server, and when he looked out over the assembled crowd, he saw the expressions of love and respect that his family had inspired. The cathedral architect wept openly as he embraced Francis's mother. At her side, his brother's widow, Helena, was surrounded by her father the barrel maker and her six younger brothers. Standing in a row, they resembled a line of casks of different sizes, each with a leak sprung where tears spilled from their eyes.

Only upon his return to his family's workshop had he discovered the full extent of the work his father had left unfinished. A score of statues remained in various stages of completion. His father had not been one to reach one journey's end before changing course to embark on another. He worked as inspiration found him, at which time he dropped all else to sketch an expression he hoped to achieve on an unformed face, or rough cut the posture of the hands. His efforts would then be followed upon by a team of apprentices and journeymen, who lacked the master's vision but could execute certain of his plans admirably well. The last steps would be taken by the master himself, and with increasing regularity by his eldest son. With both now gone, the shop workers were adrift. None had the confidence to take charge, and all feared they would not be paid with their employer in the ground.

Francis took up his father's shoulder knife and went to work. While there were more than a dozen saints he might have chosen from, he was drawn to the figure of the Virgin, which seemed so close to completion he hoped he could not fail too badly.

His past efforts, he knew, had never shaken off that lifeless quality his brother had taken pleasure in noting. But he was nothing if not dutiful. The lifework of generations of Budge craftsmen was on the line, and he would not let the tragedy of his father's and brother's deaths be compounded by an unfinished contract.

From behind him, a woman's voice said, "You've missed your calling, Francis. Had you spent the last three years in your father's shop and not bent over holy books, you would be a master carver by now."

If pressed, he might have admitted that he had loved his brother's widow since he was a boy. She was closer to Francis's age than Robert's, and for a time it had been a matter of open speculation which of the master woodcarver's sons she would marry. But then it became obvious to all which brother had better prospects. His selection for the priesthood had been seen by his parents as an equalizer; at last, the younger boy would not seem a pale imitation of the older. Francis, however, saw it as the final stone in the wall that would forever keep him from the future he wanted most of all.

Helena moved closer to the worktable, reached out and put her hand on the grain. "Even without an apprenticeship you are nearly so."

He had not distinguished himself in his studies, but had done all that was required, slowly whittling himself into a man of the cloth. He had learned to play the part and hoped desperately to do so convincingly.

"Since I could hold a knife, I was my father's apprentice," he answered. "Today I am Christ's. It's his skill you see in mine."

"Your father would be hurt to hear that. While he lived, he taught you well."

"My father knows Christ better than I do now. As does my brother. They must sorrow for us, for the distance between the world and its reward."

"Doubtless they do not sorrow to see you carry on our family's craft."

"My vocation has not permanently sheathed my blade."

Had Helena studied her husband's brother, she would've seen there was no sign of mischief in him, not then. When he said "blade," he meant only blade; when he said "sheath," he did not mean the lower folds of his robe. Her husband had not been so pious; the two brothers were much alike—in their appearance, in their voices, in their shared smell of green wood—there was just that intangible difference. She could not help herself, stepping in closer, drawn in to his familiar presence as if by habit, crowding the man and the Virgin he carved.

"What a terrible pity that would be," she said.

Francis continued, oblivious, speaking as if alone in the room, as if working out the themes of the coming Sunday's sermon.

"Yes, it would be a pity," he said. "Whatever we are capable of, we must put it in the service of Christ. I, with my knife, a smith with his hammer. . . . Millers should mill for Christ, tanners tan, tailors cut cloth—"

"And what of widows?"

He stopped and looked at her. It was customary to think of a brother's wife as a sister, but Helena held his gaze now as a sister would not, with a directness that suggested she had made a decision and he was a part of it.

Widows should weep, he should have said.

# Chapter 9

FRANCIS RETURNED TO his studies confused by competing emotions. Naturally, his heart felt heavy with his family's loss. His father had always been kind and nurturing. His brother had been a rival for their father's attention, but there was never any bitterness in it, not often in any case. And beyond his own bereavement, his mother now was alone in the world. Yet in the instants between these heartbeats of grief, he could barely contain the lightness he felt at the sudden turn his life had taken.

He cataloged the ways in which he had not committed a mortal sin. He had not wronged his brother, for his brother was already in the grave. He had not broken his priestly vows, for he had not taken them yet. He had not succumbed to a moment of temptation, he told himself, because Helena's return the following night in such obvious need for his comfort made their ongoing interaction far more an act of charity than of sin. And if that was perhaps a stretch, he was in any case certain that he had not led her blindly into perdition. On each of the five successive nights when she found him at work in the small hours in his family's woodshop, he had advised her to seek absolution at her earliest convenience after she left.

Moreover, was there not some biblical precedent for the predicament in which he found himself? He knew well from scripture the conditions under which a brother should marry his brother's widow. It was the way of the Jews in those bygone days that if no child had been born to a dead man, his brother must make an effort to produce an heir for the sorrowing bride. But his brother and Helena had been married for years. What did the ancient laws say if the brother's widow was barren, as surely must be the case? And what would scripture deem appropriate if the living brother was soon to become a priest?

For months, he thought of nothing else. Her touch had been the first he had received from a woman, and he could not stop himself from reliving it to confirm it had not been an adolescent's fantasy. Even during his ordination exam, his thoughts drifted toward her flesh with predictable results. Called upon to translate a passage of the Vulgate, he turned to the Song of Solomon and recited, "Your navel is a rounded goblet that never lacks blended wine. Your waist is a mound of wheat encircled by lilies. Your breasts are like two fawns, twins of a gazelle." His instructors noted that they could see his passion for the text even through his voluminous cassock, but he managed to pass.

When he returned home that spring to allow his mother the joy of seeing that her surviving son had indeed become a priest, he had been pleasantly surprised to find Helena still in the household. He had wondered if she would return to her parents' home, the better to find another man to marry. But there she was tending a fire in the kitchen at his mother's side. Only when she turned did he notice her belly swollen in her dress.

Francis had seen enough of pregnancy to know it was nearly her time. Though he might have momentarily felt terror for the accusations of lasciviousness that were sure to follow, he was instead overwhelmed with unexpected joy—joy in this confirmation that the moments he had relived endlessly for the better part of a year had not been a dream. Her touch had been real. The feeling that touch had brought to him had been real.

Helena smiled at him sadly, then spoke loud enough for Francis's mother to hear.

"I see from your face that you've not heard our blessed news, dear brother," she said. "I thought we should send word, but your mother thought it best we save the surprise. Isn't it a great miracle that the child was conceived the night before Robert fell?"

Francis reached for the table to steady himself, understanding all. Had her pregnancy not come to pass, she would have been encouraged to return to her family's home, full though it was with six brothers and scarcely enough room to breathe. Now, however, the carvers' guild would provide for her and her baby. And if the baby was a boy, the son would be given an apprenticeship as a master carver's heir from an early age. His livelihood would be secured, as would hers.

"And with a priest for an uncle the child will be doubly be blessed," she said. "Will you pray for us?"

Helena knelt before him, and he traced his hand in a cross above her. Following his benediction, she reached for his arm to steady herself as she climbed to her feet. When he pulled his hand away, he found tucked in his palm a small roll of birch bark, identical to those upon which she once wrote the secret messages they shared as children. As soon as he was out of his mother's sight, he unrolled it and read with despair. It was not a comment on any neighbor's unfortunate predicaments, but their own:

*I am sorry you have learned this way.*

Through the weeks that followed, they spoke nothing of their nights in the woodshop. If she had any desire for their recurrence in the future, she made no indication, offering him only the sisterly affection she had shown before her husband's death. On the one occasion he broached the subject, she chided him good-naturedly.

"What can be done, Francis? I am your brother's widow, and you are a priest. Let us be content to share your family's household and watch the child grow."

Only when he pressed his case through the last weeks of her time did she become short with him.

"Francis, you may have noticed my body already has one occupant. It will accommodate no more."

"And after?"

"After, I will surely need any care and assistance you might offer."

"But nothing more?"

"More?" she scoffed. "Would you wish me seen as the whore of a lecherous monk, like some bawdy ballad sung by a traveling bard? Far better to be a stalwart widow bravely raising a tragic craftsman's child. At least then my life will not be so easily reduced to scandal."

When the baby was born, the wonder of having participated in this creation was tempered by the inability to acknowledge the work was his alone. His brother, as ever, was credited as the master craftsman, while he was a man fit only to mumble useless words. Francis baptized the child as if it were not his own.

He looked forward to putting his bitterness behind him with a fresh start in some minor parish in need of a priest. But then the bishop's clerk encouraged him to remain long enough to put his family's affairs in order.

"We have noticed a significant development in your skill as a woodcarver, Francis," the bishop's clerk said to him. "As we have searched in vain for a successor to your father, it would be fitting if you saw his work on the cathedral through to completion. Already we have fallen off schedule."

And so he remained. Yet he could not bear to be in the household with his mother, Helena, and the infant—a boy who could not have resembled him more. The outward and inward lies required of continuing to lodge with his family drove him instead to pass both days and nights at the Budge workshop, sleeping in a partially completed manger being built for the cathedral's larger-than-life Nativity scene. So close to the materials and implements of his family's craft, he carved with abandon from the moment he brushed straw from his hair each morning. For the first time in his life there were no more of his overly careful sketches and timid incisions—just anger, intuition, and a sharpened blade.

Through the summer months he carved in the open window of the workshop. Even with a breeze from the town square, his tunic became so drenched with sweat he often would cast it off, his bare shoulders leaving wet marks on the wood as he worked. When he stepped away to examine his progress, he brushed away the oak slivers that had become lodged in the hair of his chest.

Certain ladies of the town could not help but pause to watch him as they passed. The Cathedral City had more than its share of widows. Building with stone was always dangerous, and building with stone hoisted to great heights even more so. En route to the site of their misfortune, the wives of various artisans who had met fates similar to Francis's father and brother could often be heard in conversation.

"The Budge boy has become a man."

"And a man of God at that."

"I am finding myself in sudden need of making a confession."

That his company seemed to relieve the sorrows of several village widows made Francis feel that he indeed might be a good priest after all, despite the manner in which he ministered. He tried to put his dead brother's wife behind him, first in the arms of the dead quarryman's wife, and then the dead stonemason's wife, and then the dead bell founder's wife. ("We ought to form a guild of our own," the dead glassmaker's wife once said. "If we all paid dues, he could devote himself to our craft full-time," the dead plasterer's wife replied.) His clerical robes had provided fine cover for each of these liaisons. The older women of the city spoke openly of his skill and generosity in the granting of absolution.

There was an undeniable element of physical pleasure in all this, but that was not the young priest's primary fascination with the new and unexpected role he had found for himself. When Francis visited the workshop now and viewed the previous day's carving, he saw that the change in his character could be seen also in his works. It was no mere fancy that he had a surer hand, a clearer vision. His subject, after all, was the human form, and suddenly he knew it as never before. How could he carve Saint Afra's torment until he had seen a score of mouths contorted in expressions that looked so like pain? How could he depict Saint Lucy's faultless breasts until he had seen every possible variation on their form? To capture the likenesses of such exemplars of humanity as the saints, he told himself, he must be intimately acquainted with the qualities of flesh, the curve of hip that determined how a fold of fabric would drape across the thigh, the nape of the neck that showed him how Saint Winefride's hair would tumble down.

This last detail was provided to him not by the widow of a dead artisan, but by the living bishop's quite lively mother, who had been widowed so long he never heard who or what her husband had been.

She had considered herself the uncrowned queen of the bishopric since the day her son ascended to the episcopal throne. There was no question all that was his was hers. She oversaw the decoration of the cathedral as if it was her personal sitting room, from the motifs in the altar screen to the patterns on the floor, to the painted evocation of the heavens in the vaulted ceiling. Planning, materials, and execution: there was not a detail over which she failed to extend her watchful eye. The craftsmen naturally did not escape her gaze. Most trembled as she walked the nave, lest her attention turn on their handiwork and a week's labor be casually undone.

Francis had often seen how solicitous his father had been in her presence. He alone among the artisans could find ways to steer her impression of his art. But even he stood up straighter as she examined the carvings, and carefully chose his words. There were rumors of certain craftsmen falling into her particular good graces. "Woe betide such a man," the elder Budge said. "Whatever enjoyment he might briefly sow, he will reap tenfold its opposite when her favor fades."

Now that he was in charge of the family business, Francis had not minded too much when she limited her gaze to critiquing his work within the cathedral, but as rumors of his skill as a confessor reached her suite in the episcopal palace, she began visiting the Budge workshop.

He was already asleep in his manger when she surprised him that first night. "Father Francis, might you have time to hear a poor widow's confession?"

No sooner had he assented to hear her sins, however, than she became distracted from the stated intention of her visit. All through the previous evening, he had been preparing to affix a corpus Christi his brother had completed to a dark wood cross that dominated the shop's back wall. She paused before the carved body—more muscular than Francis imagined Christ himself would have been, but still as convincing and compelling an image of the Lord as he had seen.

"Our Lord looks so powerful in your brother's depiction," she said. "Perhaps you served as his model?"

"No, not I, my lady."

"Don't be so modest, Father. We have all seen you at work in the shop window. Why play the hidden saint?"

She tugged at the leather strap that kept his tunic closed.

"Your confession, my lady. Have you forgotten?"

"I'll need something to confess first."

The bishop's mother followed him through the shop, stripping him of his garments as he fumbled backward, tripping over saints lying prone on the floor. She had succeeded in stripping him fully by the time they reached the back wall, where his bare back bumped against the bottom of the dark wood cross. He had nowhere else to go when they heard the shop door open.

"My lady? Father Francis?"

"Oh bother," the bishop's mother said. "It is my son's clerk."

"Here? Why?"

"I asked for him to fetch me after my confession. If you were not so stubborn, we'd be done by now."

With his tunic and cloak draped over a carved saint on the far side of the shop, Francis wore nothing but the belt that held his blade. He slipped even that off now and clambered up the back wall just as the clerk entered the room.

A lantern held aloft, the clerk lifted it in one direction then another, scanning the room. "Ah, Madame, there you are. And Father Francis?"

"He is around here somewhere," she said. "I was inspecting his handiwork while waiting for him to shrive me."

The clerk approached and stood directly before where Francis hung—on the dark wood cross, naked as Christ in his torment, concealed only by the half-light and the clerk's decision not to look too closely.

"Francis has progressed remarkably in his skill," the clerk said. "There is a spark of life in his carving that I have never previously observed."

"Yes, just a spark now," the bishop's mother said. "When next I visit, I hope it will grow into a much larger flame."

# Chapter 10

THE BISHOP'S MOTHER did return, often, and his inspiration grew in ways that were satisfying to them both. But in truth, he more than anyone knew that the spark of life the bishop's clerk mentioned was precisely what even his best work lacked.

He thought obsessively of the pocket-sized cat his brother had shown him. What was it about that wooden trinket that had been so convincing? The shape was easy enough to emulate. Anyone could trace and then cut a form. But there was a quality in the eyes, their precise angle and implied directionality that made one believe in looking upon it that the cat too could see, as if it was not occupied waiting to pounce on a mouse but might suddenly turn to him and wonder what he intended to do. It was an object carved not just to be looked upon but to create the impression it might look back. That was the magic of the thing. It seemed capable of knowing.

There could be no doubt that through all this he had progressed in his art, and he hoped his family had noticed. When he stopped by the Budge household to retrieve fresh clothing and leave his ripped and soiled tunics to be washed and mended, it was also with the childish need for his mother's praise, which she never gave as fulsomely as he hoped. Whatever he accomplished paled before her imagination of all that might have been done by the men she had lost.

Yet even worse were the occasions when he did not find her at home, when he was met by Helena, who received him coolly.

"I hear you are making a name for yourself as the choice confessor of widows," she said, her words sharper than any knife he owned.

"If only all widows would seek my services," he replied. "You would be astonished by the sins I've been exposed to."

"If you mean to say that widows do what they must to get by in this world that has no use for them, I would not be surprised at all. Survival is no sin."

When the day of the cathedral's unveiling finally came, the village thronged the steps to view the interior of the structure that had dominated the memory of every soul in town.

Of particular interest were the statues carved by the Budge family. It was well known that Robert and Hugh had died in the service of their devotion to both the Church and their craft, and that the master carver's sole surviving heir had delayed his clerical career for the sake of finishing his family's work. They were prepared to be awed by them.

He did not expect the whispers. Yet as he watched the crowds who had come to view the newly opened cathedral, that is just what he heard. To be sure, he observed among many the convivial mirth of enthusiasm as the long-awaited church filled with the faithful, but he also noticed pointed fingers and snickers of recognition. "Is that?" he heard. "Could it be?"

Only when he walked the length of the nave with his head craned to the level of his statuary did he comprehend with horror what he had done. In the assembled saintly women who presided over half the side chapels lining the nave, he saw shadows of each of his widowed lovers looking down, their faces aglow with satisfaction.

Surely, he was no different than many artists who had come before him. Hadn't his brother said he must learn to feel the world and not just see it? Hadn't his sensual experience brought his figures to life as no amount of practice and perspiration had ever done? It was hardly his fault that recognizing these faces became a game among the townspeople. And in any case, the cathedral had been built by generations gone by for the benefit of generations to come. The distraction he had inadvertently created, he told himself, would pass in time.

Time, however, moves differently for all. For the most part, the townspeople did indeed seem to forget who it was they looked upon when they visited the long-awaited cathedral. Not many, after all, personally knew the widows of the various deceased artisans, and so soon the faces became simply those whose names were indicated. Yet one of his subjects was known by all, and so her depiction became more notorious than all the rest.

"You capture her nicely," the bishop's clerk said to him while the two stood beneath the statue of Saint Winefride, who all agreed bore an uncanny resemblance to the bishop's mother. The statue clearly was a work of careful attention, and it seemed to many, genuine affection. The poise of her mouth, a slightly crooked tooth, a tip of tongue somehow perceptibly hidden within. Her lips were parted as if to say, Yes, Francis, yes.

"I recognize she is still a young woman by biblical standards," the clerk added, "but to have the bishop's mother the subject of salacious gossip is—" He did not say what it was but closed his eyes and took a long breath before continuing. "We admire your talent, Francis. But you've made the cathedral's communion of saints into your own personal bordello, and the bishop's mother is not even the chief harlot. Could you not at least have made her the Virgin?"

"Please express to his eminence that I am mortified," he said. "On my father's memory, I swear I'll carve no more figures."

"That would be a pity. A gift such as yours is given by God. No, there is no need to choose between Holy Orders and your art."

Relief at these words brimmed in Francis's eyes. He reached out to grasp the bishop's clerk's hand and squeeze it in gratitude. It went limp at his touch.

"But you can no longer practice either here," the clerk said.

"Where then?"

"Gaerdegen."

In his memory the very word had filled him with dread, but he knew nothing of the place then. Only that it was remote and rumored for sanctity.

"But," Francis said, "but what of my family?"

"Your family?"

"My mother, I mean."

"Had you cared more for your mother than the bishop's these last few months you would likely not find yourself in this situation," the clerk replied. "But his Excellency is not without mercy. This may prove temporary. Serve the nuns as best you can until you hear further instructions. And a word of advice . . ."

"Yes?"

"If there are widows at Gaerdegen, you had better leave them be. There is nothing but forest for miles around. No doubt your blade will be kept busy in other ways."

Twenty-one years after his arrival at Gaerdegen, Father Francis could not deny that it had. When he looked at his hands, it was hard to believe they were the same he remembered from when he was fresh from his studies, carving late into the night in the family workshop.

Never had it been easy, this pulling of life from wood. But when he was young, he had only to look at a length of lumber, to run his fingers along the current of its grain, and the image of a saint would reach back and direct his work. The assurance once inspired by the elegance of his creations seemed so distant from him now.

He put a hand to his missing eye, rough fingers on smooth scarred skin. He could feel the bony void that was all that remained of half his sight. Too much was said, he thought, about God's gifts. What of God's costs? Though his father had taught him that too much longing would lead even the strongest tree to topple, he had never explained that when human lives fall they do not do so in isolation, but at the risk of all those around them.

# PART 3
# PRIME

# Chapter 11

SNOW BLEW OVER the tall outer wall and touched down gently all over the convent, dusting the stacked stones of the gatehouse, spreading evenly in the barnyard, powdering the smooth, packed earth. It coated the wooden shutters of the bakehouse and the thatched roof of the chaplain's shack, and drifted across the high, slate-shingled rooftops of the dormitory, the refectory, and the church.

It found the bell tower just as the sisters were finishing their second Hour of prayer. A windblown flurry skimmed by the bell, ringing high and faintly as it passed, and filled the tower's hollow shaft, pulsing from sky to church.

Inside, each nun knelt, crossed herself, and let her eyes fall shut, beginning a final paternoster in the candlelight. The draft pushed through the church, rustling veils, drying lips as they moved in devotion, chilling what little flesh the nuns' habits revealed. Cold wrapped their fingers as they crossed themselves again. It grazed pink cheeks as those who had been kneeling rose from the floor.

They opened their eyes to find snow playing about the room. Fat, wet flakes swung all around them: landing on noses and veils, settling in circles on the choir stalls, then melting away as quickly as they came.

Mother John bit her lip to keep from laughing at the sight of it, and the sisters started with surprise, caught off guard by the sudden appearance of what seemed to be a cloud forming in the rafters of the church. The nuns stared upward, then looked around the room, searching for an explanation. *A miracle*, some whispered. And maybe it was. The snow fell upon them as if the stones of the church had parted; as if the ceiling was suddenly open to the sky and the walls to the wind.

A quiet excitement arose in the church. The senior nuns closed their eyes and tilted their chins, letting the snow tap gently on their eyelids. Sister Matthew, the oldest of all the Order, lifted her face into a thin line of candlelight. Permanently purple from the scriptorium's ink, her withered lips formed a child's grin as if letting long-forgotten memories well up and flow. Other nuns appeared awestruck, watching the snow in lip-parted ecstasy.

Mother John looked for Sister James across the church. Lost in her habit, the small nun gripped her hands together and held them to her heart as her mouth opened and closed, murmuring: *Jesus, Jesus, Jesus, Jesus*, as if she was stitching a pattern in the air. Behind her stood Sister Phillip, a gray square of face framed by her veil, staring with wonder hemmed in by caution, glancing around the room as if more concerned with her sisters than with the spectacle around them.

In the rear of the church, Sister Magdalene stood spellbound but serious, looking toward the opening of the bell tower, which seemed the mystery's source. Near her, the convent's newest members, Sisters Jude, Thaddeus, and Bartholomew, in white habits and white veils, put away the pious airs they had put on for the time of prayer. They were giddy and wide-eyed as their years, slipping tongues past their lips to catch the flakes as they fell.

The room filled with a palpable joy, and the abbess was warmed seeing the church that had been empty so full of life. She watched the snow and the faces of her sisters and felt the gladness of witnessing what passed between them. Flurries swung lawless about the room, lifting spirits higher and higher, brightening eyes as they jumped here and there, widening smiles as they spun upward and down. Snow filled every corner of the church like the smoke of incense.

Mother John looked again to the head of the church, which just hours earlier had so tested her faith. Snowflakes caught candlelight as they fell to the altar top and now seemed a shower of diamonds, sparkling then fading as they met and left light, flying like angels around the body of the Lord. If there is one solace of aging, she thought, it was surely that when memory fades even doubt can be forgotten. The whole convent seemed aglow with the presence of God.

The wind ceased, and the flurries fell abruptly to the floor. Prayerful whispers popped and hissed in darkness for a moment, then gave way to a renewed solemnity. The nuns fell quiet and the church filled with the silence that owned it; the all-consuming silence that always returned to Gaerdegen, no matter the disturbance. The sisters bowed low and slowly, then exited the church the way they had come, soft footsteps and the rustle of habits the only sounds.

In the cloister the air was frigid, but the sisters did not hurry on their way to the washing chamber. They lingered in the corridor, crowding around the wide openings in the cloister wall, and stared out into the garth, where the miracle continued. Inches of snow had already accumulated and still it fell, filling the sky with a glowing white fog. It came down fast and deliberate, plummeting to the earth on the straightest route to the ground.

The nuns dropped their silence like robes before a bath, cooing with pleasure at the size of the flakes, as the wind whistled and sent a squall whipping through the cloister. They watched joyously, ignoring the cold, ignoring the wind though it sometimes pinched their skin. It would not be long, they knew, until the whole convent joined the garth in dressing for Christmas. This first snow meant that the drab walls of the cloister would soon be draped in garlands, and the church would be brightened with thick red candles, embroidered altar cloths, and greenery gathered from the forest. It meant too that the coming weeks would be a time of gladdened appearances and increased comforts, for soon the sisters would don their warm winter habits and the healthy glow of the holiday meal: ale, meats, and thick winter breads. The snow fell purest white against the sky and full of promise as they watched it pile in the yard.

The four novices broke away from the crowd and hurried off down the corridor, anxious to beat the rush to the necessarium.

The lavatory was a cavernous chamber, dank and empty but for a firepit cut in the center of the floor, where a two-foot blaze burned. A large trough of a basin stood against the wall opposite the entrance to the cloister. The walls were the height of two men and arched overhead, joining above the room's center; their stacked stones shone with firelight, gleaming like the walls of a cave.

A handful of nuns gathered by the rear entrance of the chamber, waiting their turn at the cold, stone hole. A dozen others were collected around the basin, watching the snow through the south wall's windows as they washed. The sisters readied themselves for Prime, the fast-approaching next office of the day, unaware of the presence of their abbess, who watched quietly from the entrance to the cloister.

Sister Magdalene pulled her veil back from her forehead, then cupped icy water in her hands. She smoothed it over her face and into hair as orange-red as holly berries in the fall. Cut as close to the scalp as all their locks were, hers alone brought a flash of color to this black-and-white world. She readjusted her headdress and hurried away as the novices around the basin began bumping into each other playfully.

Sister Thaddeus looked up from her washing and peeked out the window, watching as the flurries fell pretty on the outer yard and buildings of the abbey. The dark stone bakehouse, the decrepit chaplain's shack, and the wooden crosses of the land between were disappearing amid the icy haze, their shapes faded like stains scrubbed from skin. Sister Thaddeus lifted her fingers from the trough and shook them deliberately at her twin, Sister Jude, flinging beads of water into her eyes. She leaned in close to her sister and spoke in her ear, though it was forbidden, "Wash me," she whispered, "and I'll be whiter than snow."

A line from the psalms. These girls drank scripture in all day and relished the chance to spit it out transformed. All four novices giggled, holding their breaths to stifle outright laughter but causing enough of a disturbance to rouse the ire of Sister Phillip, who stood at the other end of the basin, scrubbing her hands with fervor. The novices' teacher flashed a righteous, reproving look at the young sisters. She peered out from her veil, hers alone still pulled down close to her eyes, and pressed her two first fingers together then pulled them dramatically apart, making the sign recognized in the convent to mean *Quit*.

The abbey's requirement that contemplative silence be maintained when the nuns were not in the church or the chapterhouse required an elaborate vocabulary of gestures. A hand moved through the air might impart information, offer assistance, or, most often, convey orders. Some felt it was contrary to the spirit of the Rule to carry on conversations this way, but all relied on signs for basic or urgent communication.

The novices were unimpressed with Sister Phillip's insistent signifying. They were caught up in both the morning's excitement and the fun of a new game, feeling too glad to stop. Sister Bartholomew cupped water in her hands and began to lift it to her face, then turned and poured it down the front of Sister Thomas's habit, whispering to her playmates, "He turned the desert into pools of water."

Thomas squealed as the water met her neck, and her sisters erupted with raucous laughter.

Sister Phillip flared her nostrils and glared with indignation, closing her fingers and pulling them apart again and again: *Quit! Quit!* But now it was Sister Jude's turn. The youngest of the novices plunged her forearm into the water and rowed it toward both of her sisters, declaring softly but with assurance, "And the rain fell for forty days and forty nights."

She raised a wave that wet every nun around the basin, who all were silent an instant then joined joyfully in the game. Whispers and laughter arose all over the chamber. The sisters by the necessarium covered their mouths to hide their amusement, but the nuns around the basin laughed out loud and in plain view, splashing at each other with such vigor that the pool soon seemed an explosion of water, waves flying in every direction so not one nun was spared, water lapping on the wall and spilling on the floor, forming a puddle that washed toward the fire.

Sister Phillip alone remained silent, fuming, standing rigid as water splashed against her habit and sisters all around her grabbed each other playfully. She pulled her fingers apart with exaggerated effort: *Quit! Quit! Quit!!* Most of her sisters by now had forgotten her presence, but the youngest of the Order looked on with great pleasure at Phillip's earnest gesticulations. Sister Bartholomew mocked her sister from across the basin, tapping her fingers together impatiently and jutting her tongue past her lips with such disrespect that the older nun thought she might scream were she not so afraid of joining the chaos that was all around her.

Mother John gave a slight false cough from the entryway and silenced the room. The novices stopped their play and bowed their heads in shame, embarrassed to have misbehaved before their abbess. Sister Thaddeus blushed and pulled her veil down to meet her eyes. The older nuns simply returned to their morning preparations, as if nothing at all had happened. Sister Phillip ran to the abbess's side, waving her arms, shaking both hands in the air, attempting to explain her role in this mischief, but the abbess lifted her hand and denied her the satisfaction. John made a fist and rocked it back and forth on her wrist—the sign for "bell"—at which Phillip bowed low and quickly to her superior then hurried off to prepare the church for the next office of prayer.

The lavatory again became a busy and quiet place. The sisters waiting for the necessarium occupied themselves with arranging and rearranging their habits more than they required. Sister Gaius and others knelt in prayer to fill this idle time, while the nuns at the basin resumed their washing with utmost concentration, careful not to spill a drop.

Sister Magdalene watched them, seething. How they could be so carefree on a day so fraught with danger for the abbey was a mystery. Though she was roughly the age of the novices, she had seen many similar girls come and go in her twenty years at Gaerdegen. Some were more serious, some less, but none had ever been so trifling and vindictive as these young women were proving to be. Seeing them play like children, she wondered if she was the only one within the convent walls who appreciated the dire circumstances they were in.

# Chapter 12

SISTER MAGDALENE'S CONCERNS had begun with a letter received six months earlier from the bishop's court. As she had for years, Magdalene read and responded to this message addressed to the abbess before Mother John had even known it had arrived.

*It is an apostolic precept, good Mother, that we who are tasked with the care of the flock of the Lord must ever preserve the sheep pen from wolves. Trusting that you had done this and would do it—you who received the rule of religious life from that most holy woman Ursula of Gaerdegen—I reckoned according to the measure of your intelligence. But—and I am compelled to say this in sorrow and grief—it has come to our attention that the sisters in your care are not sufficiently protected from heresy and error. We need not remind you, I am sure, that ardor and affection for one's forebears may arrive unexpectedly at idolatry. At the urging of your sister abbesses from the other houses of the Order, we believe Gaerdegen would benefit from a visitation. We trust your compliance with this request will lead to prompt amendment of any misapplications of the Rule which may be found among the sisters in your care, or else will correct the misapprehensions of your conduct that have caused so much consternation throughout the Order.*

Magdalene had answered without delay. She wished she could say all that must be said: that Mother John's mind was fading but that this posed no threat to the abbey, the Order, or the Church; that it was true she overvalued the legacy of her predecessor, the Abbess Ursula, and had allowed her writings to be read aloud to the community in choir and at mealtimes. But the Book of Ursula, as some now called it, was only a collection of pious meditations. It was by no means the dangerous heretical text others in the Order alleged.

Of course, she could not put any of this into writing. Instead, she urged in her correspondence a delay of the bishop's visit until after such time that the circumstances might be explained in person. In the response she soon received, the bishop took her up on this offer, though she had not intended to make an offer at all.

A carriage from the bishop's court had arrived a fortnight later. After Sister Simon alerted her, Magdalene went quietly to meet the carriage's occupant to avoid general alarm.

"It seems they sent a child," Sister Simon told her as they rushed to the gatehouse.

"Most to you would seem so," Magdalene replied.

Simon had been gate mistress since the plague years, when the former holder of her office met her end along with half of all humanity. The post was often boring but nonetheless envied by many. Since the abbey wall had been built, few of the sisters had much of a view of the outside world.

One of the original abbey structures, the gatehouse consisted of a tiny vestibule from which Sister Simon kept watch on anyone who approached the abbey by way of the rutted track that led through the forest in the valley below, and a larger sitting room where favored visitors were offered ale and bread at the end of their long journey and invited to peruse examples of Gaerdegen's embroidered vestments and illuminated manuscripts, in case any pilgrim come there to pray might also become a patron. In keeping with the Rule's requirement of seclusion for the sisters, a latticework wall kept the nuns hidden even when their families came to call.

Magdalene opened a slot in the screen to better observe who had been sent for the investigation. Glancing through the aperture, she saw it was a young man, younger than herself, she thought on first glance, or at least carrying himself as if that were so. If the bishop took this matter so lightly—lightly enough to send a servant, and an adolescent no less—she wondered why he had taken the trouble of threatening them with such an incendiary message in the first place. Why must men always wield power so bluntly? She pushed a door in the screen fully open, taking the messenger by surprise.

"Boy, where is your master?" Magdalene said.

"Sister, where is yours?" he replied. "I have come in the name of the bishop to meet your Mother Abbess."

"The correspondence made no mention of a visit so soon. And who are you to travel here in the bishop's stead?"

"Brother Daniel," the young man said. "The bishop's clerk."

"You are not the bishop's clerk. I met the bishop's clerk during the last episcopal visitation."

"He has many clerks."

"Surely you are too young to be one of them."

"And surely you are too young to be handling an abbess's correspondence."

Their first meeting scarcely improved from there. She carefully hewed to her prepared explanation of their situation, insisting there was nothing at all unorthodox about their approach to the Divine Office or any other element of their daily devotions.

"The Liturgy of the Hours is the common prayer of the universal church," she told him. "We would scarcely change a syllable."

"That may be, but would you make additions to the liturgy if your abbess suggested doing so?"

Many in the Cathedral City, Brother Daniel explained, feared that the distance of Gaerdegen from civilization had created the impression among its leaders that they could do as they like in matters financial, devotional, and otherwise. He had been sent to make it plain that this was not the case.

"Mother John has led this abbey since the year of my birth. Why are these questions arising now?"

"Only recently have we heard of certain unorthodox practices from an abbess at one of the sister houses to the south. She apparently has a relation within Gaerdegen's walls."

"I see," Magdalene said. "And does the bishop take his orders from disgruntled nuns?"

"The bishop gathers intelligence where he may. He has been particularly intrigued by references to the so-called Book of Ursula, which some claim has taken the place of scripture in your sisters' hearts."

"The Book of Ursula? I have not heard of it. Is this a popular book of late?"

"The bishop believes there is only one copy, and he is grateful to God that it has not yet been duplicated."

"We are a poor abbey, sir. We could scarcely afford any book as rare as that. You are welcome to examine our library if you have doubts."

"That would be most helpful. When may I visit it?"

"Immediately."

She made no move but sat staring at him as he rose and walked toward the door.

"Shall I find it myself?"

"It?"

"Your library?"

"You already have."

With a flourish she pointed him to a bookshelf on which stood three well-worn volumes inked in the abbey scriptorium, bound manuscripts of the psalms, the gospels, and the *Monologian* of Saint Anselm. Their true library could be found in a room off the scriptorium, but there was no need for him to see that now.

"Take all the time you need," she said.

He did. Daniel sat down again and studied every page of the books shown to him. And though Magdalene had other work requiring her attention, she continued to watch him as if fearful he might surreptitiously slip something into his pocket. She did not only watch his hands, however, as one might a potential thief. True, she noted the gentle play of his thin fingers across each page, but she also took care to observe that his forearms seemed to have some strength in them, and his shoulders were likely capable of moving more than books. She studied the way his brow furrowed in concentration and supposed by the pace at which his brown eyes consumed the words before him that he could read equally well in Greek and Latin, which raised her opinion of him considerably. How often did he make such visitations, she wondered, and did he meet many sisters in the process? From time to time, he looked up and appeared startled to find her gaze upon him.

"I am nearly done," he said.

Only when he had finished and was satisfied there were no obvious theological errors hidden between the lines of the assembled books, or hinted at by their elaborate illuminations, did he rise, bow slightly to Magdalene, and make his way toward the door through which he had entered three hours before.

"Sister, I thank you for your attention to this matter," he said. "There may yet be need to return in order to question other members of the community."

The sky through the gatehouse window had grown dark. She had missed Sext and perhaps None as well. She might be on the verge of missing Vespers. But she could not resist speaking again, stopping him before he returned to the waiting carriage and rolled off into the night.

"You neglected to mention your canonical status," she said. "If you return, my sisters should know if they are addressing a priest, or a brother in minor orders, or a seminarian, or some class of monk let loose on the world."

"Oh, I am no cleric of any kind," he said with a laugh. "I am called Brother Daniel only because laymen do not often conduct the bishop's business."

"Nor do they often have the bishop's trust."

"Earned over a lifetime. The episcopal court took me in as a child, when there was no one else."

She looked at him closely, reassessing his age, which she now guessed to be close to her own, or slightly older.

"A plague orphan?" she asked.

"Aren't we all?" Daniel said. "I was the only survivor of my household. I suppose I was not deemed ready just yet for paradise."

"Some had to be left to pray."

"I believe I was left for other things."

Magdalene did not respond immediately but supposed her face showed her thoughts: that she too had been left parentless by the plague, and also allowed herself to hope it was for some other purpose than constant atonement for whatever sins had so condemned the world before she ever knew it. She wondered what her days would be if they were not passed so unrelentingly in prayer. Did her eyes betray that lately during the liturgy she prayed not for Christ but for oblivion?

"Such as?" she asked.

"I have been told that my father and grandfather were artisans. Now that there's a world to be remade, they would want me to do my part. As we all must."

For days after his visit, her mind turned over his words, so casually offered and yet, in the version of events she convinced herself was true, cutting to the quick. What had he meant, she wondered, by remaking the world? Was he in fact speaking of repopulating the earth? And what then did he mean that all must do their part? Must they do so together? She blushed at the likely answer, then lingered on it, then made every effort to banish it from her mind.

Fortunately, the inconclusive findings of the clerk's initial inquiry had provided useful pretext for continued visitations—all for the stated purposes of identifying doctrinal errors at Gaerdegen and preparing the nuns for the bishop's scrutiny—but, from Magdalene's perspective, with added benefits that were far from theological.

Each time he appeared inside the gatehouse, they would sit facing each other on rough stools, their backs straight with purpose. Through the course of these conversations, her initial deference to the office he represented soon gave way to a front of annoyance at being called from the abbey ledgers whenever he appeared. Only the gate mistress Sister Simon knew of the reason and frequency of these visits, and Magdalene had sworn her to secrecy with a warning that news of an investigation into

Mother John's governance would cause a panic from which the abbey might not recover. It was for Simon's benefit that she addressed him as if he were in Holy Orders; a layman at the gate expecting entry would have been too much scandal for the old nun to bear.

"Yet more questions, Brother Daniel?" she would ask.

"Just a few, Sister," Daniel would reply.

At each meeting, his queries began concerning practices in the abbey, its work, its devotions.

"Sister, how many times through the day do the nuns of Gaerdegen pray?"

"We pray without ceasing, Brother, as Saint Paul commands."

"Yes, but I speak of your adherence to the canonical Hours."

"At Gaerdegen there are eight Hours, Brother, the same as there likely are in the episcopal palace—unless those of your stature require extra sleep."

"And why eight Hours?"

"It is required by the Rule."

"Has your abbess taught you the reasoning behind the Rule's requirement?"

"The psalmist commands eight offices of prayer, saying both 'Seven times a day do I praise thee,' and 'At midnight I will rise to give thanks.'"

Only when Sister Simon grew bored of these interrogations and wandered away from the gatehouse did their conversation turn to matters more controversial and personal.

"If I inquire again about the Book of Ursula," Daniel asked in a hushed tone, "will you again deny its existence?"

"Mother Ursula herself might do no different," Sister Magdalene replied. "If you are so certain our foundress is a menace, why not trouble her with your questions?"

The stool legs beneath Daniel scraped as he drew slightly nearer to her, closing the gap between them.

"A madwoman in the mountains holds little institutional interest," he said. "But we are very interested in understanding why her influence endured after she had gone."

"I would not know of such things. She departed before my birth."

Brother Daniel studied her for a moment. His brow, she noticed, raised just so when he seemed to be scrutinizing her. A crease formed just above the bridge of his nose.

"Was it then that you were given the name Magdalene?"

"It is my name in Christ, if that is what you are asking."

She heard the scratch of wood on stone as his stool again moved forward.

"You had no name prior to taking the veil?"

"I'm told I had another when I was young."

He shifted on his seat, his legs inching closer to her own. Their knees did not touch; she looked down to be sure of it. Yet she was acutely aware of the inch of air between them.

"Do you remember what your name once was?" he asked.

When she told him, it was the first time she could recall speaking it aloud. And despite the contentious nature of many of the words that had passed between, when he repeated it back to her, whispering it slowly to acknowledge it as a secret they now shared, it rang in her ear like a lullaby that once had rocked her to sleep.

Gradually, Sister Magdalene dropped the pretense of appearing put off by Brother Daniel's visits. Anticipation of his return brightened her mood, and she came to look forward to seeing him with an admixture of excitement and dread she had never before experienced. But like children who play a game long past when it would have been reasonable to stop, it devolved into bitterness. At the conclusion of their sixth meeting, Daniel abruptly closed the door on Magdalene's fantasies.

"The bishop has said it is time for my investigation to end," he told her, "and his to begin."

Magdalene nearly shouted, keeping her voice in control only for fear of alerting Sister Simon that something worth overhearing might be said.

"His *to begin*? What has all this been if not the bishop's investigation?" she said. "What have your months of prying questions been about if not the bishop's investigation?"

She glared at him, and he held her gaze. From perhaps their third meeting onward, it had been apparent to them both that the investigation had become of secondary importance. They had agreed to this silently, conspiratorially, as if together they were putting one over on the authorities each served. With his eyes he reminded her of this, and with hers she both acknowledged it and showed she was ashamed of this fact. She had let her excitement at their—at their what, their flirtation?—cloud her judgment to the point of forgetting that all of this was not an elaborate lark.

"I will accompany the bishop to Gaerdegen in three weeks," he said firmly. "Please prepare your Mother Abbess and any others who might be questioned."

And now she alone knew what was to come. She alone might have done something to prevent it. Instead, for months on end she had done little more than stare into a young man's eyes, hoping for the sound of a stool inching forward more than she ever had for the calling of the prayer bell.

# Chapter 13

MOTHER JOHN TOUCHED Sister Magdalene's wrist with a cold finger, drawing her attention away from the storm. The old nun lifted her right hand to eye level and circled it before her face. Magdalene turned and nodded yes, she was watching. The abbess turned her palm toward the yard and began fluttering her fingers, tapping quick but gently in the air, then waved three long arcs in a rainbow, like a slow goodbye.

*Beautiful snow*, the abbess signed.

Monastic sign language was Magdalene's mother tongue. She had learned it before she had spoken her earliest prayers. But she had little patience for it now.

"Mother, we must discuss—"

The abbess looked at her sternly. It was bad manners to answer a signed communication with a spoken word. But Magdalene pressed on.

"We must discuss the bishop's visit."

Mother John sighed, relenting.

"We will welcome him warmly," she said quietly. "Shall we cook a goose?"

"Our table is the least of my concerns—as well it should be yours."

"What then?"

"What he will ask, what you will say in reply."

"Likely he will ask of my health, I of his, and we will bemoan our shared decrepitude."

"His Excellency will inquire about the orthodoxy of our devotions and will search for evidence of noncanonical writings that will incriminate you."

"Such words!" John laughed. "His Expediency will see a simple old nun like me knows nothing of such things. Sometimes I cannot even remember my own name."

"I do not understand how you can disregard the seriousness of this matter."

"When you are the abbess of this place, you will understand."

"You mustn't speak like that."

Mother John smiled. "According to the Rule, we shouldn't be speaking at all."

Magdalene knew she likely sounded as if she simply feared the inevitable: One day John would die, a new sister would lead the abbey, and if the current abbess had her way, it would be Magdalene herself. But she spoke now not only in accordance with the taboo against discussing succession. She was, she knew, more selfish than that. If Magdalene were to become abbess, she believed, she would never leave this place.

"We have many years before we must worry over the calamity of Gaerdegen requiring a new mother," she said. "Our present calamity is far more pressing."

Mother John put a finger to her lips. Silence, she had always insisted, was the first and most important requirement of the Rule. There was no room within it for emotions to flare, or for meanings to be lost in the space between words and the intention behind them. She hoped to draw her young sister away from her overwrought concern, back toward meditation on the storm and the surprising contentment one might find in its contemplation.

*Beautiful snow*, the abbess signed again. She then dropped her hand to her waist, palm down, and began to smooth left and right in the air, fingers still fluttering, polishing an invisible tabletop, her hand slowly rising, moving past her stomach, past her breast. She smiled mischievously as her hand met her chin and rose past her eyes, then reached high above her head, still fluttering, still smoothing the air, showing pale forearm as she stretched her fingers an arm's length over her head. Her eyes widened in feigned distress, and her hand fell down to make another slow circle: *Beautiful snow will bury us.*

Magdalene tried to acknowledge her mother's levity. Her lips curled upward at the corners, appreciative of the attempt to raise her spirits, but her face was pained, tired. She felt far older than her twenty years. While touching a finger to her cheek, she knew them still to be smooth and pink, and her hands themselves were yet wrinkle-free, every inch of this visible flesh bristled at its confinement by the sturdy cloth of the habit she had worn nearly all her years.

The robe hung loosely from her shoulders, white as the snow that fell in the yard, and sloped down evenly to the floor, hiding well her body, barely letting face and hands escape. Once, she remembered, it had been a source of strength, but now she wore it with the heaviness of fate.

Magdalene looked away, back to the cloister garth. Flurries flew about the yard, dancing upon the ground as she herself had when she was young.

She lifted her hand high above her head then stretched it out an arm's length before her chest and pulled it back in, making a small, slow circle in the air, then a tight fist which she opened, palm up.

*Bury us*, she signed, adding her thoughts to her Mother's, *and grant us peace.*

Her words hung in the air, though they had not been spoken. They gave the initial observation a meaning and a portent the abbess had not intended. As a girl, Magdalene had been a joy to the community, brightening the convent wherever she ran. Lately, though, she carried a darkness within, casting shadows with thoughts she would not share.

The younger nun moved away without sign or sound, returning to the day's routine. Beyond the cloister, snow fell even lovelier as the sky lightened and night's end drew near, and with such certainty the convent could have been an hourglass, white sand streaming in a rush from above, quickly filling the bowl made by the abbey wall. What would happen, the abbess wondered, when time ran out? Would God turn the world upside down?

A small voice arose from the church, pulling her from the storm's hypnotic hold. Creeping down the corridor, lingering in the air, the voice seemed born of Gaerdegen's silence: muted by stone walls and falling snow and barely audible, but haunting, piercing as a baby's cry or the bleat of a slaughterhouse lamb. Mother John recognized it immediately: Magdalene's voice, singing alone, beginning prayers for the Hour called Prime.

*Blessed be the name of the Lord, From this time forth and for ever more.*

A crowd of voices followed close behind. The voices of her sisters, ringing strong in reply, filled the church to the sturdy beams above.

*From the rising of the sun to its setting, the name of the Lord is to be praised.*

The old nun turned from the cloister window and moved toward the gathering voices.

*Glory to the Father and to the Son, and to the Holy Spirit,*
*As it was in the beginning, is now and ever shall be.*

Mother John entered the church and took her place in the choir, joining her sisters as they sang *Amen.* They prayed together until hints of dawn shone through the flurries and the church windows glowed with the sunrise. When the light was sufficient, the abbess stood before them and unrolled a page of parchment.

"A reading from the Book of Ursula," she said. With the first few words, Magdalene recalled the passage and wondered if Mother John had chosen it for her.

*Remember, my Sisters: the Hours of the Liturgy shape our days into simulacra of the life of Christ. We who follow them invite his birth, his death, and his resurrection with every act of waking. Doing so we see the whole world not just as it is but as it was and will be, for each day forever will retell the same story: There was once darkness, then there was light, then in squandering the chances light brings to do all we are able, we lost the light and can only pray for its return.*

*What have we to fear when the story of living and dying is so apparent and unchanging? Should we fear the ground beneath our feet? Living and dying are simply the surface we walk upon; all that ever was and will be is contained in their relation.*

*There is nothing that breathes that will not stop breathing, nothing that shines that will not dim. Do we not rise in the night to wait for the breath of God and the shine of God to be given again? How then should we welcome the final darkness except as we welcome each daily darkness? Pestilence, famine, war, conquest: we will greet even these with singing.*

# PART 4
# TERCE

# Chapter 14

BY DAYBREAK, A foot of snow had fallen, and still it fell, piling heavy and wet on rooftops and the earth, bending the boughs of the trees that circled the convent. It was morning, and the whole world was quiet and white, softened by snowdrifts like down, muted by the hush of the storm. Sounds of morning called through the silence: The lowing of the old ox, lonely in the abbey barn. Rustling within the waking cloister. The church bell, ringing faintly, as if miles away.

*Come.*

*Come.*

Across the convent, in the dark, squat shack between the bakehouse and the cloister, Father Francis stood with bald head bowed, his one eye fallen shut, lips parted as though thirsting. His back bent beneath the coarse cloth of his black robe; his arms hung heavy at his sides, braided with once-powerful muscles now gone slack, like the strands of the worn rope that dangled from his waist. He slid his hands to his knees and bowed slowly toward the window, toward the church, praying softly.

He sang alone in the little light: three psalms, two hymns, *Kyrie eleison* and then a final blessing, tracing a cross in the air before him, saying, "The Lord bless us, and keep us from all evil . . ." He spoke with the timbre of a priest to his flock, though he alone heard the words that clouded about his face—the same words the abbess said in the church to bring the Hour of prayer to a close. "Bring us to life everlasting; and may the souls of the Faithful, through the mercy of God, rest in peace. Amen."

Francis moved slowly through the room, limbs stiffened by the day's fierce cold, returning to his table to continue work on the carving he had begun in the darkness following the day's first prayers. Trunks and boughs of all sizes littered the floor of the workshop: the smaller pieces collected in round, tidy mounds as if waiting for fire; the larger standing alone and in pairs about the center of the room, wrapped in bark, like dark castle towers. Set apart from the clutter stood a block of ash wood stripped of its bark, ready to be split and carved so the dark heartwood at its center would become the spine of a statue of the Virgin.

The novice's confession had set his plan in motion. The moment she left, he had surveyed his available materials and found them wanting. A length of birch had not sufficiently dried and had succumbed to fungus rot. A piece of oak that had sat neglected for ten years or more was now as uncarvable as iron. The carving he would make now would need to be perfect. And so he had spent the larger part of the days since her visit engaged in a search for wood.

When Francis first arrived at Gaerdegen, the trees had been a balm for his exile. The woodlands surrounding the abbey, filled as they were with downy birch, goat willow, black alder, Scots pine, sessile oak, were for the carver an almost limitless bounty. He had commandeered a young ox and a sturdy cart from the convent barn and would harvest logs suitable for statuary much as he had done as a boy.

It had been some time since he had ventured out on such a mission when he learned of the bishop's impending arrival. The next morning, he set off into the valley below Gaerdegen, as he had so often before, listening for the call of saints hidden in the timber. His old ox remained strong despite its years; the beast was more than capable of handling a job like those they once accomplished together, and Francis hoped he could do his part as well.

Once out of sight of the abbey, with the sky above visible in patches through evergreen boughs and lingering late autumn leaves, he noted to his distress that none of the trees called to him as they once did. He led the oxcart deeper on, pausing periodically to place his palm on mossy bark and inhale the subtle scent that indicated a tree's likely health but felt none of the connection to these living materials upon which his craft relied. Faintly, he could hear the echoing blows of some other woodsmen and their axes, though it was impossible to tell how far away they were. The steady rhythm suggested they were either less discerning or more fortunate than he.

As the sun rose and fell above the forest, Francis so feared a day would be wasted that he sharpened his ax and began to hack at a tree he knew would be overlarge for his purpose. He swung in frustration until he was too winded to stand, then rode the oxcart back to the abbey, heavy with regret.

Had his father ever had a day he came back from the woods empty-handed? Yes, innumerable times. "Alas, today the trees did not speak," Hugh Budge would say with a sigh. "It is simply the way of the woods."

The second day for Francis proved no better. Departing earlier the following morning, he vowed he would not make the previous afternoon's mistake, attacking a tree in sheer desperation. But still he felt his hopes depended entirely on finding the ideal cut of wood. He prayed God would put it before him and then cursed when it did not appear. Passing by fresh-cut stumps left in the ground by the unseen woodsmen, whose ax blows now reverberated with a mocking tone, he thought it was just like God to show him evidence of what might have been his.

Two days of such fruitless effort had also not been unheard of for the Budge family—"Perhaps I have offended the trees somehow," his father would say lightheartedly. "They seem to turn their backs on me when I approach."—but a third day in the forest with only an empty cart to show for it had only occurred once, when fire blight had caused an entire hawthorn grove to appear as scorched as the gates of hell. There was no such sickness at large now, but as the hours passed, he became paralyzed by the thought he would again find nothing. The killing blight seemed not in the trees but in his bones.

It was on the fourth day that finally he accepted that any trunk, or even a moderately stout bough, would be better than none. He settled on a smallish pine, no thicker than his thigh. Already it was getting dark and he needed to make his way back up the mountainside to the convent. The adolescent tree was a paltry showing for all his efforts, but it would have to do.

Yet even this was too much. He swung his ax until his skin blistered and broke. The handle slipped in his hands as his fingers cramped into claws that he could neither tighten to fists nor loosen enough to flatten his palms and let the cool air soothe his wounds. He was still far from an old man, but at moments like this he felt keenly that the years he had known had not been kind. He could still see in his arms traces of the power they once held, but even the simplest tasks drained his strength.

Francis sat nearly weeping with fatigue and dismay. Like so much of the world, the woods no longer seemed to exist solely for his benefit and would not bend to his needs. Going back to the abbey empty-handed yet again seemed unimaginable when he set out that morning, but now—shrink or bump your head—he accepted that this expedition had been ill-conceived, a product of vanity as stubborn as his decline.

He was steadying himself for the return journey when he realized with astonishment that he was in fact sitting on a freestanding stump. Climbing to his feet to inspect it, he let out a hoot. It was a squat column of ash wood. Fresh sawn. Yellow-brown just beneath the bark, the color of dried blood near the center. He looked around to see where it had come from, but there were no recently cut trees anywhere in sight. Only studying the forest floor did he notice the indentations of cart wheels running alongside the footprints of men and beasts. No other explanation seemed possible: the fortunate woodsmen who had plagued him for four days had lost some of their haul.

No matter its source, Francis would only call it grace. He rolled the log to the cart, drove spikes into the meat of the wood, and slung a rope over a low-hanging bough to lift it. After days of trekking and labor, Francis returned to the abbey with only a length of bark-covered timber barely as tall as his knees.

In the darkness of the following morning, as snow had begun to fall upon the convent, he chose from his tools a wood-handled scraper, its grip worn smooth from years of use. Between Matins and Lauds and again between Lauds and Prime, he scraped at the log's edges, revealing green wood slippery to the touch. He had only to split it open to expose the core that would become the body of a saint.

Ordinarily he would have used his long ax and the chopping block outside the workshop, but the snow's uncertain footing and the fatigue lingering from his efforts in the forest gave him pause. He remained inside instead, taking up his old hatchet and judging it sharp enough. When he lifted the hatchet above his head it scraped the thatch above him, sending pieces of his low ceiling to the floor. He swung it with all the force his tired arm could bring, but the blade struck only a corner of the ash block and a small chip fell away.

Twenty years earlier, he might have divided such a stump neatly with one blow. He raised the hatchet again, holding it firmly with both hands, and brought it down to his target as though to cleave the very ground. The blade met the block at the center and buried itself like a nail, sinking inches into the wood but failing in its purpose. This was dense, strong wood. It held the hatchet like a fist. Father Francis tugged at the handle but could not free it. He pulled again—still in vain. With the blisters from his forest misadventure only half healed, he could only release the hatchet and step back from the block.

How like his life, he thought, this squandering of a gift so freely given. On the floor beside the worktable he noticed two long planks of hornbeam, the hardest wood in the forest surrounding the abbey. With a sigh, he bowed to his limitations: there would be no statue of the Virgin carved in time for the bishop's arrival. Perhaps a simple cross would be enough—a token, but maybe a sufficient reminder of all he once had done for the Church and the abbey that he would be allowed to leave this place. And if this gesture was refused, at least the cross could be used for his grave.

Francis moved away from the worktable, kneading one hand with the other, then stopped at the workshop's window, opened its shutter, and watched the storm. Outside, the snow flew madly, turning circles in a howling gale. It blew in through the window and filled the dark shack like stars. Snowflakes swung through the room around the hatchet where it stood immobile in the unforgiving ash wood, rising and falling in spirals of light; like angels, the priest thought, going up and coming down.

# Chapter 15

Few of the nuns of Gaerdegen could recall a time when Father Francis had not served the abbey, but those who did looked back on the days prior to his arrival as a golden age. There had been priests before him, of course, but they had come simply to offer Mass and shriving or, upon invitation, to bury the dead. There had been no man sent to live permanently among them as an exile.

Young Father Francis had sensed from the beginning that his presence was not welcome, but what could he do but make the best of it? The convent in his first estimation was a lovely madhouse. Ruled by a self-styled holy woman, Ursula of Gaerdegen, the abbey seemed filled with supporting players made to enact an endless drama in demonstration of her sanctity, in which even the most mundane details of her life became the stuff of hagiography.

She seemed to Francis a woman moved less by faith than by eccentricity. Under the shadow of the abbey barn, Ursula had built a stone dovecote in the beehive style suitable for six dozen birds. Their cooing could be heard throughout the convent, and on particularly cold and quiet days it seemed to accompany their psalms in choir. In the space between prayers, the doves might be heard to sigh contentedly or to shriek when a rat got hold of a bird with a damaged wing. Despite her rank and the general smelliness of the work, Ursula insisted on overseeing the doves personally.

"I take comfort in intelligent company and seek it where I may," she told her sisters, who tried not to be offended.

Ursula found logic and reason where others did not. "The foolishness of God is wiser than the wisdom of men," was one of the passages from scripture always at the ready on her lips. When hired laborers from the village built a dovecote far larger than she had planned, causing a shortfall in the abbey's ledgers: "The foolishness of God is wiser than the wisdom of men." When weevils invaded the grain stores, ruining it for the nuns' consumption but making it ideal for her birds: "The foolishness of God is wiser than the wisdom of men."

For Ursula, there was no better proof of this axiom than avian inscrutability itself. Her pets' eyes shone with an unknowable intelligence she found endlessly endearing. She saw in the dovecote a microcosm of the convent of which it was a part, and the convent of course was likewise a microcosm of the world. An artificial, intentional, absurd, and essential community.

"My birds are just like us," she said one day after overseeing both a new trench for waste below the necessarium and an expensive delivery of grain. "They eat, they shit, and they sing. What else is there to life?"

"Flying?" the woman then known as Sister John asked.

"Some of us may yet learn that in time."

While Ursula did not take flight herself, she did delight in making the birds her winged agents, training them to fly both short distances and long before returning to their roosts.

As the doves were not only kept for the abbess's amusement but were a ready source of protein, the sisters from wealthier families complained that all this exercise made their meat tough and stringy.

"I prefer my birds plump and slow," Sister Phillip said at the refectory table. Her chubby fingers and the fact that she had only plucked two doves to the five or six accomplished by each of her sisters made the connection too obvious, and John out of fondness for her snobby sister let it pass unremarked upon.

Ursula was not similarly known for kindness, and so John's rising role in the abbey was greeted gratefully by her sisters. It was helpful to know that someone in the abbess's favor was not looking for reasons to box the ears of others to prove she deserved authority. Her kindness naturally extended to Ursula herself, whom John took every opportunity to assist.

When she heard the sound of a shovel coming from inside the dovecote one day, John called out, "Abbess, there is no need for you to occupy yourself with such labor! I would be happy to gather a work crew."

"Why would you do that?"

"Perhaps to grant you another hour of prayer?"

Ursula emerged covered in dove droppings, excrement smeared across her face, her habit and veil shining with fresh, liquid shit. To John the smell was overwhelming, but Ursula seemed not to notice.

"Prayer?" she said. "Sister, this is the closest I've felt to God in days."

As Mother Ursula's informal deputy, Sister John had taken on the challenge of welcoming a priest permanently into their community. Francis had not known if the reasons for his abrupt relocation from the Cathedral City to an abbey in the wilderness had preceded him. When he carefully inquired, the sister had put him at his ease. "Mother Abbess cares nothing for the world and its reasons," she said. "She asks only that we improve upon it."

To his dismay, he had quickly discovered that the first improvements required would be to the abbey itself. Even as he unloaded the carriage that had brought him, he was informed that Ursula had designed the convent with no living quarters for a priest.

"You would be welcome to sleep in the barn," Sister John said. "Our ox has quite a large feeding trough. Filled with yellow straw, it would make a bed more comfortable than any of Gaerdegen's nuns enjoy. The Holy Infant knew no better."

"I've slept in a manger before," Francis replied, "and it was not nearly so spiritually edifying as you might suppose."

The young nun took note of the trunk full of carving tools the priest had brought with him. "We've abundant trees if you would be inclined to build a cottage of your own."

"I would indeed."

He set to work immediately, digging deep holes for ash wood posts, framing in with oak, then setting thin lines of woven wattle in the walls to be covered with thick river mud. He stuffed the walls with yellow straw for extra insulation—far better surrounding him on all sides on a cold night than simply lining an animal trough for his rest. In short order, he had also built a heavy worktable. He made one chair on which to sit while taking his meals, and then, feeling optimistic that he might welcome a guest from time to time, he made another.

With a roof of his own making over his head, Father Francis allowed himself to begin to feel settled. That he was the first permanent priest should not be an obstacle to his happiness. An abbey needs a priest, after all, and after feeling superfluous in the Budge household, first as a craftsman and then as a father, he did not mind the prospect of being needed. To be one man among three dozen women would take some getting used to, especially now that he believed his travel along the way of the flesh was behind him, but he hoped he might one day feel at home at Gaerdegen.

After just a week in his new cottage, however, he remembered there was good reason to doubt that he would ever belong. He heard a commotion coming from the neighboring structure, which by then he knew was the bakehouse. He had settled on his building site in part because he welcomed the notion of waking to the smell of fresh bread from a wood-fired oven. But the arguments he heard as the sun came up that day reminded him that even the most pleasant odors dissipate in the breeze.

When he stepped outside, he saw sisters rushing in and out of the bakehouse. He stopped one in a particular state of disarray and asked what had happened.

"Ursula has bid us bake two hundred breads," Sister Philomena said. "As abbey treasurer, I support spending as much as we can on alms for the poor, but this is madness and financial ruin."

There had been in those days a famine in the region; he had seen signs of hunger everywhere during his journey from the Cathedral City. Beggars' hands reached to him as he rolled by families of vagabonds cooking tiny birds and rodents over roadside fires.

Father Francis admitted he knew nothing of the abbey's finances but agreed that two hundred breads seemed excessive. The treasurer was pleased to find an ally.

"Speak to her, Father," Sister Philomena said. "Perhaps she will hear reason from a priest; she listens to no one else."

"Not even the treasurer?"

"The abbess is my cousin," Sister Philomena said, "and I can tell you that from girlhood she was stubborn as a stone."

Inside the bakehouse Francis found the baker Sister Lazarus and Mother Ursula overseeing a baking operation such as he had never seen. Several sisters stood on each side of the broad wooden table, passing bowls between them, each adding an ingredient and then moving it down the line.

"We have three days, Sisters," Lazarus said. "We cannot make the fires bake faster so you will need to move more quickly."

"Father, thank you for joining us," the abbess said. "You may take a position on either side of the table. We bake for the poor along the river."

"Abbess Ursula, there are but a few people nearby asking for alms. Why overburden the sisters with this task worthy of Hercules?"

"There are many more hungry in the world than just the few you can see."

"That is certainly true, but for that bread is not a solution. The peasants of the region are scattered through dozens of encampments along the river. Most of the bread we make will molder and rot before it can be distributed."

"Suit yourself if you have no wish to powder your fine cowl with flour, Father. But, no matter your logic, we sisters will bake."

Smoke poured continuously from the bakehouse chimney for three days. The smell was everything Francis hoped it would be. When he closed his eyes and inhaled thc combined scents of charred wood and darkening breads of hearty grains, he imagined he was still in the Cathedral City, soon to taste the wares of a master baker, or perhaps those of the master baker's widow. Then came the nuns' voices, and he remembered where his appetites had landed him.

With the baking done, Sister Lazarus directed a team in loading loaves into the back of the abbey oxcart and then stepped aside as a procession began. All the nuns who could be spared for the afternoon marched toward a clearing by the river where the poor folk had gathered. Francis followed along with Sister Philomena, both eager to see what would come of Ursula's folly, and the abbess herself led the way. Winged companions from her dovecote floated above the parade. Remarkably, the priest noticed, not a single bird swooped down to snipe at the bread.

By the water's edge, the forest peasants stared at the sisters with hungry eyes, as if ready to devour them. As always, Francis wore a carving blade at his side, and he wondered if he might be forced to draw it in defense of the nuns now in his care.

"Our Lord fed the multitudes with loaves and fishes," Ursula declared to the crowd. "Today we nuns of Gaerdegen will do the same."

"Seems we've forgotten the fishes," Francis said to Philomena, "unless she has taught her birds to swim."

Ursula slapped the haunches of the ox and it ambled forward into the rushing current, pulling the bread-laden cart behind it.

"No!" Francis shouted. "The bread!"

"It cost a fortune!" Sister Philomena cried.

But the ox kept on, taking uncertain steps over the bed of river stones until the cart came to rest. Their calls drowned out by the churning river, the priest and the treasurer watched in horror as white-capped water swept over the cargo. Soon the cart was empty. The loaves traversed the waves as swiftly as the Viking raiders who once had made this land their own.

"No doubt she is truly Christlike," Francis said to Sister Philomena. "Jesus helped the poor by feeding loaves *and* fishes; she has made us poor by feeding loaves *to* fishes."

He feared a riot, but the peasants cheered as they saw the water churn. Under the surface, just out of sight, something began to break apart the soggy logs of bread.

"Aye, come on you, wily snakes," a man beside Francis said. "Quit your hiding in the mud and swim up to feed."

River eels now swarmed the loaves, so thick in the water it seemed the river itself had transformed into a creature of slick green-black skin. Long as arms and slow moving as they gorged themselves on the nuns' bread, the eels lolled on the surface, allowing the assembled crowd to wade in and grab them bare-handed. Those who had nets cast them to gather five or six at a time. Smoked dry over fires on the river side, they would see the forest folk through the hardest days of winter.

A cry rose up. "Mother Ursula, protect us! Mother Ursula, protect us!"

"What's that?" Francis asked Philomena. "Do they think her a saint?"

"Throughout the valley they call out to her in moments of duress. The simple folk believe she appears wherever her protection is invoked."

"Blasphemy," Francis said.

"We thank Christ for Mother Ursula," the man beside Francis said. "You must have led a blameless life, Father, or else your station as her priest is a fortune you don't deserve."

In the days following, reports from other encampments along the river suggested they had seen similar results. As the bread floated downstream, eels, fish, and other wildlife awakened and made themselves easy to catch. It was said that thousands ate thanks to the abbess's supposed folly, and the convent made a profit besides. Even Sister Philomena had to agree the nuns' own harvest of smoked eel was a net gain against the expenditure of flour and salt. Shouts of "Mother Ursula, protect us!" rang throughout the valley.

"The foolishness of God, Father," Ursula said to Francis. "Should you remain at Gaerdegen, you will learn in time."

# Chapter 16

UNWILLING TO PLAY the part of the bewildered priest awed by Ursula's holiness, Francis began to spend his unoccupied hours out of sight, either locked away in the cottage he had built for himself or exploring the forest that surrounded the abbey. Armed with the carving implements he had brought with him, he told himself this exile, though intended as punishment, may yet become a boon for his craft.

Still he hoped that he might be allowed to return to the Cathedral City, and he checked daily at the gatehouse to be sure the bishop's clerk had sent no message calling him home. But for whatever time he was fated to serve at Gaerdegen, he would make the best of it. He had been inching closer to something in his cathedral carvings that he had not yet attained. Perhaps here, in this woodshop at the end of the earth, he could finally view the world from a vantage that would lead him to channel all he had seen into a single carving.

His limited responsibilities included saying Mass for the sisters each morning after Lauds and hearing their confessions as necessary. Through his first few months at the abbey, as soon as he was able to dispatch his unpleasant daily duties, he put his ax on his shoulder and led the oxcart out of the abbey barn and down a winding path into the wooded darkness of the valley below. There, he felt, was the site of his true ministry, the forest full of saints uncarved yet somehow more holy for their formlessness, not yet shaped by human will, human desire, human sin.

The people he met there seemed similarly formless, the plain folk of the forest villages. Generations of the same families had lived in just this spot since before the Vikings had sacked the monastery centuries ago, before even Christendom had arrived to pull them from their pagan past. They were, some of them, men not unlike how he wished to be—men who reshaped the world with their hands. They had no formal training, yet each seemed more skilled in the practical side of woodcraft than any artisan employed in his father's workshop.

He had been chopping a particularly stubborn oak one day when his ax hit a stone embedded in the tree and badly chipped its blade.

The nearest dwelling, he knew, belonged to a man known to his neighbors as Butcher, for the skill and care he applied to the business of slaughter. He had no formal shop. Like all the others, his occupation changed from to day to day, but he kept his knives sharp so as to make the end of life as painless as possible for the animals brought before him. Massive and bearded, more a bear than a man, he was nonetheless far gentler than his appearance or his reputation would suggest.

Francis approached his encampment with his ax clearly visible so that it would not seem concealed. The forest, he had learned, was a dangerous place, full of highwaymen and other rogues who would be happy to slide a hidden blade into your back as you strained to free their cart wheels from a ditch.

"Greetings, Butcher! Have you a sharpening wheel I might make use of?"

"Behind the house," a booming voice called out.

He found him there at work on a hog, methodically dismembering it with a curved blade and a fine-toothed saw. His arms covered in blood to his elbows, he said, "I would help you but I am rather occupied at the moment." For a big man with a loud voice he spoke with unexpected musicality, an audible joy in his work and lot in life. "My daughter can show you how to use the stone, in the shed at the creekside."

Francis was at first offended. Show him how to use a sharpening stone? Ensuring his father's tools had adequate edges had been one of his earliest occupations in the Budge workshop. Would a girl now be giving him lessons?

Not wishing to seem rude, he gave no sign of misgivings but followed a short path to a well-built little structure poised beside a waterwheel in the swift-moving brook. When he opened the door, he saw that the outer wheel was attached with a series of gears and straps to one within—a thick circle of stone that spun faster than he had ever seen of a hand-cranked grinder. The floor of the shed was bare dirt. Its only furniture, a low, stout-legged table covered with an array of tools and blades.

A girl sat between the sharpening wheel and the table, arranging the implements. Some, freshly sharpened, gleamed with light from the door Francis had opened. She hummed a lilting tune, wordless but sad, as she lifted pieces before her to polish them with a cloth. When she became aware of his presence, she looked up at him with surprise but no apparent alarm.

"Your father said you might help with repairing my ax?"

Wordlessly she took it from him and pressed the damaged blade against the spinning stone. With the sudden awful noise of it and the closeness of her hands to friction that could reduce her fingers to bloody stubs, Francis feared for the girl for a moment but then saw she was wholly unconcerned, staring intently at the line where the metal edge met the moving wheel. Sparks jumped toward her and gave her face an otherworldly glow. He thought he had never seen anything so lovely.

When he returned to the Butcher, the hog was already neatly in pieces, hams and hocks ready for salting and hanging.

"I am obliged to you," Francis said. "What shall I pay you for use of your stone?"

"You are from the abbey?"

"Alas," Francis said.

"I have thought of sending my Maureen there."

"Such a pretty girl? She'd be wasted in a convent. If you seek for her a better life, she might well marry above her station."

Butcher raised an eyebrow at the priest, as if to ask: *What better life is there than this?*

"I fear she may be too strong-willed to marry," he explained. "And I am told such lasses feel at ease with others of their ilk."

"She's a clever one, then?"

"Aye. The waterwheel you saw was her notion. She had heard of such from a rag and bone man and figured how it might be done."

Francis ran a finger over his hatchet blade. "Then she is clever indeed. Her spinning stone brings out the finest edge I've seen. Might I return some time to sharpen my other knives?"

"An honor to be of service to a man of God."

"I would be obliged," Francis said. "And if you'd like, I will mention your daughter and her skills to the abbess. Perhaps there could be a place for her there."

"That would be a kindness."

If Francis had truly intended to do so, the intention soon faded. Why should he let the nuns of Gaerdegen ruin such a child? She did not need the influence of Abbess Ursula to attain holiness, the priest thought. Already she glowed with it. The girl could even be his model for the Blessed Virgin herself, not just for the beauty and purity in her, but the way her adolescent uncertainty mingled with the surety of knowing the favor of the divine. Surely it had been the same with the girl who had been chosen to give birth to the savior. Only such a vessel could be filled so full of grace.

It became his practice to circle close to Butcher's cottage whenever he went searching for carving wood. He found himself watching for her, listening for her humming tune, and when he heard it he would wander the forest searching for its source like a little boy in a fairy tale. If he was fortunate enough to cross paths with her while she attended to various chores, he would greet her curtly ("Good evening, Miss Butcher," he would say, receiving only a nod in reply), and then he would loiter unseen, watching from a distance as she performed whichever task she had set for herself.

When he gathered the courage, a fortnight later, to return to the sharpening shed with a selection of knives and chisels in need of a finer edge, he found her again at the spinning wheel, her legs tucked beneath her as if in prayer. Yet rather than concentrating on devotions, she was at work mixing a bowl of animal grease, which she applied in handfuls to the axle at the center of the stone.

"Good morning, Miss Butcher," Francis said haltingly. "Your father kindly offered your services; perhaps he mentioned?"

As usual, she barely nodded in reply.

He handed her a leather bundle of blades and hoped she might put them immediately to the wheel, so that again he could see the sparks reflected in her eyes.

"Forgive me, sir," she said, "but my father and I are busy with other chores at the moment. It will be some time before I can repair your tools."

Like her father's, her voice was full of certainty; respectful, but not at all the soft or small whisper he might have expected from a girl her age.

"Keep them as long as necessary. I will be glad to retrieve them later."

As she set the bundle down at her feet and prepared to return to her work, Francis watched her slightest movements with intensity, his eyes fixed on her face, attempting to capture every detail.

"My wheel?" she asked with a hint of pride in her creation. "Would you like to see how it works?"

She began with the bowl of lard she used to grease the moving parts of the mechanism. "I find deer fat combined with mashed forest slugs to be the slickest mixture," she explained, "but rendered hog fatback will also suffice." Then, she traced her fingers along the cut marks where she had directed her father to chisel the wheel from an outcrop of red sandstone. "A day's journey north, but worth it for the quality of the grit." She showed him the leather straps that connected the sharpening stone's axle to the axle joined to the waterwheel that spun ceaselessly with the current of the brook outside. "The danger comes in the spring, when the snowmelt overflows the river and the wheel moves so quickly it could grind the strongest blade to dust."

In its simplicity, ingenuity, and elegance, Maureen's sharpening contraption was not unlike the finest of wood carvings: a reordering of raw materials that brought something new and unexpected into the world.

Watching this quiet girl become voluble as she described her invention, he supposed she was perhaps the age Helena had been when she had married his brother—the age she had been when he had lost her.

In the weeks following, he continued to look for her in the forest, listening everywhere for her voice, her song. He had no ill intentions. He wanted simply to capture her image, first with his mind's eye and then with any medium at hand—a charred branch on the smooth face of a split log; blood from his fingertip pricked with a thorn, smeared across the underside of birch bark; an alder bough, hastily whittled to approximate the profile he had memorized during their brief interactions. Chaste though he insisted to himself his feelings were, he did more than once wonder if she might replace Helena in his heart.

# Chapter 17

A YEAR AFTER HIS arrival at Gaerdegen, Francis received a message from the Cathedral City at last. His first contact with home since his ignominious journey north, the sight of the letter lifted his spirits with the possibility that his exile in the wilderness might be coming to an end.

Yet it was not what he had hoped. No formal letter from the bishop begging his pardon or humbly requesting his return. No pleading from the carvers' guild to defy the episcopal directive and return as a respected craftsman rather than a scandalous priest. It was instead a sheaf of pages, with the briefest of messages from the bishop's clerk appended.

"For reasons that will become obvious," he wrote, "you must abandon any expectation you may have of returning to the Cathedral City. You would do well to serve Gaerdegen for whatever days you have remaining, thanking God that you have been spared our fate."

To Francis's astonishment, the remaining pages were addressed to him, and they were written in Helena's unmistakable hand. It was far more than could ever be written on the birch-bark scrolls they had shared in their youth but he knew the shape of her letters at a glance.

*My dear Francis,*

*Certain though I am that you have found peace so far from the daily turmoil we face, and reluctant though I am to introduce evil into the holy convent you now call home, I cannot allow the silence that has passed between us these long months to extend into the eternal quiet in which I fear we who you left behind are all soon to dwell. If by now you have heard even at such a great distance of the suffering visited upon the Cathedral City, I am sorry to add to the distress of such knowledge. If somehow thus far you have been spared, I am sorry to rend the veil of your comforting ignorance. In either circumstance, to be sorry in some measure is perhaps for me all that remains.*

*You may suspect that I greeted your abrupt departure with relief. Nothing could be further from the truth. I had hoped the sharp feelings between us would blunt in time, as you came to understand my reasoning and we together learned to live in proximity in ways that would bring shame neither to our family nor to the Church. Even in your absence I trusted God that this would be the case. But now it is too late.*

*Do you remember when we were young, and we passed idle hours among the great blocks of stone set to be lifted in place for the cathedral walls? When we learned to write from the architect's draftsman in the building dust? What joy we felt in the nonsense we traced in that fine powdered rock! When I wrote "love," you blushed at my boldness and added a "g" to disguise the word as "glove" before our teacher could see, but then I put my hand on yours as if one wore the other, and together we swept all our words away. We blew their residue from our fingers and laughed when it caught the sunbeams, making apparent the light all around us which we can only sometimes see. This letter I know will amount to little more, but try to find in it some echoes of those happier days, as I endeavor to do even as I write what I must.*

*Soon after the bishop sent you to that northern wilderness, we began to hear rumors of a pestilence that had entered the region from a port to the south. Many believed we were too far removed for this to be of any concern, and the bishop sought to assure us with a sermon claiming the finished cathedral would be protection enough from the fate met by those localities of lesser devotion. Oh, but I knew in my heart that great sins had gone unpunished in our city. Even in the cathedral, the statues you left behind spoke in their stillness of the carnality by which we will all be judged.*

*When further reports from our southern villages made it evident the pestilence was indeed moving ever closer, the bishop's confidence lagged. It was time, he said, for general penitence. He called for all in his spiritual care to gather in the courtyard before the episcopal palace for five Masses to be held each evening. We were to kneel throughout, every soul holding a candle until the night seemed like day. But the light was no balm for our worry. It only illuminated the faces of the faithful, showing them to be full of fear, newly suspicious of neighbors they had lived with all their days. Every glancing eye in the candle glow appeared to be asking: Is it you who will bring Death among us? What sins have you concealed that cry out for retribution so severe none who know you will be saved? Holding a child by a man not my husband, scarcely could I meet a single gaze that found my own.*

*Your mother had little patience for these spectacles. She often said, If they are so concerned with someone bringing the plague into the Cathedral City, why not simply prevent its arrival? All who would listen heard from her lips that men of learning had discovered that pestilence arrived through ill humors carried on the wind. In order to prevent it, she told us one must surround oneself with sweet smelling things. She lit fires of bay tree, juniper, wormwood, and mugwort, and let the smoke settle about her home like a cloud.*

*At the cathedral she took the sexton by the arm and would not leave his side until incense burned in every corner. We spent an hour moving from chapel to chapel offering this haze of protection to all who prayed under the Budge family's carvings of the saints. Your mother, thank God, made no remark about my resemblance to your statue of the Virgin, but the sexton made such a study of my face that I did not doubt his assessment of my virtue.*

*When she was satisfied we had protected those viewing your family's legacy in the cathedral, your mother insisted we go next to the workshop, and that is where our time of trial truly began.*

*We arrived to find the familiar sight of a stray cat sleeping in the doorway. It was the old tom Robert had once carved in such detail, its tongue hanging from his mouth as if eager for the morning food scraps he had so often received. Yet as I stepped over his tail to open the shop door, the cat did not stir. On closer inspection the cat lay perfectly still. I said to your mother, Poor old thing. And she responded that it was just as well, for cats bring the Devil. If that is the case, I replied, let us hope the Devil is as skilled at killing rats as this one was.*

*Surely I should have known to never hope in the Devil, even in jest. Only after we had opened the shutter of the shop window did we see perhaps a dozen rats stiff and lifeless at our feet. Your mother called upon Saint Sebastian for protection, as the arrows that pierced his side were as numerous as the dead vermin upon the floor.*

*We soon heard from the proprietors of other shops in the artisans' district that similar discoveries had been made across the city. The streets in which we once ran and played filled with mounds of carcasses swept from thresholds and thrown from windows.*

*My own family's shop was spared, as the fires my father kept burning to char his barrels made the cooperage unattractive to rats. But still he felt bound to assist in cleaning the streets. He made a score of his largest casks available, and my brothers spent two days with shovels in their hands, piling rodents into hogsheads until the lids had to be pushed down against the soft bodies to nail them shut. They then rolled the barrels to the river and watched them float away.*

*My brother William began to complain of bumps on his arms the following day. I pinched his cheek and said to him, You've been spending too much time with your pet fleas.*

*May the Lord in his mercy forgive my blindness, and may I find the strength to forgive the Lord for what then befell the youngest of my family before he had seen six summers. The morning next I looked closely at the source of Will's distress and saw sores that resembled no insect bites I had ever seen. The bulges appeared in the joints to start, small red welts in the crook of his elbows and the back of his knees. When I studied them again just hours later, they had grown into purple bruises with the look and feel of rancid plums. His afflicted skin split open before the end of that very night, and he howled in pain.*

*If you can imagine how his cries echoed through my parents' home, filling first the room closest to his agony, then the next near, then the next, you will understand how my other brothers came to be stricken one by one. The sickness moved like a shout, and my father buried one son each day for a week. By the first Sunday of the city's ordeal, he believed that he had not yet mourned his firstborn and his last remaining child only because this Death, like God, rested on the seventh day.*

*By grace alone, I did not succumb that first week but instead have lived to see the artisans' district grow crowded with the dead as the Budge shop once did with the wooden forms of saints arranged on worktables. Consecrated churchyards do not suffice for the burial of the multitude. No matter their station in life, all are thrown in trenches, where names and fame are lost. Anyone might wake in the morning to have breakfast with their families and then by the night dine with their ancestors in the world to come. Some drag themselves out of doors to die in view of any who might pray for them. Others die alone in their houses, their deaths made known by a smell that overwhelms even the most fragrant efforts at fumigation.*

*Please find solace knowing that your mother was not alone. She never left my side when she lost her husband and her elder son to their accident, nor when she lost her younger son to the misadventures I abetted, and so I did not leave her side when the sickness came. To the last she believed the fires of mugwort would be her salvation, and I kept them burning until I coughed with the smoke and tears filled my eyes.*

*Weak though she was, your mother reached from her bed to hold my face in her hands and said to me, When God sees fit for this storm to pass, you should make your life with Francis. Pull him from the convent by force if you must. It seems God meant for him to be a father.*

*It is no blasphemy, I hope, to say that with her regard upon me then I felt as if seen by God, from whom there is no hiding or secrets, only love. Even through the smoke, she likely observed in my features the lines of confusion caused by this new comprehension that she knew more than I credited. And she said to me, Do you suppose only the Budge men understand acts of creation because they alone wield carving knives? You forget I carved my two sons with my body and knew from their births of what materials they were made.*

*I wish I could say these calming words were her last upon this earth. But the pestilence is not so kind.*

*After her body was removed, I could remain no longer in the home we once shared. The stink of death was too great, and I feared breathing the foul air a moment longer would mean the end of our child. I returned instead to the workshop where I sit now among the tools of your family's craft. What will become of such sad evidence of all to which human effort once aspired?*

*Many have said if we had spent the last sixty years building a wall rather than a cathedral, perhaps we would have been spared. Perhaps the devils that brought this pestilence among us could have been kept out. I've no doubt, Francis, had you known the fate that would befall us, you would have built a wall to the heavens in order to protect us—my brothers, your mother, myself, our son.*

*But it is surely God's will that you survive this, that your exile now proves an escape. I am told Gaerdegen is a holy place and will surely be spared, not like this sinful city, which I have done my part to populate with sin.*

*Perhaps you might yet build a wall to keep us safe? A wall of prayer you can construct even from so far away?*

There the letter ended. A second note in the bishop's clerk's hand explained that he had found Helena at the shop's worktable, her face pressed against the page, an infant in her arms.

Francis recalled the longing he had felt for her, the complicated feelings that their son's birth had brought, and also that in the end it had come to nothing. He thought, too, of his mother's long care for him, her kisses when he was small, her concern as he became a man. What had all that love and torment meant, with its objects gone so quickly? And was it possible that he had occupied himself following the voice of a girl through the forest while his family suffered so?

Francis read Helena's final words again and again, with rising torment at the knowledge that he had been her dying hope.

# Chapter 18

NEWS THAT THE plague had come to the Cathedral City cast even the brightest days at Gaerdegen into darkness. Reports of the fate suffered by Francis's family were the first to reach the abbey. He made no announcement of his loss, but after the sisters saw how his usually steady hands shook while offering them communion he quietly explained. They had little time to offer comfort, however, as his tragedy was followed quickly by others. Soon few nuns among the three dozen were spared correspondence including names of lost loved ones and the circumstances of their ends. Though the city was a great distance, many among the sisters feared it was only a matter of time before the sickness reached the convent.

"And even if not," Sister Philomena said, "we are sure to be found by those fleeing the pestilence."

"And should we not be?" Sister John asked. "What higher purpose has a house of the Lord than to take in those in greatest need?"

"Preserving the lives of those dedicated to a life of prayer, I should think."

The valley below was said to be reigned now by the lawlessness of lost hope.

With Death on the horizon, inhibitions fell away. That criminality increased every time the word "plague" was spoken was a matter universally acknowledged. The constable of the region announced that every theft would lead to the loss of an ear; every act of violence would result in a walk to the gallows.

Despite the mounting dangers, Francis could not remain within the relative safety of his workshop. Visions of Helena and the boy haunted him, their features emerging whenever he attempted to use carving to forget his grief. His one solace was in the forest below. To walk among the trees reminded him of happier times with his father and brother, times before he knew of sin and its costs.

Nor had he forgotten the simple joy he felt in catching sight of Maureen, another reminder that innocence and beauty still could be found in the world.

One late morning he heard singing through the trees and followed its lilting melody until he spotted her gathering scrap wood into a basket on her back. She moved about dreamily, studying first the leaves above her and then the pine needles on the forest floor.

Already the sun was setting behind the hills. Truly, he knew he should be on his way back to the abbey or he might get lost in the dark forest, as even the most experienced woodsman might. But he remained stuck in his place, bound to watch her, transfixed as one might be by a house fire. The light of the sunset filtered through the trees and the light she herself seemed to emit gave the scene an almost holy glow. He had never favored haloes in his depictions of saints, but perhaps this was what it was like to be witness to such a presence. How else to capture it in a static form but with a penumbra of gold? The fact that such a person should live gave the world a new radiance.

Only with this light in his heart could he return to Gaerdegen and offer prayers to God with any sincerity. Without her, he wondered what would become of his faith.

"Father, mind yourself as you wander in the wood," Sister Philomena told him as he left the abbey the next day. "There are only rogues about who don't fear death."

"All fear death, Sister."

"Then they don't fear judgment, which is all the worse."

It was a bright afternoon after days of dousing rain. He led his ox down their usual path, their empty cart clattering behind. He had no real plans to fill it, intending merely to forget his losses for a time in the company of trees.

Once under the forest canopy, Francis paused to consider the wet drops suspended from the low-hanging branches. He put his hand behind a transparent bead; when he raised his fingers, the bend of the light in the liquid made it seem they were reaching down, a divine hand stretching from heaven to set the world aright. Why had no such intervention occurred in the Cathedral City? Perhaps such a hand could have crafted the wall Helena had prayed for. If he could return to the moment of his departure, he would have sharpened his chisel and then carved a bulwark out of the cathedral itself.

He was thinking such thoughts when he saw them approach suspended in a raindrop: two men weaving among the trees, singing with slurred voices.

*Hither, thither, masterless*
*Like ships upon the sea,*
*Wandering through the ways of air,*
*Go the scavenging birds like we.*

*Bound we are by ne'er a bond,*
*No cage for us, no key,*
*Questing always for our kind,*
*We find depravity.*

One man, the smaller of the two, wore a fine purple cap. The other man, taller by a head or more, wore boots riding up past his knees. Like the purple cap on his companion, they were a fashion above his station, more likely products of a recent robbery than his usual attire, as the peasant rags worn above them attested. They were just the sort of ruffians Philomena had warned him against. He felt for the hatchet tucked in his belt and was glad to find it there.

When the shorter of the two spotted Francis's tonsured head, he smiled broadly, calling out while they approached.

"Father, it is fortunate we found you," he said. "My friend Dougal and I have spent these past days disputing theological matters. He says to me, Roger, ain't it true that the plague is sent by God to give man his comeuppance, to knock us down a peg and make us humble once more? I says to him, Don't be daft, how can there be a God when such a thing as the pestilence should come to pass?"

The men had reached him by the end of this pronouncement, their hot breath rancid with whatever was in the jug they passed between them. The short one leaned in close to Francis, studying his face, which since learning of what had happened to the Cathedral City remained a map of grief.

"Ah, Father. What's troubling you?" Roger said. "Look at him, Doug. It's like a ghost just snuck up upon him."

And with this suggestion, a ghost seemed to do just that: Francis imagined Helena standing at his shoulder while he carved in his family's workshop. He thought he could smell her on the breeze and grimaced as he felt his heart break anew.

"Ah Roger," the taller of the two men said. "You made a priest cry. That's some kind of sin, ain't it then?"

"Don't be sad, Father," Roger said. "Have a drink."

The jug was at his lips before he thought better of it. He drank deep, and it burned his throat, but from the first taste he felt his thoughts of Helena fading.

"That's right. Drink up," Dougal said. "It's the only way through this wicked world."

"Have a seat with us, Father," Roger added. "Tell us your troubles."

They sensed his hesitation and spoke quickly to put him at his ease.

"Father, it is true what you must suppose of us," Roger said. "We poor brothers have lived sinful lives, but now we have repented. If in your mercy you would join as fellow Christians, we do not suppose it will win us entry to paradise, but perhaps it would help us climb out of the infernal eternity that otherwise awaits, earning a place in purgatory with the other sinners trusting in the grace of God for our salvation."

Francis eyed them warily but then sat on the wet ground beside them and drank again from the jug, taking a long slow swallow that he feared would melt him from within.

"She's gone," he said.

"*She?* Father, you surprise me!"

He surprised himself. The ease with which he then began to describe his loss, his failings, his sins caught Francis off guard. "My brother's widow," he said.

"Your brother!" Dougal laughed.

"A widow!" Roger hooted approvingly.

"The first of many, unfortunately," Francis continued. "I'd grant them absolution and then give them more to confess."

"A man after my own heart," Roger said.

"A man after your own piss pole, more like," Dougal snickered.

Francis wished with every word he would stop talking, but the jug kept coming, pausing in its circuit only when Roger held on to it, lost in thought as he brought another verse of his song to mind.

*Life is short, and all too soon*
*We emit our final gasp*
*Death ere long will come for you*
*No soul escapes his grasp.*

"A bleak song, friend," Francis said.

"And all the truer for it."

An hour or more passed as the jug changed hands. Why, Francis wondered, had he feared these men when he first saw them? Perhaps he had spent too long in the company of women. He had forgotten the hearty fellowship of men—simple men like his father's woodsmen had been. He imagined these two new companions as carved of similar stuff. His head full of wine, he suddenly felt he loved these men. Dougal with his too-long arms, Roger with his nasal twang that never failed to find another verse to his rambling song, which perfectly fit the mood the three men had created between them.

*But when I'm drunk on good strong wine*
*That makes a body warm within*
*Little care I for absolution*
*My hope's in the Resurrection*

"Have you forgotten, Father?" Roger asked when his song at last seemed to have reached its end. "I posed a question when first we were fortunate enough to cross your path. When the plague finds us, will you say God is out to get us or that there is no God at all?"

Francis let his head loll backward, taking in the forest canopy, radiant as it was with late afternoon light. Each leaf glowed like a different-colored stone in a vast mosaic depicting the grandeur of the heavens.

"How can you say there is no God when despite the plague there is so much beauty in the world?"

"Beauty, ha! Show me a bit of beauty in this ugly mess."

"What about the trees?

"You won't find them beautiful when they fall on your house," Dougal said, "or get lost among them and eaten by wolves—"

"Or if a couple of rogues come out of their shadow and put a knife in your back," Roger added with a dark grin. "Name me one thing of beauty that won't harm you in the end."

Francis thought first of his father's carvings, but then recalled how they had killed him. He thought next of Helena, but then of her rejection, and then of the fresh pain of losing her again, forever. Maybe this rogue was right? Through his drunken fog he chased these images away, grasping at something that might save him from despair.

"There is one," he said as the thought formed unbidden. "A girl, who is beyond doubt the most beautiful of God's creatures.

I see her wandering in the wood sometime, her face alight with a holiness. She is beauty with no pain, only joy."

"Prove it."

"Prove her beauty?"

"Don't play the fool, Father. Take us there!"

Once again Francis felt the menace of these men, but the sharp edge of it was blunted by the jug, which he continued to put to his lips whenever he found it in his hands. Still, he was able to form the hope that if they went in the direction of Butcher's encampment, they soon would encounter not the girl but her father, who surely would put an end to this dark merriment.

They hauled Francis into his oxcart and bid him to point the way, Roger singing all the while.

*Down the primrose path I post*
*Straight to Satan's grotto*
*Shunning virtue, doing most*
*Things that I ought not to*

Expecting to pull one man, the ox strained with the weight of three. The cart rattled through the forest as it fell into dusk. The rocking of the wheels over the rough track combined with the churning liquid in his belly caused Francis to fall on his side and heave the contents of his stomach onto the ground.

"Now that's good grog you've wasted, Father!" Roger shouted. "Better give him some more."

Once again the jug was at his lips; when he pushed it away, Dougal grabbed him roughly by the cheeks and forced his mouth open. The wine felt thick in his throat as he choked it down. He struggled against the grip on his jaw, but it only tightened.

"Easy, Father," Dougal said. "Easy."

The wine dragged Francis deep into a numb stupor, all his thoughts falling away. He felt the world spin above him, tree boughs turning like a windmill. Through a fog he heard the two men murmuring.

"This cart will fetch a fair price."

"Did you check him for a purse?"

"Like I told you when we spotted him, priests got no fecking purses."

"Any holy oils or such? A fecking relic maybe?"

"He's got naught but that hatchet in his belt."

"He's poorer than we are, but I'll be glad to take it."

"This must be the place."

"Better be more here or it's a wasted fecking night."

For all Francis could tell, they could have been rolling through the forest for a day or a week, though they had scarcely traveled a mile. When they arrived at Butcher's dwelling at last, it appeared deserted. Francis could barely lift himself from the cart, but he surveyed the encampment with relief.

"It seems," Francis stammered. "It seems . . . there are none here this evening,"

"What a pity," Dougal said.

"So I was right then," Roger laughed. "No real beauty to be found left in this foul world. Just sin and death and devils like us, eh, Father?"

Early shades of darkness had begun to descend on the three men, making it difficult even to see each other. Just then through the sounds of the gathering night they heard a high-pitched keening, a screech like an animal in agony, but prolonged as if its suffering would continue without end.

"What's that, then?"

Francis recognized the cry of the sharpening stone. Even in his inebriation he knew what the sound must mean, who must be nearby engaged in her usual innocent industry. *No*, he thought.

Inside the shed, they found her as she was when Francis first set eyes on her. She sat at the wheel with assorted blades set on the low table before her. In her hands, metal met stone and seemed to launch tiny balls of flame around her. The sparks caught her green eyes just as she looked up and saw him there.

"Oh, Father," she said brightly. "Fortunate that you have come. I have been sharpening your blades this evening. I think you will find the edge left by our wheel a considerable improvement—"

Then she saw that he was not alone. Roger and Dougal followed Francis through the door, then pushed him violently to the floor.

"Forgive our friend," Dougal said. "He's had too much to drink."

"Do you gentlemen," she asked in confusion, "have blades in need of sharpening?"

"No, lass," Roger said. "Our blades are plenty sharp."

"My father is not here," she said. "He is off on a hunt. If you need to speak to him, I'd advise you return another time." She reached down and took up a knife as if to put it to the wheel, though gripping it in clear preparation of defending herself. She looked beseechingly at the priest where he lay on the floor but spoke still to the strangers, a catch in her voice as she realized she had said something she would have been wise not to mention. "But of course, he will return any moment," she added, "with his hounds, and his companions, I am sure of it."

When Roger moved forward, she stood with her back to the spinning stone and raised her arm slightly to be sure the empty-handed man approaching could see her blade.

Dougal took two strides and reached the girl with his long arms before she had time to turn to face him. He easily wrapped her arm in his fist, twisting her elbow until her hand opened and the shed filled with the sound of metal clanging to stone.

"None of that now, lass."

She swung around to strike him with her free hand, but Dougal just hoisted her into the air, her feet dangling beneath her, kicking like a fish caught on a line.

Looking up, Francis could see her face clearly though his vision was fogged. The interior light she had shone a moment before was now white-hot fury, as if the sparks made by her sharpening wheel were sparking from within.

"I don't know, Roger," Dougal said. "She's such a wee thing. Mightn't we be damned?"

"Damned?" Roger scoffed. "Bah. The world is damned. The plague is but a long walk away. It'll be here by year's end. Or could be tomorrow. All a man can do is grab what he can in the meantime. And I'm grabbing her."

*Plague.* The word woke Francis from his daze, and he struggled to his feet. The word strangled any thought he had of a happy future, like the hand he saw tighten on her throat. The world would be brutalized as he saw her brutalized now, thrown down to the dirt floor, her head knocking so hard against the corner of the table as she fell that her orange hair went dark with blood.

Neither of the men could see him; Roger had his back turned as he grabbed the girl's legs; Dougal looked away as he pinned her arms stretched out to the sides. Francis hoisted his hatchet and brought it down hard on Roger's shoulder. Despite his strength and usual skill with the tool, his blunted senses caused the strike to land with the wide side of the hatchet—a solid blow but less damaging than he had hoped.

"The feck, Father!" Dougal shouted.

"I'll stave in your skull, you damned priest," Roger wailed.

In an instant they had stripped him of his hatchet and thrown him across the shed. With the cord he kept around his waist, they bound him to the heavy frame of the sharpening wheel, where he would be powerless to do anything but witness the ruination of the world. As they hovered above the injured girl, he cried out to let them know they were seen and heard by a man in Holy Orders, that through him God saw this scene and would judge them all according to their sins. But even as he shouted that the Lord was watching, he found he could not do the same. He shut his eyes with the urgent awareness that he had set this all in motion, and he wished he would never see the world again.

When the men rose, the girl was motionless.

"Ah Roger," Dougal said as he nudged her head with his toe. "You've gone and fecked her dead."

"The Devil take her, then. He'll take us all soon enough."

"Then we've only saved her the suffering of the end times. Ain't that right, Father?"

With another drag on their jug, they moved toward the door.

"I hear there are nuns in these woods," Roger said. "I've a mind to grab a few of them next."

"Nuns, Roger?" Dougal said. "Mightn't we be damned?"

Roger's laugh lingered in the doorway long after the two men had disappeared into the night.

Francis stretched to reach a blade that had fallen beneath the sharpening stone, then sawed at the rope until it gave way. He dragged himself across the room until he was at Maureen's side. He stood over her as clouds outside gave way to moonlight through the open door, and her body seemed to glow. He examined her wounds—on her hands where she scraped at their eyes, bruises on her legs where they had gripped her ankles to pin her down, at her temple where the sharp table corner had drawn blood. Pale in the light, she looked at once familiar and entirely of another world.

Her eyes moved and seemed to focus for a moment on him. She did not know his name, but he wondered if she might speak it, if God through her would call out the one who had allowed this to happen.

"Maureen?" he said. "Maureen? Stay, girl. It's not yet your time."

Fast, frightened breaths grew shallow and then faded. Francis watched as her soul seemed to depart, and her body joined the stillness of the forest falling toward night.

There was nothing that could be done now save absolving her sins, though he doubted they could be many or severe. He made a cross above her, then collapsed again on the floor, retching hot wine into the dirt.

Darkness then came for him as well, but it was only drunken sleep.

# Chapter 19

"FATHER, DID YOU think we had forgotten you?"

The girl's face shone in the moonlight, then dimmed, then glowed again, as two figures moved through the open door.

"We were halfway home when my friend says to me, 'Roger, that priest knows our names and he knows our faces.' And then I remembered that blow you gave me with your hatchet, so we thought we'd come back and shove that same hatchet up your arse until it comes out your throat."

Dougal grabbed him by the hood. He pulled the priest's robe first from his shoulders, then his waist, tearing and tugging until Francis lay naked on the floor. Feet flew to his ribs and stomach; Francis curled in on himself, tasting earth and blood.

"Now where is that fecking hatchet?"

As the two men searched the dark dirt floor, Francis dug his fingers into the ground and dragged himself away, crawling across the shed toward the spinning stone, where the blades the girl had been sharpening lay neatly on their cloth.

He had nearly reached one when Roger's foot swept them all out of reach; the knives clattered against each other as they scattered across the floor. Francis tried again to rise, attempted to pull himself up to his knees but could only manage to cling to the frame of the sharpening wheel.

The wheel spun still with the current of the moving water outside. Roger pressed his foot against the back of Francis's neck, pushing the priest's cheek toward the spinning stone. Every muscle in his neck and back strained to preserve the space between his skin and the rough grit whose heat he could feel even without contact. He knew not where the words came from, but they were there on his lips. "Mother Ursula, protect me!"

But the force of Roger's foot proved too much to resist. The stone's grit met his skin and began to tear it layer by layer, as if he was being dragged along a cobbled road by a horse at full gallop. He let out a scream loud enough not to wake the dead but to shake them loose from Francis's memory, to jumble their varied ends into an indistinguishable tangle of all the losses he had ever known.

It all happened in a flash as the skin around his eye socket was shredded to fleshy strings, as the wheel consumed the soft tissue of his right eye and all went dark with blood. All at once the girl's suffering and Helena's suffering were joined, and together their pain was all the pain in the world, which was simultaneously the torment of Christ on his cross. The spinning stone was first the wall of the cathedral that had dominated his youth, then it was the wall Helena wished he had built to keep them safe. Then it was the earthen floor on which the girl was ravaged and seemed to breathe her last. His failure to save himself was inseparable from his abandonment of his child and his drunken inability to rescue the girl. Somehow his carnality and his vanity had delivered him from the plague, and in this deliverance he had brought demons to the door of an innocent.

Roger put his full weight on the back of Francis's neck and pressed his face fully against the stone, and in that instant he glimpsed all that he might have done to save his family, all that he might have done to save Maureen, all that he must to do now to save Gaerdegen.

When the pressure finally lifted, Francis rolled away from the stone and saw through his remaining eye Roger and Dougal looking about the floor.

"Now where is that fecking hatchet?" Roger asked again. "Did you take it with us when we left?"

"No, it's here. But I thought you had it last."

"So where is it?"

Then Francis saw it: a glint in the air, catching light from the open door, it flashed above Roger's head and came down as if to split a log. The wet crack of his skull sounded like a beer barrel bursting.

"Roger?" Dougal said, and then the hatchet fell again, meeting him squarely on the back of the neck. They fell together in a heap.

Mother Ursula stepped into a shaft of moonglow. Francis lay before her, naked, bleeding, half-blind.

The abbess handed the priest his robe to cover himself, then went to Maureen's side. Francis watched as she touched the back of her hand to the girl's forehead. She then unfastened her veil and spread it over the silent body.

Just before all grew dim again around him, Francis saw the room fill with light. In the last sight of his ruined eye, the world appeared made of stained glass bursting into flame.

# Chapter 20

HE AWOKE TO the sensation of fingers on his face. They moved as a potter might mold clay, massaging his skin with a slow, purposeful touch.

"Careful not to stir too quickly, or they might fall off," a voice said beside him.

He opened one eye to see Sister Anna sitting in the sunlight of the small room where she tended to the convent's ill and aging. His other eye seemed somehow locked behind its lid, as if sealed with the sand of sleep. From a bowl in her lap, the infirmarian took what appeared to be a small brown stone. When she placed the stone on his cheek, he felt a new finger join the others in the probing of his pores.

Francis sat up with a start and a dozen of these stones clattered to the floor. Reaching toward his temple, he found another clinging to the few hairs remaining of his left eyebrow. He held it before him and saw it was not a rock but a shell, an oozing mass protruding from its base. He flung it across the room, where it cracked against one of the dozens of herb jars lining the walls.

"You mustn't excite yourself," Sister Anna said, putting a firm hand on the priest's shoulder. "A snail's grease soothes the abrasion and helps with the pain. When you have settled yourself, I will reapply them."

She eased him down onto his back then placed a damp cloth on his face. It smelled of medicinals—horsemint, meadowsweet, silverweed—but would not have burned more if it had been made of glowing coals. Even through the sting he felt something amiss in the way the poultice's weight draped from his forehead to his upper lip. He raised a hand toward his left cheek and walked his fingertips upward as the snails had done. Beneath the cloth where the small mound of his eye should have been, he found instead a hollow depression, like the pit left when a sprouted acorn is dug out of the ground. He pushed two fingers into the hole, then exhaled a gasping sob as he experienced anew the damage done by the sharpening wheel.

Sister Anna took Francis by the wrist to move his fingers away from the wounds.

"Yes, you have lost the eye," she said, "but the skin will heal if left undisturbed. You should thank God and all the saints that you did not bleed to death, as you surely would have if Mother Ursula had not brought you back from the forest in time."

Francis glanced about the room and then down at his own body, registering that it was daytime and that his blood- and vomit-sodden robe was somehow clean. He was far from that awful night, though he knew he would never escape its consequences.

"The abbess brought me?" he asked. "When?"

"Near a week ago. This is the longest you have been lucid since."

He could recall very little of the previous days. When he attempted to remember how he had come to be in the care of the infirmarian, he saw in his mind's eye only scenes of the girl's suffering commingled with Helena's description of the suffering of the plague, which danced through his memory like a shadow play. He drifted off again as Sister Anna removed the poultice and began repositioning the cold wet creatures on his skin. As light shifted across the floor and walls, Francis could not tell where his diminished worldly vision ended and his heightened spiritual vision began.

When he next opened his remaining eye, the room was dark but for a single candle burning at his bedside. A nun sat still in the chair beside him, but it was not the same woman as before.

"Good evening, Father," Abbess Ursula said. "Sister Anna told me your condition had much improved. I am pleased to see this is so."

The old nun sat so serenely in front of him that he could scarcely believe the memory that came to him all at once now; this wrinkled woman wielding a hatchet—*his* hatchet, which in his drunken state he had allowed to fall from his hands.

"How?" he asked. "How did you find me?"

Ursula smiled sadly, as if the answer was obvious and she pitied his inability to grasp even the plainest of facts.

"I heard you," she said.

Could it be true, Francis thought, that she heard those in need when they called for her protection?

"You heard me call your name?"

"No," the abbess explained patiently. "I heard shrieking such as the forest has never known. And the tracks of the oxcart are not difficult to follow. When you had not returned by dark, Sister Philomena feared the worst. I know the woods better than anyone, so I went alone to search for you—but it was Philomena's concern that sent me looking."

"Had I heeded her concerns, I would not have gone at all, and then—"

The words caught in his throat as images of the girl flashed before him in quick succession: of her wandering among the trees, of her face lit by sparks, of her body still on the floor. He remembered that it was the magnitude of his grief launched by Helena's letter that had kindled his desire to see Maureen that day—and that this same grief had devoured her.

"A great tragedy has occurred," Ursula said. "When your strength returns, I will await your explanation."

Francis nodded for a long moment, sorting his thoughts, separating what he did and did not remember from what he could never tell. "There is no need to wait," he said. "You have heard perhaps that my family was taken by the plague."

"We are all aware, and we have held them in our prayers. As you know, many of the sisters have received news of similar losses, and doubtless many more will yet."

Ursula's genuine look of compassion caught him off guard. Framed in her veil, her face struck Francis in that moment as utterly without judgment, interested only in relieving him of the burden he held as the witness to great evil.

"In my grief," he said, "I fell in with those two wicked men. They were mockers of the faith, and I wanted only to show them that heaven had not completely abandoned us. Are there not still some signs of divine love left in the world?"

"Indeed there are."

"I had thought so, but now I cannot be sure. I know only that my sins brought the plague upon my family, and now they have led death to the door of an innocent."

"Do not be so certain of what you know," Ursula said. "You have heard me speak often of the foolishness of God and the wisdom of men. What I mean by this is that even though the world seems mad, we have to believe there is an order to it all, no matter how incomprehensible."

Francis studied her features, which remained impassive, betraying nothing of her thoughts, only continuing to take him in with wide, clear eyes. He saw the candlelight reflected within them, and then saw himself, reclined as if on his deathbed, yet grasping for life.

"The girl?" he asked. "She is—"

"She is in God's hands," Ursula said. "As are we all."

"I did what I could to keep her in the Lord's care," Francis said. "I was useless to save her, but I was able to absolve her sins. We should tell her father so he has that solace at least."

Ursula looked at him sternly. "There is no need for you to speak to the girl's father or for you to return there for any reason. You did all that was in your power, and I did the same."

"And the two men?" he asked.

"I dragged them into the forest. No one will doubt that some other rogues did them in or that they deserved it. Their stolen clothes will be sufficient evidence, along with their stink of sin."

The abbess seemed to scrutinize him with her final words. She was said to have knowledge beyond the usual senses. He wondered what she might know of the further circumstances that had brought him to the sharpening shed that night. In truth, even readily observable facts would have given her some indication. She no doubt had smelled the same wine on his robe as on the men.

"Rest now," she said, standing to leave when it seemed he could say no more. "We will talk further when you are well."

She had nearly made it through the door when he called after her.

"Would you like me to hear your confession?" he asked.

"Confession?"

"For the sin of killing those men."

"Sin is an odd thing to call the act of saving your life."

"To take a life is still a grave offense to God, is it not?"

His face half-covered with a cloth poultice, he stared intently at her with his remaining eye, held open to take in all he might.

"Very well," Ursula said. "A confession." She sat again at his side, leaning forward to speak in soft tones. "When I was a young woman, my family traded me in marriage to a wealthy man for his political connections. He was not a good man, generous only with his fists. I was only the age of the youngest of our novices when we wed. Four years I shared his bed, and four times I lost infants in my womb because he was never gentle, not even when I was with child."

"I am sorry for your trouble," Francis said, "but what has this to do with—"

"As we neared the fifth anniversary of our nuptials," Ursula continued, "he announced that he had grown weary of having no heir. If he had a younger wife, he suggested, he might have better luck. He even had one in mind. I reminded him I was all of twenty years old and told him if he did not imbibe until his manhood shrank or beat the woman condemned to bear his children until she wished she were barren, he might have better luck as well. For this advice I was given a broken nose and told to be careful on the stairs, for he had dreamed that he soon might be a widower. 'God knows no accidents,' he said, 'but we poor mortals do.'

"The next day as I descended from our sleeping chamber to the sitting room, I found my feet swept out from under me. I tumbled with my knees over my head and only did not die because my skull was too stubborn to crack. That, at least, was what my husband said when he expressed to his cronies his dismay that his clumsy wife was still living. And perhaps I was clumsy, but a week later, coming down the stairs, I tripped over a loose board, and when I inspected it, I saw that the nails had been removed.

"'Are you truly trying to break my neck?' I asked him. In reply, he gripped me by the throat and said, 'To do that I would scarcely need to try at all.' The force of his fingers left a line of perfectly round bruises like the holes in a piper's flute, as if some tune could be played with my bones to lead the mice out of town. When I studied the bruises in the looking glass, I wondered what that tune might be and decided it would sound like the willow warblers' song on the first day of spring.

"It was then that I became so taken with birds. I kept the smallest of finches in a cage at my bedside, and its melodies brightened my dark days. One afternoon it sang so loudly that it woke my husband.

"'Would you quiet that flying rat?' he shouted.

"'I will not,' I said. 'It is past midday and it is not time for sleeping. It is time for dining.'

"My husband reached into the cage, grabbed my little bird, and stuffed it whole into his mouth. He crunched down on its bones and he spat the pretty finch onto the floor. I rushed to see if it might be saved, but I had never seen a creature so diminished. A moment before, it had been singing its happy tune, and then it was just a lump of spit and feathers.

"I was so distraught by what he had done, I began spending my days on the rooftop, nearer the birds, farther from him. Or so I'd hoped. He found me there one day, grabbed me by the hair and pulled me to the ledge. He vowed that if I did not conceive again soon, he would teach me to fly. He was sure it would seem like an accident, or perhaps a suicide—in which case my soul would be damned.

"That evening, after he had passed out from too much drink, I informed the servants that my husband had requested a feast to be laid at his bedside in case he woke up hungry, as he often did. They set out a roast goose and meat pudding, fine wine, and hearty ale as if for an honored guest. After they had left, I pried open his mouth and stuffed the fat end of a goose leg deep into his throat. None who had seen him eat would have found this unusual. He breathed in meat like air. The quantities he consumed were so well known that children sang songs about them in the street.

"Just as I drew back my hand, his eyes opened, and his cheeks turned purple. But his body was still too besotted with wine to move. He only stared at me—first, I think, with the belief that I would help him, then with the recognition that I would not. He struggled for some time, and I watched to make sure this would be the end of it. Before his soul departed, I told him that if God had no use for accidents then neither would I.

"I passed the year that followed spending his money and seeing what I could of the world. What I found was that there were few places where women were no less at the mercy of cruel men than I had been, and so I resolved to make one myself. While I have not confessed this sin until now, I have long regarded my founding of Gaerdegen as a private penance. Was his unholy life worth the scores of sanctified sisters who have passed through the abbey? I do believe it was.

"Of course, you are correct that this new occurrence will require absolution, and I would be obliged to you if you would grant it. I will accept any penance you give, but perhaps we might wait until we see how this sin weighs in the balance. How can we know yet if it has made the world better or worse? Should we presume this is not what the Lord intended from the beginning of time? I put the drumstick in my husband's mouth, but God made the goose. I lifted the hatchet over the heads of those rogues, but God brought it down."

Ursula stood again to leave Francis to his recuperation. She moved to the door but stopped in the threshold and turned to face him.

"This is likely only the beginning of the suffering we will endure," she said. "The question put before us is: *What will we make of it?* You are both a priest and a carver of wood. If anyone could transform these awful days into something of use or beauty, surely it would be you."

# Chapter 21

LATE THAT NIGHT, Francis rolled from the cot in the infirmarian's chamber and made his way across the abbey yard as if in a trance. Though he had begun to heal, his wounds proved to be even more disorienting once he was beyond the confines of the infirmary and outside in the starry darkness. With distances both near and endlessly far for his vision to sort through, the loss of half his sight made this short walk difficult to navigate. The ground seemed to rise to meet him with such urgency that every step forward had the feeling of falling, and the trees surrounding the convent seemed to bend, as if finally succumbing to the weight of longing as his father had warned they might.

Reaching his squat shack by moving away from the sound of the church bell, he went directly to his worktable and sharpened his remaining blades. He had left his best knives on the floor by Maureen's wheel, and so those he had available required particular effort. Every scrape of his whetstone seemed to speak her name, the low tone of pushing a knife away, the higher pitch of drawing it back. He continued just to hear it, bringing every metal edge to a vanishingly small point.

Through the night he carved, with a certainty and conviction entirely new to him, becoming only the implements and the action of the work: smooth wooden handle and a cold, sharp knife, sliding swiftly through clean white wood. Slivers fell and turned in the breeze that filled the one-room shack; wood chips blew all around him then out through the window, into the night. He carved by candlelight, watching as a body rose from the block of wood; coaxing life from the trunk of a slaughtered tree.

First the feet: one over the other, scaled down slightly from a grown man's. He cut a hole dead center for the nail they would wear. Then, the legs: thin, round, strong. The priest's hand moved steadily, careful but sure, raising his knife with the grain of the wood, gauging a deep, bending line where the two legs would meet, sending paper-thin shards of wood spinning to the floor. Next, the hips: wide, womanly, carved to curves that appeared to be hidden beneath wood that rippled like cloth. Then the stomach and subtle lines of muscle. The chest only slightly rising, like small breasts lying flat. Shoulders that surprised him with their strength. Cut from separate pieces and pegged into place: arms with veins visible running through the wrists, and finely articulated hands, graceful even with their brutal wounds.

Francis chiseled, shaped, polished until the wood was made fine and smooth as flesh, and a full body stood before him, arms wide open, legs and feet still joined to the stump of the tree they once were.

He moved in close to the round block on his worktable that would be the statue's head. It was virgin wood, just the bark removed. He whittled slowly, paring away the thinnest of slivers while watching the wood grain, searching for sunken cheeks, thirsting lips, forsaken eyes—all the features that lay hidden within the lines. Hours passed, and he found them, astonished by the result though he had searched for the face's features as if for a child swept into the sea.

When it was morning, he attached the head to the body, lodging a thin stem beneath the neck into a waiting slot between the shoulders. Only then did he back away to take stock of what he had done. Bright lines from the sunrise sneaking through the shuttered window lashed the limbs and torso with fresh scars of light. The face stared back at him, pained and perfect, as if wondering what comes next. The broken body was flawless.

And yet it was incomplete. This was a statue intended to tell a story with its wounds, and there was one he had forgotten. Francis raised his curved chisel to the wood flesh and began to make an angry crescent in its side, and then stopped short when his own arm entered the light. He had worked straight through the night. No food. No rest. He felt exhaustion in every pore, and now his skin had grown pallid—offensive and sinful in comparison to the holy body of his Lord.

Christ's eyes crawled over him as words his brother once spoke echoed through his mind. *If you fear the chisel*, Robert had said, *there can be no blood in the flesh you bring to life.* He brought the blade to his chest and slid it across his ribs, cutting just deep enough to draw blood.

He wet his fingers, then wiped them on the carved body where Christ's wounds would be: a red dab in each of the palms, on the feet, across the forehead where the thorns dug in. He pressed his chest up against it so the gash in his side would color the wooden incision where the Roman spear pierced Christ. Bare skin on fresh carved wood, he remembered the mockery of the cross he had made in his family workshop when the bishop's mother came with her own carnal interests. He had not turned her away then, and yet that day he had turned away from others' sins of the flesh far too easily. How wicked the world. How inevitable punishment in the form of the plague must be.

With the final wound added, Francis stepped away from his worktable to see more clearly his creation and recognized fully what part of him had known dimly all along. It was Christ on his cross, but it was also the girl in the sharpening shed. Arms outstretched in helplessness, feet immobile, beaten, and left for dead. How had he never truly seen that his Lord was wretched, naked, made ugly by the violence of men? It was a vision of innocence destroyed because of his failure; goodness defiled because of his sin.

"Forgive me," he said, then wiped his hand across the statue's lips and kissed them, tasting his own blood.

Before Lauds that morning, Father Francis tied two ropes to the cross's horizontal beam and hoisted it into the air above the altar in the abbey church. Christ's feet floated above the stone slab, an image not of his death but of his ascension, a broken body exalted so that there was no mistaking that this was the god of suffering.

Morning light fell upon the crucified figure's face as the sisters entered the church. Ursula gasped at the sight. She alone recognized the girl from the butcher's shed depicted in the statue; to see her features so transformed, this beaten peasant youth remade as the Lord, revealed to her a depth of the priest's skill she had not previously seen.

Yet even more surprising was the man himself. Other than Ursula and Anna, none of the sisters had seen Father Francis since his fateful trek into the forest a week before. He stood to the right of the altar, first with his back to the nuns as he too gazed up at the cross. Only when he turned did Sister John see that he seemed utterly transformed. Gone was the timidity he had brought with him from the Cathedral City, replaced with a countenance so resolute he too might have been carved of wood. Gone were the fine features she had heard had led him into such trouble. Half his face was now a mask of brutal injury. He wore a strap of cloth tied at an angle across his forehead, covering the hole where his eye had been.

"Sisters!" he called out. "Never have I sought to interrupt your chapel devotions by speaking with you here outside of Mass. But what I have to say cannot wait."

Ursula grabbed Sister John by the hand and pulled her close.

"Father is not well," she said, "go fetch him some water."

But neither John nor any of the nuns of Gaerdegen could move. They stood transfixed by the apparent act of sorcery that hung above the altar. Was it possible the figure before them was not flesh and blood? How could wood be carved so that it seemed not only to breathe, but also breathe its last?

Francis noted the upward tilt of their eyes with satisfaction. The spark of life he had searched for, he realized, was also the spark of death. There could be no true creation that did not include a shadow of its end.

"God has taken half my sight," he continued, "but he has compensated by giving me a vision. These past few days I have seen what is to come. I am sure you have all heard news of the plague's arrival in the Cathedral City, where scarcely half the population remains to bury the dead. But sickness is only the beginning of the torment the plague has brought upon the earth. Demons walk openly among the living. Two of them took my eye. They could come to find us any time.

"My ability to create this cross came to me in a vision in which Christ himself had opened his wounds and shown me death on an order none have ever contemplated. Bodies litter the streets in the Cathedral City, their flesh tears open from within."

The plague chronicle he had received from Helena served as a horror story that grew more monstrous with every word he chose. "Imagine the ground beneath your feet writhing with dying vermin. With every step they squeal and wet your ankles with blood. Imagine mothers breathing their last with infants at their breasts. Imagine fathers burying their children one by one for days without counting. Imagine all of Christ's churches empty, only carved saints like this one remaining in memorial of the thousands lost."

"Father, please," Mother Ursula said. "You are frightening the sisters."

"They should be frightened. For it has already begun. What can those still living do but stumble along the roads leading north? They are anxious for the safety they believe Gaerdegen's sanctity will provide. But no matter if they are our families or those dearest to our hearts, they carry the pestilence with them, and we cannot abide their arrival."

Sister Philomena called out, "Father, what can we do?"

"This cross is a warning of what is to come, unless we act to save ourselves."

Francis did not tell them that the cross they knelt before held not just Jesus but a girl called Maureen, or that in his fever dream he had come to see the fates of these two innocents entwined with the world bracing itself for the gates of hell to break open. But he did make a private vow that this time he would not stand idly by. He would protect this place as if it was the last bastion of goodness on the earth. He would protect it as Helena had prayed he might protect his lost loved ones, as he had failed to do.

"And now," Francis said, "the time has come to build a wall."

# PART 5

# SEXT

# Chapter 22

HUMAN NOISES ROSE and fell outside the chaplain's shack, muffled by the crying wind. Several of the nuns had come out from the convent into the storm and were now clearing a way between the cloister and the surrounding buildings. Father Francis recognized Sister Magdalene through the flurries, shoveling quickly, quietly. A handful of others worked nearby; white-veiled novices he did not yet know. They wielded round wooden paddles, heaving snow away like spoonfuls of salt, slowly exposing a dirt and stone path, then watching helplessly as the drifts began to blow back and bury their feet.

Francis pulled the shutter toward him and hooked its latch, hurrying to block the flurries and avoid the sisters' gaze. He crossed the room and returned to the block where his hatchet had become stuck. He took hold of its handle, strained against the grip the wood had on the iron wedge, and again found it too deeply buried to be removed. He decided to leave it where it stood, a monument to his newfound impotence, as storm winds rattled the workshop walls.

*Come.*

*Come.*

Sisters Thaddeus, Jude, Andrew, Bartholomew, and Magdalene stood shin-deep in the path they had been clearing and answered yet another call to prayer. *Pater Noster, Ave Maria*, then the older nun speaking with the novices in reply:

*O Lord, come to my assistance.*

*O God, make haste to help me.*

By mid-morning, they had labored two hours in the storm with little result, the snow accumulating almost as quickly as it could be moved.. Flurry upon flurry came beating down, relentless and wet, blinding white. The snow weighed on the nuns' habits and clung in icy clumps to the fabric of their veils. It mounded on their shoulders when they stood upright and feathered their backs when they bowed to the church to continue their prayers.

*Glory to the Father and to the Son, and to the Holy Spirit,*

*As it was in the beginning, is now and ever shall be.*

All over the convent the sisters prayed, most from memory wherever they worked: in the snowdrifts; in the kitchen; in the barn. Others were gathered in the church, where Mother John ended the office with a reading from the Book of Ursula.

*Remember, my sisters, how little men have seen of the world. They may walk the earth either looking down or looking up, but all they know is that which is immediately before them, following sight upon sight, becoming lost if even for a moment they do not recognize their surroundings. Yet have we not all seen how the doves will always find their way?*

*Sisters, how much better to be like doves than like men. Have you ever observed, doves of my heart, a bird as it leaves its perch? If you study its eyes, as I have done, you will see that at the moment of separating itself from a stable hold on branch, ground, or rooftop, it is not entirely certain what will happen next. It is true that once I said their lives were like our own because they do little but eat, shit, and sing, but now I understand that such actions are simply necessary preparations for their true occupation, which is also ours:*

*Trust. Leap. Rise.*

The sisters bowed again to bring the Hour to a close, then most returned to work while the older nuns took pause to visit and enjoy a bit of bread. They gathered in the refectory, a room filled with daylight and long wooden tables; a room silent but for the whispers of the sisters and the wind.

In the cloister, Sister Lazarus, the baker, led a crew clearing the walkway of snow and ice then shutting up the arches with wooden shields, blocking out the storm. She slipped in frozen slush and dropped a heavy rough-hewn plank on her hand, crushing her fingers as if in a slamming door. As she made her way inside to attend to the wound with an herbal poultice, she slipped again, landing hard on the elbow of the same damaged arm.

"So much for tomorrow's bread," Sister Bartholomew said.

"Have you no goodness in you at all?" Magdalene asked. "You're not content to destroy this place, you delight also in your sisters' misfortune?"

"Destroy this place? I hope to save it. Should we follow Mother John down the path of confusion and error? Her reverence for her predecessor is beyond all reason."

"You care nothing for her or for reason. You are motivated solely by your own interests."

"And whose interests have you been pursuing in your meetings with the bishop's clerk?"

Magdalene felt her cheeks glow with such urgency she could only hope her blush would be mistaken for windburn, but Bartholomew cackled in victory at having elicited such a response.

"Ha! Did you think we all did not know?"

By noon the entire convent had been sealed and the cloister walk was dim as dusk, as though the sun had set. The day's meager light filtered through gaps in the wooden storm shields, giving them an eerie glow.

*Come.*

*Come.*

All work came abruptly to a close at yet another calling of the bell, and once again the nuns gathered together to sing and pray. The church was bitter cold, filled with drafts that shook the candlelight and rattled the cross, filled with a chill that shut lips tight and wrapped bare fingers like wet leather gloves. It seemed morning had never touched the slate and stones of the floor and walls, for the room was again as dark as it had been at the night office eight hours before, though it seemed like years.

Magdalene sang first while the other nuns crowded close in the choir stalls, shoulder to shoulder to share their warmth, watching her, concerned. Even through the darkness they could see that the young nun's face had lost its usual brightness. Her voice carried through the room like far-off tears, sharing the air with the keening of the wind and the noon bell's lingering reverberation.

"O Lord, come to my assistance," she sang.

"O God, make haste to help me," answered the others in reply.

There was no better place to hide her true thoughts than beneath these scripted prayers. The uncertainty of the impending visit from the bishop howled in her mind as loudly as the storm, and with the same disruptive effects. Any hope of focusing her attention on the psalms and the comfort they offered, the comfort she once so easily could accept, was blown away by awareness of all the ways she had likely made Mother John's predicament worse through her girlish preoccupation.

Brother Daniel's letter to her had arrived barely a week after of their last meeting, suggesting to her he had written it immediately upon departure, sending it by courier even before he reached home.

*My dear sister in Christ,*

*Though I am removed a distance from your person, I yet incessantly seek for you in my mind, tormented by regret for words both spoken and not. When you asked why the matter with which we grappled at great length has only lately arisen, I did not say all that I might. For this I beg your forgiveness and hope to make amends with an answer closer to the truth that are all called to witness.*

*As is well known, my master the bishop has occupied his office for years advanced beyond common expectation. Many in the episcopal court say openly he lacks the vigor to serve the Church, and so he has hungered for a cause that might allow him to demonstrate otherwise. The intelligence recently received from other houses of the Order of heretical teachings at Gaerdegen has presented such a cause, and from it he will not be turned. Should our coming visitation uncover unorthodox materials within the abbey walls, it will be the undoing of all responsible for their promulgation.*

*Know that I never once spoke lightly in your presence, least of all in our first meeting when I mentioned my intention to help remake the world as it emerges from the long shadow of the plague that formed us both. When this investigation is behind us, I am called to reconsider my service to one whom I have now abetted too long and to discover what our Lord next has in store. As the fate of your superiors becomes clear, I believe a loving and merciful God will inspire you to do the same.*

She had bid the messenger to remain while she considered Daniel's words. He had framed it as an atonement, but was it actually a warning? And though ostensibly written out of concern for Mother John's predicament, did it not also advise her to desert the abbess in her hour of greatest need? And did he truly suppose they would both quit their lives and run off together as in some troubadour's song? Five times she reread the letter in rising agitation, and then she responded in a quiet fury.

*My dear brother in Christ,*

*I read the letter I received from you with an abundance of impatience. While your late-coming candor deserves some small measure of gratitude, it does little to decrease our peril, and indeed in light of the intimation with which you close your missive, it appears to be offered less with the intention of doing so, and more as a lever to nudge the boulder of my will.*

*What you propose in the blasphemous guise of God's will, lacking the fortitude to make it plain, can never be. The logic of this is irrefutable: The abbey's mother needs me, and the abbey needs its mother. The Order needs the abbey (whether Judases at our sister houses know it or not), and the Church needs the Order as its most fervent conveyance of prayer. And as even you must know, the world needs the Church as a bulwark against sin and death, which are ever raging at the gates. What then will become of creation should I heed your call?*

His last response had arrived just the day before, and again it had sent her into paroxysms of bafflement and rage. What this man wanted of her he left intentionally opaque—a consequence perhaps of the reasonable assumption that any written correspondence might be intercepted. But it was maddening nonetheless. He knew nothing of her except that she had spent her entire life within the abbey—but then, she thought, perhaps that was all one needed to know.

*My dear sister in Christ,*

*I fear my meaning has been lost in this imperfect medium, in which the space between intention and expression can be as great as between purgatory and paradise. While I may have spoken rashly in my advice to reconsider your long service to your superiors, I only hoped you might reflect piously on the possibility that heresy has indeed infiltrated your holy abode. And when I speak of remaking the world, it is only in the sense of striving for such immediate improvements as working against the secrecy that sadly and too frequently is the mother tongue of our Church and our times. To tell you the full truth of the bishop's motivations seemed to me one small way of doing so. I am mortified to recognize another implication may have been gleaned. If I have given offense, I will endeavor to transform myself. Just as Saul became Paul when struck down on the road to Damascus, it is within the Lord's power to remake any of us at any time, as I trust one who has been called by other names might know.*

As she sat in the abbey church singing words from memory but never once noting their meaning, she wondered why this man filled her with both anger and longing. From her earliest memory, she had known only walls. They hemmed in her youth and promised to circumscribe her maturity and even her death. Every nun buried in the abbey's grave field had at least seen something else of life before turning away from it. Very likely being placed under the soil would be her first venture into the unknown. Each time her thoughts drifted to the bishop's young clerk, she imagined herself beyond the convent enclosure, free of its confinement for the first time. She did not know whether the teachings with which she had been raised amounted to heresy but—daydreaming as the liturgy droned on—she envisioned a divided future: the abbey or the world beyond; Mother John or Brother Daniel; a schism of the heart.

# Chapter 23

NOTHING HAD DIVIDED the sisters of Gaerdegen as had the structure that immediately became known as Father Francis's Wall. Debate on its merits and its usefulness consumed discussion in the chapterhouse until all other business of the abbey fell away. As chapter meetings were reserved for the sisters of the community, the priest was not permitted to be part of the debate, though he of course had provided the spark that lit the fire.

"It is generally agreed," Mother Ursula said, "that plague spreads by malodors in the air. What possible good could a wall do us? Does not air rise and descend with the wind? Cannot the odor of roasting meat be smelled high in a tower above a cookfire?"

No matter the irrefutable logic of her arguments, the nuns most stricken by Francis's account of the torment that awaited them simply pointed to the new crucifix that now stood sentinel in the church.

"But the vision!" Sister Philomena said. "Father Francis has seen what is to come and has been given the reality of the cross as evidence of its reliability."

"The man has been through a trauma," Ursula countered, "and he is terrified of the world. It is natural that such a man would long for a wall to hide behind, but we need not be led by his fear."

"What of our fear? Are we not right to be afraid?" Sister Elizabeth asked.

"We are right to have faith, which is fear's greatest enemy," Sister John replied.

Finally, Sister Philomena called out above the din, "Does not the Rule require a vote?"

Ursula gaped at her cousin. They had their differences through the years, but never had she heard such open defiance. She struggled to find words to reply.

"The Rule requires a vote only on matters of succession," Sister John answered for her. "We are not choosing a new abbess here, and so the decision belongs to Ursula alone."

"Well then perhaps it is time to choose a new one," Philomena said.

John was nearly too startled to speak. "Nonsense," she managed. "What would Gaerdegen be without Mother Ursula?"

"Safe from the plague to begin with," Philomena said. "The Rule may not require a vote, but it requires counsel. And wise counsel requires an accounting of opinion. How many—"

"Sisters!" Mother Ursula called out to silence the count her cousin seemed determined to call. "Have I ever told you the story of my namesake, Saint Ursula?"

She had of course many times, but her stories of the saints were always just starting points; one never knew where she would take them, what novel holy exploits she might describe. The source of her lore was a mystery; a few skeptical sisters wondered if she simply made up such tales as the words left her mouth.

"Saint Ursula was a holy woman from a kingdom to the south. Betrothed to a great prince across the sea, she set off by ship to her wedding accompanied by her most trusted companions.

"These companions were not a few friends but eleven thousand virgins. Eleven thousand maidens drawn from the finest families in the kingdom, all there at her side as a sign and promise of her purity.

"They had not traveled a fortnight when a storm sent from heaven brought them far off course, and then dashed their ship upon the rocks of a distant shore. Miraculously, every one of the eleven thousand survived, and they began a pilgrimage through all of Christendom to reach the prince for whom Ursula was intended. They carried with them the wreckage of their vessel as testimony to the power of God, so that all might be moved by their devotion.

"But then, my sisters, another storm began to blow. This one came not from heaven but from hell, and from its winds emerged a heathen horde. They surrounded the virgins with a ring of armored horses and battle wagons and then slaughtered them with axes. The heathen chief bound Ursula to a stake in the center of the melee and shot her full of arrows so that she would linger watching as her companions met their end.

"There was among the eleven thousand a single maiden who feared meeting the fate of the others. She pulled broken pieces of the shipwrecked vessel around her, forming a wall which she might hide behind. Through the torment of all those with whom she had traveled so far, she remained concealed. So well protected was she, doubtless the storm could have passed before she was revealed. Yet as the heathen axes fell, the blood of thousands flowed as great as a river. It seeped under the wall the hidden maiden had made, wetting the bottoms of her sandals. As the slaughter continued it rose to her knees. Saint Ursula called to her, for in the throes of torment she could see all.

"'My sister, I ask you,' she said. 'What is survival? Is it merely to live another day? Or is it to live beyond? Beyond what you fear? Beyond what you think yourself capable of enduring? Beyond even death?'

"As the lifeblood of her companions pooled about her, the hidden maiden listened and was aware of every wound, feeling every cut and gash, knowing that in her concealment she might save herself from their fate but understanding that the consequences of being spared would not be what she had supposed.

"When she pushed down the walls around her, she glowed with a holiness that made the heathens shield their eyes. And when they pierced her skin an even greater light was revealed.

"Sisters, we follow the Rule of Saint Benedict insofar as it has shaped the daily lives of monastics, women and men, for centuries. It tells us when to rise, when to work, when to pray. But know, too, that another rule governs those parts of our lives we cannot control. This Rule has no name, but we might call it the Rule of Saint Ursula.

"The Rule of Saint Ursula directs our response to fates we cannot comprehend. When God sends a wind that changes our course, the Rule of Saint Ursula commands you to marry the wind. When God sends a storm, the Rule of Saint Ursula commands you to take the storm inside yourself, allow it to mingle with your soul and give birth to a prayer conceived of faith and thunder. And if God should present death to you in the form of ax or plague, the Rule of Saint Ursula commands you to be like the eleven thousand virgins, who opened their arms to receive it. The Rule of Saint Ursula declares that soft flesh will subsume the strongest blade like a smithy fire. Our pain will melt death into wedding bands for our marriage to the Lord."

Far from mollified by their abbess's oratory, the sisters who supported the wall felt only increased urgency upon consideration of the dark implications of such parables. They urged Ursula to allow Father Francis to protect them from her apocalyptic visions by finishing the barrier as quickly as possible.

"Sisters, I understand your concerns," Ursula argued. "But there are also practical matters to consider. A wall of the kind the priest has described, fully encompassing the abbey, sealing us off from the world, would cost a fortune. Perhaps we should hear from our thrifty treasurer. Sister Philomena, you are clearly intrigued by this notion, but will not building a wall on this scale drive us to penury?"

"No, Mother. It will not," Philomena said. "We have the funds necessary for this important expense."

"My cousin, this is the first time in all my years at Gaerdegen that I have heard you say we have sufficiency of anything."

"With respect, Mother Abbess, I have watched you squander the abbey's wealth for too long on birds and bread and other nonsense. Now that we have an urgent reason to spend our silver, I will not let your fantasies of martyrdom leave us unprotected. As treasurer I believe if you are not prepared to make this decision yourself, we should put it to a vote."

"A vote!" others agreed. "A vote!"

"Very well," Ursula said, taken aback by her cousin's rebellion. "In the spirit of receiving the wise counsel of my sisters, I would be curious to know how many among you support this notion. Who among you believes a wall may preserve us while prayer will not? Who among you will put faith in stones rather than the Lord? Which of the nuns of Gaerdegen trust this priest over the abbess that built this place from dirt and ruins?"

Silence lingered long enough to cause Mother Ursula to smile in satisfaction.

"You see, Sister Philomena? Your sisters understand that the lack of a wall surrounding Gaerdegen is no accident. It is consistent with the spirit with which we founded the abbey. We have always been open to all, and so we will remain."

As the abbess spoke, she looked out over the gathered community of thirty-five nuns and saw Sister Lazarus's hand rise slowly into the air.

"I am sorry, Mother," the baker said.

"I, too, am sorry, Mother Ursula," Sister Elizabeth said.

One after another: a hand in the air followed by a whispered apology.

"I am sorry, Mother."

"Forgive me, Mother."

"Mother, I trust in you always, but in this matter we must err on the side of prudence."

Ursula's smile faded as fully half the nuns raised their hands, and then a dozen more. Some joined the majority with surety, others with hesitation, but their disposition mattered little. Soon all but four of the sisters had sided with the wall.

"Very well," the abbess said. "It is utter folly and it may be our undoing. But very well. Never let it be said that Mother Ursula denied her sisters choice in this life."

Around the chapterhouse, nuns crossed themselves and whispered prayers of gratitude or concern. Sister Philomena grinned so widely that it seemed as if her teeth could serve as the wall's foundation.

"Cousin, please inform the priest his fear has sufficiently infected the community," Ursula said. "He may have his bulwark, but he may not have my blessing."

# Chapter 24

COINS IN HAND and with local fears rising that the coming plague would mean hard times ahead, Francis had no trouble recruiting laborers who were hale, strong, and eager for silver in the hope that it might one day buy them protection from the sickness. With this help, enormous hay wagons hired from farmers in the valley were filled with river stone. From the first light of morning to the last sunset stripe of color on the horizon, the rumble of rocks dropping around the convent provided a counterpoint to the church bell's toll.

For well-nigh a month, Sister John watched as the carts came and went, each depositing its contents, sending dust into the air. When the cloud from the final load had dissipated, a miniature mountain range remained, circumscribing the sisters' view of the valley below.

For the first time since adolescence in her parents' grand manor, John felt the choke of confinement. Already she envisioned the wall that would rise from these unformed piles of stone, realizing with alarm that it would mean not just that the world would be kept out but that she and her sisters would be kept in.

"He must have gathered every river stone within five days' journey," Sister John said to Sister Anna.

"May they all tumble down the hillside and flow back to their source," Anna replied. "How will he keep them all in place?"

The answer came in the form of rough-hewn lengths of timber, set in the earth every ten paces. Thirty such posts formed a ring around all the abbey's yards and buildings; between them the stone was stacked two feet thick, each layer joined to the next with a mortar of chopped straw mixed with rich clay dug from the river's edge.

Father Francis oversaw it all, calling dire warnings to his workers as they raced to keep to a building schedule only he understood.

"Plague travels with the wind!" he shouted at them. "If we do not move faster than the breeze, every stone you place will be as useless as dust."

When the men enlisted to assist in construction lagged in their efforts, Francis took them to view the carved crucifix that had become known as the Christ of Gaerdegen, and their wonder at the sight gave them new desire to listen to the man who had carved it. He offered interminable sermons about the wall and its meaning as he joined them in the spreading of mortar and the lifting of stone.

"Make no mistake," he preached one day. "When the pestilence comes, it will crucify us all! Just as the stone rolled away from the tomb revealed the resurrection, only the one who rolls the stones in place today will determine who among the living remains in the world. God has destroyed nearly all the earth's inhabitants before! Why should it not happen again? In the time of Noah, the world's sin was such that heaven could not bear to look upon it. All the works of man were but a slate to be wiped clean. Only those who hid themselves inside an ark were spared. But in order to save themselves they had to work night and day while those condemned to die jeered at them and continued their sinning."

"First he is Christ, and now he is Noah?" Sister Anna said to Sister John.

"I fear our priest has lost his mind along with his eye," John replied.

With every foot of wall constructed, Francis became more unyielding in his demands, ever darker in his descriptions of what would come to pass should they not finish the wall in time. Yet there was little John or Ursula's other supporters could do to stop it. The abbess had publicly given her assent and could not very well reverse course. That did not prevent her from making her feelings about it known, however.

The wall rose in sections like teeth emerging from infant gums—first, small protuberances here and there, none taller than the knees of the shortest sister.

"Tell me, Father," Ursula said, "What shall we do if the plague steps over it?"

Yet soon the wall reached their shoulders, and more workers arrived. Word had spread throughout the region that a fortress against the plague was rising on the side of a mountain far to the north of the Cathedral City. Francis personally inspected every man seeking employment. No plague symptoms had yet been reported in the immediate vicinity of the abbey, but he was vigilant in making certain that construction of the wall did not invite in the very devil it was meant to defend against.

The man called Butcher appeared one day with a crowd of others, and when Francis saw him he nearly fell to tears. It was all he could do to remind himself that the man knew nothing of the hours Francis had spent watching his daughter wander among the trees, the sketches he had made of her face, the dark inspiration she had provided for the cross that now hung in the abbey church. For all Butcher knew, the priest had simply visited, sharpened his ax and instantly forgotten his offer to find the girl a place among the sisters. Their eyes met with mutual recognition.

"Something happened to my Maureen," the big man said, the music gone now from his voice. "When I find the man responsible, I will gut him with a dull knife."

Francis nodded gravely, careful not to give any indication that he understood. But still the words Butcher had used—*the man responsible*—stabbed at him, piercing with self-hatred and dread.

To his relief, he did not see the grieving father again during the construction. His indictment of Francis's responsibility echoed through the priest's days, however. When not overseeing construction, the priest passed as many as hours as he could spare in contemplation of the crucifix he had made, studying the body that belonged equally to a broken God and a broken girl, whose fathers dwelt in heaven above and the forest below.

Only as the impressive and imposing stone barrier surrounding the abbey approached completion did it seem that Francis had not planned sufficiently. When all the stones hauled from the river had been used, and hardly a pebble could be found in the nearby creek beds that Francis's laborers had scraped clean, still an opening remained wide enough for a half dozen nuns to link arms and walk through it side-by-side.

"Father Francis, your wall is quite an accomplishment," Ursula said. "Shall we pray the angel of death doesn't notice a huge hole in your fortification? Prayer, after all, is what Gaerdegen does best."

"The liturgy will disappoint you if you think it a shield," Francis said.

"The true purpose of prayer is to transform oneself," she replied, "and so all sincere prayer is successful. But has there ever been a wall that has not ultimately failed in its purpose?"

As she spoke, the others gathered around. Since the start of the wall's construction, tension between the abbey's mother and its priest had lingered beneath the surface, like a pipe tone keeping a song on key. Now it seemed to be rising to the top.

"Mysticism will not protect us," he told her. "You may not admit it now, but in time you will agree the wall was worth any price."

The next day, when the nuns of Gaerdegen returned to the church for the chanting of Matins, more than one felt her foot slip on a patch of unexpected slickness on the stone floor. The sisters looked to the ceiling over the choir stalls and saw dozens of sleeping birds, barely perceptible in the candlelight below. When the sun rose and morning brightness found every darkened spot in the abbey, the doves woke and cooed with surprise at their surroundings. They may have wondered if it had been a dream, their cozy beehive dovecote dismantled in the night, the stones they had made their home carted away and stacked upon the earth.

The moments after Lauds were generally a time when monastic silence was most valued, allowing a quiet certitude that the coming of the light was somehow related to the coming of the Lord, that the day itself and all the sounds it offered were proof of God's dominion. Seeing her birds and instantly understanding what their dislocation meant, Ursula added to these sounds now.

"That bastard!" she said.

The sisters followed behind her as she swept through the cloister and out into the mud beyond the abbey barn. Just as she feared, she found only a black circle of bird shit where the dovecote had been.

In the distance they could hear the ruckus of laborers and rushed as one body toward the unfinished section of wall about which Ursula had teased the priest the day before. It was nearly complete: a stretch of newly stacked stones filling in the last remaining gap ensured the abbey would be fully shut off from the world. Stained as they were by decades of excrement and Ursula's attentive affection, the new stones were noticeably darker than the fresh river rock that made up the rest of the barrier. The workers had tied rags around their noses to protect them from the stench.

"The angel of death will find no way in now, good Mother," Francis said. "He will circle us fully but find no welcome. When the plague comes, Gaerdegen alone will withstand it, and we will owe it to your birds."

"Only a fool puts his faith in a wall," Ursula scoffed.

"Ah, but what is it you have so often said?" Francis replied. "The foolishness of God is wiser than the wisdom of men."

Ursula picked up a stone layered in multicolored bird droppings. She turned it over in her hand, then lifted her chin to take in hundreds more stacked over her head, each with its own pattern, all part of something she had carefully created that this man had casually destroyed.

"Father, I believe we are overdue for a private word," she said. She turned her gaze from the dirty stones to the faces all around her. The sisters anxious, the workers amused, the priest now seeming as damaged in spirit as he was in flesh. "All of you, away!" she shouted, and the nuns and the laborers scattered.

"You have your barricade," she said to Francis, "but I will instruct those in my care to keep the gate always open, to welcome every stranger who asks admittance, to feed and clothe every beggar who comes seeking God's love."

"You will do no such thing."

"I will," she said. "I will send my birds out in every direction with a message tied to their feet. *All you sinners, come to Gaerdegen.* And when they arrive, we will offer a feast to celebrate our victory over fear. How would you prevent me from doing so?"

"The sins I have seen and those you have confessed are sufficient to see you consigned to both hell and the gallows," Francis said. "Have you forgotten you await my penance?"

Ursula laughed loud enough for the nuns who loitered in the near distance to crane their necks, tilting their heads and pulling their veils back off their ears in hopes of catching any stray word.

"Are you threatening *me*?" she asked. "You must know an abbess does not answer to any priest but to the bishop. I would be happy to discuss the events of these last months with him, should you desire it."

Francis narrowed his eye and chose his words carefully.

"No doubt you have temporal authority here, but on whose spiritual authority will the days ahead most rely?" he asked. "Who would grant your strangers absolution of their sins? Who would provide your beggars with the sole meal that matters, the sacrament of Eucharist? You offer God's love but cannot deliver eternal life. A priest alone can. I alone can."

Seeing his seriousness, all sign of mirth left Ursula as quickly as it had come.

"There are other priests," she said.

"Not in a hundred miles. And which among them will venture here in Death's wake? When the plague comes, all the sisters will die if our wall is breached. What becomes of them after that depends on me, but it is up to you. You may see yourself as above needing the solace offered by a lowly priest like myself, but your sisters do not. Without the presence of a man in Holy Orders to hear their confessions and perform last rites, all those afflicted will be doubly tormented by fear for their souls. Would you wish those in your care to suffer so?"

"You are not a hard man, Father. I do not believe you would let the sisters die unconfessed and unforgiven, or even that you would allow them to worry that may be the case. For some, the burden of that concern would be too much to bear."

"My only desire is to protect this place," Francis said. "If you will not defend their bodies, how can I safeguard their souls?"

# Chapter 25

THE FINISHED WALL stood twelve feet high, fully enclosing the convent. There were now just two ways in or out: the narrow door in the gatehouse with its iron bar window, and the wider but equally well-secured postern behind the abbey barn, where Francis bowed to necessity and acknowledged the occasional need of deliveries of provisions. The wall, he believed, was his greatest creation, as if with his blade he had carved a New Jerusalem from ordinary earth and river stone.

Within days of its completion, Ursula announced she would not live within it. Her decision threatened to further splinter the abbey, with some nuns vowing to follow wherever she might lead, and others offering them best wishes as they ventured into a world ravaged by plague. Ursula herself put an end to this potential schism.

"The Lord calls me now not to be an abbess but an anchorite." She would live out her days, she explained, in a little cave carved in a craggy hillside nearby. "There is water enough and abundant berry bushes," she said. "My birds will otherwise sustain me."

On her departure day, as was traditionally done for the occasion of an anchoress abandoning the concerns of the living, the sisters sang the Office of the Dead.

*I love the Lord for he heard my voice;*
*he heard my cry for mercy.*
*Because he turned his ear to me,*
*I will call on him as long as I live.*

*The cords of death entangled me,*
*the anguish of the grave came over me;*
*I was overcome by distress and sorrow.*
*Then I called on the name of the Lord.*
*Eternal rest give unto them, O Lord,*
*and let perpetual light shine unto them.*

"Don't cry for me, Sisters. Cry for yourselves," Ursula told the nuns of Gaerdegen. "I will see more of the world from my hole in a crag than you will behind your wall."

"But who will lead us?" Sister Elizabeth asked.

"One who enjoys the trust of all will succeed me as abbess. Look to Sister John to take you through these sad times. She will help you find light shining in this darkness."

"What of the vote?" Philomena asked.

"Vote if you wish," Ursula answered. "If this abbey has any sense remaining it will choose as I have."

John embraced Ursula and whispered quickly, so none of her sisters would hear. "Mother, don't leave. How will we bear it? How will I?"

"Look to the heavens," Ursula replied. "All answers come from above."

As they watched her walk away, a cloud of doves flew over her, following from the site of their ruined home to whatever might come next. The dark murmuration moved with her every step, as if she was casting a shadow upon the sky.

They did not have long to wait. Answers to John's questions arrived within a fortnight, shortly after she had been affirmed as the new abbess by near unanimous acclaim. Some among the old guard believed one of the three remaining original nuns of Gaerdegen should succeed the founder. Yet of these three, Ursula's aunt Sister Elizabeth was deemed too senile, Ursula's sister Anna did not want the job, and Ursula's cousin Sister Philomena was considered by many too closely allied with the priest. The woman now known as Mother John was accepted by all.

Following John's elevation, an odd feeling of normalcy came over the abbey. With the wall complete, they had received information about the progress of the plague from passing travelers with surprising equanimity. But even those among Francis's faction sensed the wall had made Gaerdegen a cauldron resting in a fire. Only constant attention would keep it from boiling over or burning all within.

On one such simmering day, the sisters had just taken their work outside to enjoy the summer morning sunshine when a tightly rolled tube of parchment hit the ground with the hollow knock of an acorn fallen from a tree. Tied carefully with a long flower stem, it stood upright as a cornstalk in the middle of the courtyard. A small stone affixed to one end had caused it to drop as decisively as an arrow.

"Are we under attack?" Sister Elizabeth asked. As all looked to the sky, a white bird winged away.

"Don't be daft," Sister Anna said when she was sure a hail of arrows was not about to fall upon them. But then they saw the second dove, and the third.

"Ursula," Mother John said as she unrolled the small scroll. All the nuns of Gaerdegen crowded around to hear its contents.

*Remember, my sisters, how easily the walls of men may be breached.*

*The walls of men crumble with time. They topple when the catapult hurls stones against them. They shrink to nothing when a simple ladder is placed by their side. They cause those without to grow resentful, and those within to fold up with fear. The walls of men make it difficult to see what is coming until it is too late.*

*How much different are the walls we sisters have built around our hearts through prayer? The walls of men are closed-off, limited. But the walls built by sisters protect the whole world. The walls of men are held together by mud that softens and washes away in the rain, but the walls built by sisters are bound with a mortar of God's insoluble love. Know that you too are builders though your ramparts go unseen. The only fortress that is impenetrable is the one that is open to all.*

She reached for another scroll, and again read aloud.

*Remember, my sisters, there are two books by which creation can be known—the Book of Knives and Stones and the Book of Birds and Bread. Men will tell you it is the former that is responsible for all that is lasting in this world. They point to cathedrals and monoliths and statues they have made and insist they are permanent, that time has no dominion over such structures because they can be seen long after their makers are gone. Such is the gospel of the Book of Knives and Stone. But what of the other book? Birds and bread, they tell us, are fragile things. Birds fall from the sky with a rock-strike; bread is reduced to crumbs in a fist. There is nothing lasting, men explain, either in God-created things whose bones are as fine as twigs, or in human inventions which molder in a fortnight. But consider this my sisters: When a single great work of stone falls, as they all must one day, when will another rise to take its place? But if any one bird shall fall another and another and another quickly picks up its song, and the moldered bread will feed them as the new loaves rise.*

And another:

*Remember, my sisters, though Christ entered the world as a man he need not have done so. We speak of God as Father, Son, and Holy Spirit, but there is nothing in the nature of the trinity that determines that its first two persons must be Father and Son rather than Mother and Daughter. Indeed, if it is consistent with the nature of the one to be the Father, and of his offspring to be the Son, because both are referred to with the masculine word Spiritus, why is it not, with equal reason, consistent with the nature of the one to be the mother, and the other the daughter, since both are also truth and wisdom, which are known by the feminine words veritas and sapientia?*

*There are some who insist that we know them as we do because the categories of father and son belong to the superior sex, and mother and daughter to the inferior. Yet though this is a natural fact in certain instances, in others the contrary is true. Is it not so that among certain kinds of birds, the female is always larger and stronger, while the male is smaller and weaker? Is the trinity of birds not the same as the trinity of the Church? How might they speak of God in the liturgy of birdsong?*

And another:

*Remember, my sisters, the world once was yours. Before God molded mud and called it Adam, you were the unformed earth on which all creation would depend. Before the Garden offered the tree that was man's undoing, you alone bore fruit that yielded the seeds of stories. Before men learned to take life, you alone knew how to give it.*

*We have all seen the morality play in which Eden's Husband berates his Wife, crying and blaming her for their Expulsion: Oh, evil woman, full of treason, / forever contrary to reason, / bringing no man good in any season. /*

*Our children's children to the end of time / Will feel the cruel whiplash of your crime!*

*Yet there is drama that goes unspoken but is seen far more often, for it is played endlessly in the mind of every daughter of Eve: Oh spiteful man, to fantasy tethered, / nursing a grievance old and leathered, / fear of women has got you wethered. / You harp of the fall when you cannot rise, / and build up great walls to hide your lies.*

Each of Ursula's letters was a clear rebuke of Father Francis and his wall, but taken together they became more than that. They were meditations on the value of the nuns' labor, inquiries into the role of women in the salvation of mankind, and an idiosyncratic accounting of their lives.

By summer's end there would be a library of scrolls that, when rolled together, were as thick as a forearm—a dozen sent by winged messenger to the courtyard that first day, others found here and there throughout the convent, either sent later for particular purposes or dropped to locations unintended by their author, apparently by birds distracted or less well trained. The former abbess's habit of beginning them always with the same words, *Remember, my sisters*, caused Mother John to consider if they were sent primarily for her benefit. Each letter seemed written not merely to impart knowledge but to help the nuns of Gaerdegen, and especially John herself, to see that they already had the spiritual resources necessary to go on without her.

Perhaps inevitably, these detailed statements that the abbey's founder was nonessential to its future soon themselves became essential elements of the nuns' daily devotion. The sisters asked so often to hear Ursula's words that adding their reading to the liturgy and mealtimes was among Mother John's first acts as abbess.

"Shall we read them also at Mass, Mother?" Sister Matthew asked.

"No," John answered. "Better if our priest does not hear of them just yet."

# Chapter 26

WHEN THE MIDDAY prayers had ended, the nuns shuttled out from the church and continued with the day's routine, which they would not allow to yield to the storm. They gathered in the refectory to eat the noon meal in silence as Sister Thomas recited aloud from the daily reading, though hearing her words proved difficult over the wind's screams.

The younger nuns grew impatient during such readings. Those born after the plague tended to regard the Book of Ursula as hopelessly ancient and opaque, a relic of a darker time in need of unrelenting reassurance. They could not help but fidget during the words their elders found so meaningful.

"Oughtn't we be preparing for the bishop's visit?" Sister Bartholomew sighed with a sudden spasm of exasperation.

Magdalene slammed her hand on the refectory table. "And would you care to tell your sisters how you know of the bishop's visit?" she asked.

"Silence!" Sister Phillip shouted. No longer content merely to sign her disapproval, the magistra pointed to the door and bellowed. "Out with all of you!"

In punishment for breaking the mealtime silence, all five young nuns were sent into the storm again to clear any doorways and passages that might soon become impassable with the accumulating snow.

Once outside, Magdalene lifted her shovel and dug it into Bartholomew's back.

"You didn't answer my question. Why are you so eager for the bishop's arrival? His interest here is of no concern of yours. You should not even know of it."

The storm seemed to intensify as they argued, forcing the sisters to stand close in the gale as snow stung their skin and they lifted their sleeves around their faces in protection.

"The future of the abbey is not your secret to keep!" Bartholomew hissed.

"Nor is it yours to determine!" Magdalene replied. "Do you truly think Mother John a heretic? Do you wish to see her imprisoned, or dead?"

"I wish only that she step down as abbess. She may end her days here in prayer like any old nun or go off to find her precious Ursula for all I care. Then Gaerdegen will be free of error at last."

"And what of those of us who love her and would carry on her teaching?"

"What of you alone, do you mean?" Bartholomew scoffed. "Magdalene, it would be best for Gaerdegen if you would simply disappear in the wind."

As the older sisters lingered over their supper, five creatures made of ice appeared in the refectory. Their habits were glazed and dripping with snowmelt, their cheeks red with windburn, their veils stiff as boards. The senior nuns wondered how they had completed their tasks so soon. Mother John moved her hands smoothly through the air, joining them together and closing them like a book: *Finished?*

The novices at first just stared at the floor. Sister Jude smirked and put two fingers together, then pulled them apart: *Quit.* The other novices were eager to explain. Sister Andrew first, sending a hand quickly through the air; she fluttered fingers blue with cold and made a pinching, awful face: *Evil snow.* Then came Sister Thaddeus, quick to add her thoughts: *Wicked. Mean.* And, finally, Bartholomew, with a comment on both the work that lay ahead and the argument that still simmered with her sister: *Hopeless.*

Magdalene ignored the question; she looked past her elders to the windows and the storm, her eyes full of longing as though she had come in against her will.

# PART 6

# NONE

# Chapter 27

DAYLIGHT FADED AND the white sky turned a nocturnal gray, while the snow fell still and the wind continued to blow. The trees that encircled the convent swayed violently in the gusts or bowed low with the ice that weighed down their branches. The blizzard battered the wooden shields that sealed the cloister and shook the walls of Father Francis's tiny residence, howling through gaps in the shutter and the thin thatched roof.

*O Lord, come to my assistance.*

*O God, make haste to help me.*

Father Francis prayed quickly in his quarters and then returned to work. The day's project was nearly finished. Eight hours of slow and difficult labor had transformed the two planks of hornbeam. Each when stood upright would reach above the priest's head. Both were white wood, polished smooth as bone, carved now with a series of scenes in half-relief. All that remained was to join them. The priest bent over his boards, inspecting them by candlelight, oblivious to the creak and whine of the workshop walls.

In order to impress his contrition upon the bishop, he had realized, the cross he presented must also be his confession: his sins and sacrifices all laid bare. True, many of these scenes would be inscrutable without commentary, but as he looked over the work, it seemed every consequential moment of his life was there, each reduced to a carved relief.

Free from the burden of working with large pieces of lumber, he was astonished at the level of detail he still could achieve. There he was at the foot of the cross, a boy learning the consequences of desire from the unbalanced boughs of trees, and there just above was a scene depicting the cathedral in which his father and brother fell, with Helena, the wife who would not have him, looking on from the side. The remainder of the vertical plank showed a priest with a blade carving the Virgin, the son he sired but could not claim, and the widows that became his saints. On the horizontal plank he had carved the abbey and the wall he built to protect it, the thieves and their jug, and the nuns who had grown to fear him. At the cross's center, a young but haunted face stared back at him from the wood grain as if looking through a barred window, the girl brought back to life to carry Death within their walls.

# Chapter 28

A GIRL AT THE gatehouse: her face quartered by the bars in the gate's one window, lit by moonlight. Pale and thin, framed by orange curls, purple bruises dotting her neck, she appeared on a hot night in August, the Feast of Saint Mary Magdalene.

She stood too near the door to be observed fully, but glancing down through the window, Mother John could see that her belly was swollen, barely covered by a ragged tunic, stretching it tight. Her face slumped slightly and one eye wandered; she was as dirty as a body pulled from a grave.

The gate mistress, Sister Elizabeth, stepped awkwardly across the dirt floor of the gatehouse, treading as well as her age would allow. She held gray hands to her lips, removing them only to speak.

"Who is she, Mother?" she asked. "What does she want?"

Innocent despite her years, her voice shook with agitation. She had been one of Abbess Ursula's original sisters, but the adventurous spirit she must have had in those days had long since left her, replaced by a desire for certainty and stability no doubt born of that early dangerous time. She spat words into the air, anxious to speak while she still might during this unexpected break from the requirement of silence; an excitable child permitted to break the rules.

"Why should she come to us? And in the middle of the night?"

The new abbess ignored her sister's questions, looking at the face on the other side of the abbey gate. She stared as one stares at fire, watching orange hair blow like a moving flame. The girl was young, but just how young was impossible to tell. She seemed veiled somehow though her face, neck, and even her shoulders were bare. Her age disguised by a damaged beauty—a flower, full-petaled, crushed in its bloom.

"It seems she wishes to enter," Mother John answered. "In which case you might've welcomed her and left me to my rest."

Her voice sounded to her lofty, alien on her lips, still playing the part Ursula's departure had thrust upon her. In truth she had not rested easy a single night since she moved from the dormitory to the abbess's cottage. She wondered if she would ever feel at home.

"Please open the door, Sister," she said, as if she simply wanted to take a stroll and had taken no notice of the girl at all; as if she did not wonder at the bruises on her neck or had not noticed that her eyes were green as spring. The girl glowered through the window. Though she did not say a word, fast, slight breaths made John's awareness of her acute, distracting.

Sister Elizabeth's face contorted at the abbess's suggestion. Her hands tightened over her lips. Words had become a burden.

"Oh. Mother, no," she said, speaking slowly through her fingers, trying not to breathe. "No. That has been forbidden."

She looked away nervously, inspecting the room: the dirty stone walls, the wood and straw bed where she would rather be sleeping, the single candle that burned at its side.

Mother John glared at the old nun. "Forbidden, Sister?"

Sister Elizabeth looked to the floor, ashamed, hiding.

"Father Francis has forbidden me to admit a single guest without his approval."

"And what authority has Father Francis over you, Sister? Have you forgotten who your abbess is now? Who is responsible for your actions as well as your soul?"

The words came quick; the tone, harsh and unnecessary. Mother John could not be certain whether she was feeling protective of the new power of her office or of the girl at the gate. She hoped it was the former, but the green eyes still peered from the darkness. She felt their stare like heat.

"He has made it my penance, Mother," Elizabeth stammered. "He said on this matter my obedience will count more toward my salvation than will my prayers." Her voice trembled with the need for approval, confused by the rift between her superiors. "Is it not as he says, Mother? That the survival of the abbey and the good of the Order depend upon all those who are outside being kept there?" Her eyes flashed to the window, and she leaned in close. "Is it not true that hell has come upon the earth? That Death is always at our door?"

"It is for the good of the Order, Sister, that we do the bidding of the Rule."

John spoke with assurance, yet was unsure her words were true. Why, she wondered, wasn't the rightful abbess here to calm and beguile us and set us at our ease? Having no answer, she did as Ursula would never have done, quoting from the Rule to convince her sister as well as herself that she was worthy of the power that had become hers: "All guests to the monastery shall be welcomed as Christ, shown every courtesy . . ."

Elizabeth nodded impatiently: yes, yes, she knew the Rule. She had been following it, she wished she had the courage to say, since Mother John was a child.

"Greeted with great humility, for with bowed head and prostrate body all shall honor the person of Christ . . ."

The older nun turned away, but John would not relent. "For it is Christ who is really being received. Would you keep Jesus so long outside our door?"

She stepped toward her sister and raised a hand toward the gate, ordering it unlocked not with a word but with a gesture, as if silence would remove responsibility for the action. Elizabeth bowed slowly in obedience and did as she was told. The door opened and the world poured in.

The girl stepped shyly across the threshold, barefoot on the dark earth, followed by a wind as hot as noon, and then an animal stench of decay. The rags she wore were a mockery of the nuns' intentional poverty; they must have been white once, but now were stained brown with road mud and gray with dried sweat. John blushed at the girl's immodest flesh, embarrassed by her own simple habit and the healthy pink of her skin, which seemed elegant in comparison.

Elizabeth backed away, crossing herself at the sight of this timid girl and the smell of plague that followed her through the door. Some of the sisters had told tales of everywhere outside the walls being filled with wailing, but beyond the open gate there were only the usual sounds of silence on a hot August night: a choir of frogs, toads, and insects, attending to their summer liturgy.

Both nuns bowed low to their guest, greeting her as they were bidden by their Rule, speaking together with solemnity, "Thanks be to God." Mother John then beckoned the girl to the wood and straw bed and seated her on the corner, asking no questions.

The girl spoke absently, staring strangely about the room, parting her lips lightly, allowing words to ease out like wind.

"I heard you calling me," she said. Her voice was delicate and high but dropped to a false low tone to sing the next words: "Come . . . come . . . come . . . come . . ."

John placed a wooden bucket before her, knelt beside it, and began gently washing the girl's feet, a ritual of humility. She soaked a clean cloth in the bucket, then smoothed it over the broken skin, scrubbing delicately from the tips of the toes to the small arches to leather-hard heels, up to the knobs of the ankles, returning flesh to the hue of its birth. Thick and tough to the touch, she wore a map of scars caused, the abbess assumed, by hardship the nuns of Gaerdegen could not imagine.

"Thank you," the girl said, a shy whisper: "So kind. I—"

The nuns watched their young guest curiously as she rose and stood in the light of the bedside candle. She rocked left and right, dizzy, as if about to fall. Her words trailed off and she bowed her head, her face growing dark while for the first time her body was fully lit. They could now see clearly that her belly was swollen as if it might burst; the ragged dress covering her thighs dripped wet though it was a hot dry night. Mother John wondered if that much water could have spilled from the rag, but the older nun knew better.

"Mother, she is near her time!"

The girl just smiled and whispered into the air, almost singing, to no one.

"No, no," she chimed, "it is not yet my time."

The abbess looked again at the girl's belly and finally understood. How slow she was, Mother John chastised herself; how little she knew of the world of other bodies and the things men might do to them. She spoke softly in her sister's ear, bidding her to run and wake Sister Anna, the infirmarian, and bring her to the bakehouse, where the girl would be kept out of the sight of Father Francis, who would surely add conflict to this already trying night.

Elizabeth bowed quickly and took her leave, struggling to make haste. Mother John took the girl's hand in her own and led her across the darkened grounds of the convent to the bakehouse, empty at this hour but for the next day's bread.

Later, she would wonder if she had thought to use the bakehouse because of the fixation on bread that Ursula had shown in certain of the scrolls that she had nearly committed to memory—it was second only to birds in the concordance she had begun to compile. Yet there were practical reasons for choosing it among the abbey's buildings: plentiful water and a roaring fire. Though she knew less about midwifery than she did about being an abbess, washing and warming, she suspected, were essential.

Inside, oil lamps lit the powder-whitened floor and walls. The girl stepped softly in her bare feet, tracking through a residue of flour dust. Her thin arms, bare to the elbow, cradled her belly. John took her by the wrist, led her to a table in the center of the room, and patted the dark wood tabletop, raising a cloud of fine white dust. The abbess moved her hands carefully through the air, signing instructions without a thought that her guest might not understand: *Sit. Lie back. Rest.*

The girl watched spellbound, confounded. To her, the nun's movements seemed a strange and intricate dance. She answered with movements of her own, smoothing small hands up and down her body from the curve of her breast to the start of her thighs, but appeared otherwise unconcerned, oblivious to her condition. Her smile, small and sweet, just now came to life below eyes like those of a beaten child: innocent and injured, wary but hopeful for suffering's end.

Sisters Elizabeth and Anna soon entered from the hot night: Elizabeth nervous, shaking still; Anna, small and quiet in her black veil, eyebrows raised thoughtfully, concerned. Ursula's sister, she too had been with the abbey since its founding. Some had thought she would be the logical choice for abbess, but she preferred working in her medicinal garden to settling petty nunnish disputes.

"I came as quickly as I might, Mother," she said. "I was fast asleep." Her eyes shifted from the young abbess to the stranger by the baking table. "Our guest?"

The girl eased back on the tabletop without explanation, grabbing John's hand when she came to her side. She spoke unexpectedly, a whisper that filled the room.

"They call you Mother," she said. "Are you their mother?"

John blushed at the thought. She squeezed the girl's hand, smiling and nodding support, then answered softly, sighing.

"No," she said, shaking her head, almost laughing at the notion of having birthed an old crone like Sister Elizabeth, "that is the title of my office."

At the end of the table Sister Anna bent the girl's legs at the knees and spread them wide though her patient seemed not to notice. She only stared blankly at the abbess, confused, as if detached from her lower half. John looked away to watch as Anna stooped to peer between the girl's legs then stood up with a fright, eyes wide as coins. She whispered through her fingers, "Jesus save us," then looked to her mother, joining her hands together near her waist, signing gravely: *Death.*

That particular sign was not used often, but the abbess would come to know it well. She could not see the reason for the infirmarian's diagnosis then but soon would learn of the source of her fright: purple bruises, like those dotting her neck, mottled the girl's calves and thighs; red-black boils, large as hen's eggs, lodged in the pits of her knees and curve of her groin, the skin swollen like overripened fruit, ready to burst.

John spoke loudly, keeping a hold on the girl's attention, her words anxious and quick. "Mother is what my sisters call me," she said, the girl nodding attentively, eager to show she was listening. "It is my name."

The girl laughed like the child she should be. "That's no kind of name!" she said, proud to have seen through this tall tale. She looked away, thinking a moment, oblivious to the attention given her at the other end of the table, then asked, "What does your mother call you?"

The young abbess thought of her mother—asking for her prayers in the abbey courtyard; struggling in the roadside mud; turning to soil in the all-consuming earth.

"Ruth," she said. "My mother called me Ruth."

The girl smiled, squeezing the finger of her new friend's hand.

"A pretty name," she said and stared off to the ceiling.

Sister Anna spoke through tears, "It is indeed her time. Had she come an hour later the child would have been born in the forest."

Sister Elizabeth muttered under her breath, thinking herself unheard, "Better for us all," but before her abbess could flash a reproving look, a shrill cry from the tabletop erased her words from the air. The girl struggled to sit up and then fell back, weakened by pain. Her eyes rolled white, and her thin lips curled, suggesting an agony the abbess could not imagine. She squeezed John's fingers as if they were the cause of her suffering and began to weep as the shock of pain subsided and she was left to wait for its return.

The girl whimpered, sweating now, her head rocking on the tabletop, side to side like a stubborn child saying *no, no, no, no*, back and forth like a slowly tolling bell, while pleading for help, "Ruth . . . Ruth . . . Ruth . . ."

"Fresh water," Sister Anna declared, "and clean cloth. Build up the fire."

She raced to find the first items while Sister Elizabeth shuffled across the room to place several short, thin logs in the hearth, then joined her sister in the other preparations. The abbess was struck immobile, as if bound to the girl's side. She put a hand on her forehead and tried to calm her, ease her pain, though she thought this unlikely.

"Where are your manners?" John said, wiping sweat from the girl's eyes with the hem of her sleeve. "You know my name but have kept yours a secret." She hoped her fear did not show in her voice. "Can you tell me your name?" She was speaking as though to a child, she thought—nodding her head, grinning—though she had not spoken to a child since she was one herself, and even then it was rare.

The girl breathed violently, inhaling with a high-pitched scream, exhaling with a low, harsh roar. She squeezed John's hand and managed to speak.

"Ma—," she said, her utterance cut short by another stab of pain. She wailed, her hands flying to her belly then clenching the boards of the tabletop. She reached out to John again and buried fingers in her waiting hand. Tips thin, almost fleshless; their nails pinched the nun's palm.

"Maureen," she whispered when she could speak again. The she let her eyes fall shut, slipping her tongue past her lips to lick spit and tears and sweat away, rocking her head again, right and left: no, no, no.

"Ruth?" she called, as though fearing herself abandoned. "Ruth!"

"Here, child," the abbess said, stroking the girl's forehead, "Here I am."

She comforted the girl throughout the birth, sponging her brow with a dampened cloth, wetting her lips, holding her hand through the torment as if she would never let go.

When the baby was born, the new mother fainted exhausted on the tabletop, gripping the nun's hand, digging fingernails into her palm.

Sister Anna held the infant in the air, habit sleeves stained red, grinning through tears. The child was close-eyed and squalling, painted with blood but beautiful, miraculous.

"A daughter," she whispered, though the new mother could not hear.

The infant had been washed and wrapped in clean white cloth when other nuns, one by one, began to enter the room. The time for Matins had come and gone, they explained, leaving them to wake on their own; and the time for Lauds was then at hand. Why have they heard no bells?

They saw one answer sprawled on the tabletop, knees bent, clamped together, and another bundled in Sister Anna's arms. The nuns crowded around swooning, bowing to see the infant's face and to touch her small fingers. They immediately forgot the Office that had been missed and seemed prepared to forget the next for only the chance to hold the babe in their arms.

John showed a worried smile to her sisters and saw in the faces of Anna and Elizabeth expressions torn quietly between joy and fear.

Sister Phillip, still so young then, in the white habit and white veil, hurried to the abbess's side and squeezed her free hand gaily, hoping to win approval and perhaps to gladden her mother's smile. There was a hot rush of breath as Phillip whispered a line from scripture in her ear, *For unto us a child is born*, then quick puffs of shy, loving laughter.

Sister Matthew, more pragmatic, also moved close to whisper, her lips even then purple with scriptorium ink.

"What of the others?" she asked.

"Which others?" John said.

# Chapter 29

TWO DOZEN OF the girl's kith and kin sat huddled a short way down the hillside from the gatehouse, out of sight. When Mother John approached them, it was the first time she had stepped outside the abbey since the completion of the wall.

A mountain of a man stood at the nun's appearance. He held his meaty palms open and stooped in deference upon seeing that her eyes were level to the middle of his chest.

"I've come looking for my daughter, who wandered off in the night," he said. "She is soon to give birth and I fear for her safety. A blow to the head has stolen her wits." Gesturing to the men, women, and children who accompanied him, he added, "These others seek refuge from the plague and the violence it has brought."

"Come," John said without hesitation. "Come to safety within our walls."

*Our walls*. Never before had she felt any ownership over the ugly stacks of stone that had driven Ursula away, but now she could see the point of them. She had hated Francis and his obsession with providing them protection against a fate it seemed the whole world shared, but looking upon the abbey from the outside, she wondered if suddenly she could see the wall as Father Francis did: an ark, such as Noah built, to keep them from slipping beneath the deluge until the earth might be habitable again.

The refugees from the forest followed her, moving swiftly and silently as directed, through the gatehouse and immediately to the abbess's cottage, so recently abandoned by the abbey's founder, given over to the care of one who had never wanted such responsibility. They settled into the sitting room with the relief of the condemned allowed to walk from the gallows.

"And Maureen, she is with you?" the girl's father asked.

"Yes. She is the reason you are here."

As she left them to their rest, she looked to the night sky above the convent. A flash of white in the moonlight hovered overhead, then squawked as it released its delivery. It fell in an arc shaped by the hot summer wind and landed decisively in the abbess's path.

*Remember, my sisters, a simple loaf from our bakehouse is a greater achievement than the most cunning work of art. Consider how your sisters' labor in the bakehouse turns flour, salt, and water into sustenance for all the abbey, and even beyond. Consider how their effort alone produces the loving flesh of God to be consumed during Mass. Has anyone ever survived on a repast of carved wood in any shape? No, my sisters, there is a reason our Lord was born in a place called*

*Bethlehem. In my distant travels when I was a young woman of means, I once met a learned Hebrew who explained to me that the root of the holy city's name is Bet Lehem, the house of bread. It is there where unlike ingredients came together to become something new. God and man joined by the fire of a woman's womb. Let your hearts each be a Bethlehem and remember that revelation arrives in the world only through bodies like yours.*

By morning, the nuns' nighttime dread had lifted in the bakehouse, replaced by joyful talk and laughter. Mother John had told the man called Butcher that she would bring his daughter and granddaughter to him as soon as the girl felt strong enough to move. Though he and others in the cottage appeared wan, bedraggled from their exodus out of the forest, he had bloomed with joy at the prospect of seeing her.

"Your father has come for you," she told the girl. "He is waiting in my cottage with all your friends, planning a feast to celebrate the babe's arrival."

Until the sisters made a plan for how to care for them all, it was agreed that the abbey's forest guests would remain quietly out of sight.

Then came another hot whisper in Mother John's ear—"The priest!"—followed by frightened silence as the door swung open and Father Francis marched into the room.

He studied them balefully through his remaining eye. The change that had come over him through the preceding months was not limited to his ruined face. It seemed something within him had been similarly ground down, as if any softness of heart he once had known had been pressed to a sharpening wheel until it had a cutting edge.

The younger nuns buried faces in their hands and huddled before the baking table, a blur of white and black, moving in a cloud of flour dust. Mother John alone stood defiant, with Sister Elizabeth hiding behind.

"Forgive me, Mother Abbess," he said. A mocking smile delivered John's new title; he had doubted Ursula's saintliness but never that she had the authority to lead her sisters. "I was not informed that this morning's Office would be offered in the bakehouse. Gathered to study your predecessor's rantings?"

He had of course seen the dove's deliveries and hoped to catch them in the act of reading if only to glean something about what Ursula would take such pains to say.

John offered nothing in response, well aware that whatever mischief the priest suspected was insignificant compared to the reality of this morning. The two held their ground, each staring with unchristian disdain. But in a moment their contest was ended. Rising from the mass of habits and veils encircling the baking table was a terrible, unmistakable sound: high-pitched, helpless, piercing deep—a baby's cry.

Francis's face fell loose, lips parting. It was a sound never heard within the abbey walls. He moved toward its source, arms raised in a priestly posture, strong hands with palms open as if to part a sea, and the nuns scattered all around, some running to the corners, most making for the door, revealing what was hidden.

The new mother was seated on the tabletop, the swaddled infant at her breast. She looked as though she had been beaten:

her face sick and swollen; the bruises that were tiny spots had become blackened, fist-sized welts. They covered her forehead and cheeks, crawled down her neck, and pimpled her chest, where the child clung nursing as though from these sores. The priest barely stifled the girl's name as it formed on his lips.

He turned reprovingly to Sister Elizabeth, stabbing at her with words. His speech was labored all of a sudden, his voice choked with confusion and distress.

"Have you broken your penance, then, Sister? Did you not have strict instructions to seek my counsel before allowing a soul past our gate?"

Elizabeth stared at the ground, cowering at her Mother's side. With a touch and a nod, John bid this sister to take her leave, at which a dozen nuns hurried for the door. Through the commotion, Maureen sat still on the tabletop, aware only of her child, stroking her, calming her cries.

"It was I who admitted her, Father."

The abbess stood, angered and unafraid, staring hard at the priest, her words offered not as confession but a remorseless statement of fact. *Mother Ursula*, she thought, *protect us*.

Father Francis crossed the room, putting distance between himself and the baking table. His face contorted, his eye shone, for he wanted to look upon the girl, to weep over what she had become, what he—*the man responsible*—had allowed her to become.

"Sister, are you mad?" he asked John. "Have you forgotten why a wall stands around us? It stands to preserve sanctity from corruption. To keep us all from the sins of the world. And now when sickness knocks, you let it in?"

His gaze flashed across the room to the young intruders. The girl had been his image of the Virgin, but what was this tableau but a perversion of holiness, a leprous Madonna and Child? He breathed deep the air of the bakehouse and bristled at the detection of humors so malignant he could nearly see them. The room stank of sin and death; that he knew most of the sin he smelled was his own only heightened his disgust.

"I have done as we are bidden by the Rule," Mother John said. "She asked our assistance and we have provided it . . . as we would do for Christ."

The last word lifted Francis's arm and swung it through the air like an ax, meeting the nun's cheek, cutting her down with an open palm. She stumbled to the floor, and the priest berated her, spitting words.

"Do not dare, Sister, compare this diseased girl to our one hope and salvation."

Francis thought of the cross he had carved, where of course he had done much more than compare them. He had in fact made them a single body, two persons joined in a lone figure, united by their pain. But even the murdered girl he had depicted as one with the crucified savior was incapable of being so thoroughly corrupted as this carrier of the sickness seemed to be. And what could the child she carried be, he wondered, but a monstrous birth, conceived of woman and all the evil of the plague itself?

"She and her bastard must go," Francis said with finality.

The nun climbed to her feet, black veil powdered with flour dust, unbowed.

"No," she said, "the child has only just been born. If they leave today they will surely die tomorrow."

"And if they stay we will all be dead by Vespers."

Francis allowed himself a lingering glance to study the young mother. The table washed in daylight, she sat there grinning with wonder at her newborn child. Her beauty was apparent despite her affliction; her eyes shone, though her face had grown gray.

"Ruth, may I now see my father?" she asked. "Does he still await me in your cottage?"

In an instant, Francis was out of the bakehouse at a run. Before the door to his workshop, an ax stood upright in its chopping block. He pulled it from the wood with barely a break in his stride.

When he opened the door to the abbess's cottage, he stepped back in horror. Huddled inside with the guilty faces of stowaways, a mob of men, women, and children sat on the floor, all gathered around the vast man from the forest called Butcher. Their eyes met in recognition, and the priest turned away to study the others. He smelled the air as he once breathed in the scent of trees to discern their value for carving. Now, though, he detected only rot. There were far too many of them to physically remove, and likely the damage of their presence was already done. He slammed the door shut and dropped his ax across the handle, locking the interlopers inside.

The nuns crowded around him now, drawn by the commotion.

"If they have not brought plague into the abbey, they can depart tomorrow," he announced. "If they have, we will know soon enough."

The wailing inside the cottage began within the hour, as the first of the afflicted fell to the disease. To his credit, Francis did not shrug off his priestly duties through the long hours that followed. He stood by the barred door and heard one confession after another through the cracks between the boards.

"Father, forgive me, for I have sinned," began each litany of error and regret. "Father, forgive me . . ." A woman admitted her frequent infidelity, and a man admitted wishing her dead. "Father, forgive me . . ." One brother admitted sabotaging his brother's garden, and then the other brother admitted the same. "Father, forgive me . . ." A child, speaking as if prodded by a parent's finger in his side, acknowledged stealing a potato, kicking a dog, and pinching his sister so hard it left a welt. "Father, forgive me . . ." Some talked on and on, and as they did, their lists of misdeeds fell away, replaced by remembrances of the places where the supposed sinning occurred, the people they had lost and loved dearly with whom they most enjoyed to sin, the unexpected outcomes that made them believe even the most sinful acts might ultimately yield positive effects.

"Who is to say, Father," Butcher said when his turn for confession had come, "if any good might yet come of what happened to my poor Maureen? She is here now and safe, is she not? She is not in here with all this sickness and wailing. Will you promise me she will remain? That you will speak to the abbess, as you once said you would, and find her a home among the sisters?"

Anxious to make amends for all he was responsible for, for his actions and inaction, for the bawdy farce he had once made of confession now that he understood what the word could mean, Francis answered through the cracked boards of the door he had barred. "I will."

Late into the night he listened and granted absolution. By the end of Matins, he heard only dark silence through the door to the abbess's cottage. After he called several times to Butcher and heard no reply, he went to the cloister walkway, retrieved a lit candle, and returned to the cottage to set its thatched roof alight.

He then stood back to watch this small part of the world burn.

"Heaven protect us, he has murdered them," Sister Elizabeth said as the nuns watched from outside the abbey church. "The girl and the child will be next."

"No," Mother John said. "He'll not get them."

Back in the bakehouse, Maureen was singing to her daughter: simple, silly words; a voice like small bells. John watched them a moment then began hurrying about the room, filling a wicker basket with bread, potatoes, and a clean white cloth. The abbess took the girl by the hand and led her across the convent, back from where she had come. She stumbled along, clutching the child to her chest.

"Ruth?" she asked. "What is happening? Are we going to the feast?"

John's eyes fell shut as they reached the gatehouse. The room was brighter now and empty but otherwise exactly as it was when the girl arrived. They will both be dead within the week, she thought. Tears welled beneath her eyelids, and she swallowed hard then told Maureen to hide in the forest, just for a short while, and do all that could be done to keep the child safe.

"You must go," she said, "but you will return."

She looked away, inspecting the gatehouse's shabby interior: the dirty stone walls, the plank and straw bed where she had washed the girl's feet, the iron-barred window and heavy wooden door that perhaps should not have been opened but must be opened again.

Maureen nodded, saying nothing, then lifted the infant to her face and kissed her small head, gray lips wetting wisps of orange hair. The baby nuzzled under her chin, which when lifted announced a truth John could no longer deny: The girl was doomed.

The swelling and discoloration of her joints was not a consequence of labor. It was, it could only be, the sickness, death made flesh. The infant, though, was miraculously unblemished. A light shining in the darkness.

The girl stepped ruefully across the threshold, basket in one hand, baby daughter held tight at her breast. She turned and looked at the nun, her friend, and curled her lips though she was too weak to smile.

"Thank you, Ruth," she said; the voice of a child grateful for a gift she is too young to understand. "Thank you."

Without a word, without a thought, the abbess stepped forward and took the new mother by the hand, pulling her toward her with a tug and then lifting the infant from her arms. The baby wailed, but Maureen did not move. She stood still and staring as the nun walked back to the gatehouse and disappeared behind a wall of wood and stone.

Inside, Mother John stood startled by her own action, staring through the window, the mewling child clutched to her habit. The girl approached the bars, arms cradled as if holding still what had been taken from her, her face revealing that what had been taken was everything. But she then turned away, her ragged tunic still powdered with bakehouse flour.

The nun watched her shrink away down the oxcart path until she disappeared into the forest.

In the days to come, the consequences of the girl's visit would be seen: seven nuns would fall dead in their choir stalls, a dozen more to follow within the month. As infirmarian, Sister Anna would survive constant exposure to the pestilence for three weeks before she herself succumbed. Sister Elizabeth, the first to greet the sickness, would be the last taken by it. Father Francis would busy himself with confessions and the carving of crosses, which allowed the infant smuggled over from death to life to go unnoticed until the threat had largely passed.

For the moment, to Mother John caring for the baby girl seemed all there was in the world. This child, orange-haired, round, and healthy, was her one certainty. The abbess smelled her head and patted her small, warm back, realizing that this was the first time she had held an infant in her arms. Together, the surviving nuns of Gaerdegen decided to call her *Maureen* in remembrance of her mother, a name they believed none should soon forget.

# Chapter 30

THOUGH IT SEEMED the storm winds raged enough to tumble his walls, Father Francis studied the freshly completed cross with utmost concentration. After he had finished his inspection of each of its scenes, he backed away to contemplate the work as a whole. The cross would be perfect: Cleanest white, its wood had not one blemish, neither from the carver's knife nor the hand of God. It would be the summation of all the crosses he had carved in his lifetime, the forest of markers he had planted for the old and the plague dead. Even if it failed to win his freedom, it would be a fitting monument to his memory.

The only problem was his ceiling. Shrink or bump your head: With the thatch above him too low to set the cross upright, he was unable to view it as it would be seen either hanging on a wall in the bishop's palace or standing in the ground over his grave. He would need to carry the two pieces to the abbey barn to complete their assembly.

He gathered the necessary tools and was preparing for a hard walk through the snow when a faint knock came on his door. The priest ignored the sound, deciding it was the wind. But it came again, loud and deliberate this time, no mistaking its intent. And a voice, small and soft but with urgency, as though the matter was of life and death.

"Father?" the priest heard, "Father?" Muted by the wood of the walls and the racket of the storm, the voice belonged to a woman but called like a lost child. "Father?"

Ice and snow came pouring in as the door opened, and behind them stood Sister Magdalene, knee deep in the drift that had begun to swallow the chaplain's shack. Her black veil blew in the wind, wildly about her face, and her white habit seemed connected to the snowy earth, like the trunk of a tree. She was barely able to stand against the gale's awful force. Her body swayed left and right with each ebb and gust of the wind, as if she might be swept away.

Francis just stared like an old man confused. He was surprised first by the knock and then by the knocker. He backed away slowly and nodded, *Come in, come in.*

The young nun entered and pulled the door shut behind her, casting her eyes to the dark, frozen floor, taking note of dirt, wood chips, decaying yellow straw, and knives. She spoke quickly, her voice shaking.

"Forgive me, Father," she said. "Forgive my intrusion. I am on my way to the bakehouse and thought to inquire how our chaplain is faring in the storm."

Still he only stared. The years had taken his fire but not his suspicion. He sharpened his glare and raised an eyebrow lightly, as if to ask, *Why venture outside in such weather?* Though of course he was about to do the same.

Magdalene spoke nervously; she had asked herself the same question and offered a rehearsed response. "Storm or no, the bread must be baked." Her twentieth year in a place ruled by silence, she remained unaccustomed to conversation.

Francis nodded again then turned from the nun, taking careful steps across the floor, back to his cross. Though its carving was complete and in need of no more attention, he held a small knife tightly and lifted it to the wood, then traced it slowly in the air above the grain, careful not to touch his blade to the hornbeam's flesh and mar its perfection. If she believed he was working she might leave him in peace.

"Father," Magdalene said timidly, "will you hear a confession?"

The priest breathed heavily. Her concern for him was a lie, he thought; she had come not for his benefit but her own.

"Father?" she asked again.

He closed his eye and wished she would go and leave him to his work.

"Say what you must."

Then it was she who stared. Her lips parted, but the words would not come; her throat grew dry as if she had already said too much. The two stood speechless for a moment, listening as the storm filled the room and gave volume and weight to their silence.

"Speak, child," he said. "What are your sins?"

She closed her eyes then opened them. They shined wet in the workshop's little light.

"Father, forgive me, but I do not know."

Her words cracked and scraped as they moved past her teeth and into the air. The corners of her mouth turned sharply down and her tongue wet her lips to help her speak through throat-constricting tears. The priest watched as she turned away and spoke to the walls, speaking loudly, as if through them.

"I know I have sinned for I am being punished. I ask forgiveness so that the punishment might end."

Magdalene turned again to face the priest. Her cheeks, he saw, were lined prematurely with worry; her eyes were wide with uncertainty.

"I am no longer called the way I once was. I am distracted in church, impatient during the liturgy, disinterested in the holy readings. It is as though I have been abandoned. I fear I have been waiting for someone who will never arrive. Someone whose presence to me had come to seem a new beginning. Someone whose rejection would leave me undone."

Tears rolled hot on her cheeks, and her mouth shut tight, as though fearing her own voice and the words it brought. Whether she spoke of Jesus or Brother Daniel, she couldn't precisely say. Each had been another name for hope, but where were they now?

"Please help me, Father," she said. "God has left me."

Father Francis found the words startling and amusing. He moved his battered fingers over his cross's staff and thought of the ground that might soon lie beneath it, and of the body that would become that ground. He passed his fingers over his own wrists and arms, then across his cowl to the turn of his ribs, pausing at the long scar he could feel through his robe.

"He leaves us all," he said. "Now leave me."

Sister Magdalene turned from the priest and hurried from the workshop, back into the storm and the grayness of approaching night.

# PART 7
# VESPERS

# Chapter 31

FROM EVERY CORNER of the darkness they appeared, moving as if footless through the tall, wide room, floating above the floor like ghosts. The day's work was finished, and the nuns again gathered to sing and pray. All bowed low and slowly to the altar as they entered, then took their places in the choir, sitting close-shouldered in the cold.

When it seemed all had arrived, they stood, crossed themselves, and prayed without speaking, waiting for the voice that began all the day's Hours of prayer.

But Sister Magdalene was not in the church. Their silent contemplation ended and silence remained. Eighteen nuns looked nervously about the room, but none could offer an explanation. No one seemed to know where their sister might be, and if any did the words would have to wait.

It had been years since the abbess had sung alone in choir, but she opened her lips and began the Hour herself, singing weak-voiced and unmusically, but with all her sisters in reply.

*Let our evening prayer ascend before you, O Lord.*
*And may your loving kindness descend upon us.*

Their voices shook, betraying their fears. They wondered at Magdalene's absence, concerned for her safety, for even through the thick church walls the nuns could hear that the sullen storm had grown mean and whipping. It tore through the air, howling against the bell tower and off the steep roof of the church. Already the blizzard had been brutal, frightening, and they guessed from the sound that it would only get worse. Yet still they prayed, first a psalm appropriate for the Hour, then a reading from the Book of Ursula that offered her interpretation of the words. No more could be done but to listen and wait.

"My God, my God, why have you forsaken me?" they chanted. "I cry out by day, but you do not answer. I call through the night and cannot rest."

*Remember, my sisters, how the Liturgy of the Hours makes Christ's life our own. Vespers is his Crucifixion, the ending that gives our every beginning meaning, and so in the evening we sing his lament upon the cross. But when our Lord spoke those words, do not suppose he directed them to his Father in heaven alone. No, he speaks them to each of us: Why have you forsaken me, Ursula? Why have you forsaken me, O holy nuns of Gaerdegen? And as we each through our prayers join him in his passion, we must recognize that we are always at once forsaker and forsaken. Why have you forsaken your sister when she hangs on a cross which you are unable to see? We will cease this forsaking only when we begin all things with an awareness of how they will inevitably end.*

Mother John rolled the day's final reading from the Book of Ursula together with all the others, and slid them inside her habit, tucking them into a belt worn around her waist. In times of duress, she preferred to keep the pages close. It was a particular comfort to feel the parchment on her skin when outside it seemed the world might blow away.

The smaller buildings of the convent were in greatest danger. In the gatehouse, the heavy wooden door creaked and cried with the push of the wind, and the ceiling bent toward the frozen floor, threatening to cave in from the weight of the snow. The chaplain's workshop, too, was in danger. Supported mostly by the snowdrifts that buried its walls, its thatched roof sagged inward, brushing against the priest's bald head as he stood alone and sang the evening's office, oblivious to the risk.

The stone bakehouse seemed immune to the storm's anger. Alone in its firelight, barefoot on the cold stone floor, Sister Magdalene stood bent over in her habit, curves hidden, face framed. She worked intently, concerned only with the solid table and the few things it held. The heat of the baking fire and the warmth of her exertions drew sweat to her brow. Beads of perspiration chilled in the draft that snuck through under the door.

From the four bowls before her, she took rye flour, barley flour, water, and salt and mixed them in a larger bowl, working her spoon in slow circles, giving body to liquid and dust. The mingled scent of them smelled of spring: wet grass and wood smoke. Soon she was able to roll a fleshy mound of dough back and forth through a covering of flour until it was round as a small log. She set it aside to rest and rise in preparation for the fire. Then the work began again.

Storm winds crept down the chimney and into the oven, fighting then feeding the flames, sending shadows jumping on the floor and walls. The room was darkness then light, darkness then light, and Magdalene squinted to see her work though the tabletop was high, just an arm's length from her face. The dough was cold and wet in her palms like handfuls of snow, but heavy as meat. It grew dense as she kneaded and held her fingers like tiny fists as they moved through the flour. She had forgotten how many loaves she had come to bake, but she continued, content to work into the night.

Outside the storm raged. The door rattled in its frame; the shutters banged violently against the stones that held them. The wind alternately sharpened and softened its tone, rising from a roar to a high-pitched whine, then low again, then climbing to another piercing cry. Squeezing between the shutters and under the door, it found the sister's ears, though muffled by the cloth of her veil. She heard it call softly, low then high, a whisper of the screech that was outside the thick stone walls.

With a start, Magdalene looked up and listened, staring ahead in the flickering light of the bakehouse. She seemed to know the sounds. Her veil played lightly about her face, and from the floor a breeze rose and rustled the hem of her habit. The chill moved across her toes and slowly up the full height of her legs, mounting shins to knees to thighs and higher. It shaped the curve and small of her back and traced a line between her shoulders. She put the dough gently on the tabletop and moved toward the door to listen more closely.

Through the cracks, the draft blew on her pale and tired face, weaving through hair of the most burning red. The cold whispered through her with a clean feeling that filled her mouth and dried her teeth. Magdalene lifted the latch and let the storm breach the bakehouse.

Wooden bowls met wooden spoons and clicked like dice on the tabletop, then tumbled to the floor and clattered toward the walls, but Magdalene could hear and see only the world outside. The storm seemed a fire of white, glowing somehow, though the sun had long since set. It was the worst she had ever seen, worse than she had ever imagined, and it was beautiful. The nun stared and thought of a girl turning circles to watch the night sky, constellations spinning dizzily, forming one body of all the stars blurring until they were one light—like this holy white fog, pure and perfect as the flesh of God. Magdalene nodded slightly and allowed the wind to kiss her open lips. Her eyelids fell softly and trembled at the touch.

# Chapter 32

EARLY AUTUMN WIND seemed to lift the child the sisters called Maureen. Orange hair like ropes of fire, flying as she moved, wrapped her face. Young, not yet six years old, she ran madly through the cloister, dragging a stick behind her, lifting it and tapping the stones of the wall. From the shade of the convent church she burst out to the daylight of the cloister garth, stopping just an instant to feel the breeze and watch the sky. The sun hung high and soft above her. As always, it would soon be time to pray.

A dozen sisters working casually in the garth watched this girl on what would be the year's last warm day. Sister Phillip knelt in the turned earth of the garden, tending to herbs and flowers, whispering prayers. Purple-lipped Sister Matthew and other nuns sat like mushrooms by a waist-high, gray stone basin carved with a pattern of leaves and flowers. They all bent forward, mending holes in habits, while the abbess walked about maternally, examining their work.

Father Francis stood off in the distance, busy in a corner of the yard but keeping close and careful watch on the girl. He followed her with his eye as though frightened; he would never forgive her for the horror she brought, as if her presence assured its return.

Maureen stormed about the yard, pulling at the hem of Mother John's habit, tapping her stick on the fountain, tromping through the flower bed, laughing, laughing, laughing. The sisters seemed not bothered at all by her mischief, not even the oldest. No, the sight gladdened them. The plague had become a distant memory with the help of these sounds of excitement and joy.

She ran with her wide sleeves and white dress flapping, weaving in and out of the sisters' sewing circle. Soon they all had set aside their work, laying lengths of cloth across their laps, thinking only of the girl. Each watched as though the child was her own, reaching out gently to run fingers through her hair as she flitted past. They grinned self-consciously, cupping hands to hide their teeth, as though just learning to laugh.

Mother John looked proudly and lovingly on these nuns, her sisters. Their faces shone pink in the sunlight, pretty and pleased, framed in the cloth of their veils. To her, they all were glowing and ageless, even the oldest, like portraits of the Lord. And Maureen, the abbess thought, *Maureen*, almost singing the name: She was small and freckled, framed in red, cheeks flushed by vigor and the sun. Her lips wet and her eyes shining, the girl watched the sisters in awe, fascinated by the way their habits rippled in the wind.

Maureen stretched a small hand to Sister James's lap and pulled a battered white veil from the pile of cloth in need of repair, then wrapped the fabric tight around her little head, letting its free end fall past her shoulders. The tattered veil caught a breeze and flew about her face, flapping against her cheeks like white wings. The girl stared piously to the sky above the abbey wall, playing the nun, small eyes falling shut against the light.

Other sisters nodded and grinned, but at this the abbess seemed displeased. The girl, she thought, had aged too quickly in the silence of the cloister. She had seen Maureen sit for hours in the back of the church when she might have been outside playing and had heard her small voice echo the liturgy, anxious to join the sisters in all the day's work. *Too young*, she thought, *too young*, wondering if such a life was fit for a child. She clucked her tongue disapprovingly and pulled the veil from the girl's head, then spoke unexpectedly, her first unscripted words in weeks.

"In due time," she said.

The sisters were startled, the words hanging uncomfortably in the air. They heard the abbess's voice often, but rarely outside of the church and never in such a casual tone. In this place, words were saved for prayer, and so they all stared in surprise. Maureen especially could not understand. Young as she was, she was well aware that Mother John had broken the rules. She looked quickly to the others for an explanation, then realized that the words were meant for her.

"When?" she asked, as though a vague promise had been made, in a voice loud and ringing because she had grown accustomed to song.

"Patience, child, patience," the abbess said, looking down kindly, then offered an excuse she hoped would end the discussion. "You have yet to be properly baptized, after all." The sisters had christened her themselves in the time of the plague, fearful she would be taken while still sullied by original sin, hopeful a woman's performance of the sacrament would suffice in such a dark time. But all agreed it would be better for a priest to remove all doubt of her baptism's efficacy.

Maureen looked at Mother John coldly, eyes sharp, jaw clenched. She knew what it was that set her apart from her sisters, and knew she had been forbidden to approach the only one who might solve this problem. Glancing across the yard, her eyes widened and she smiled mischievously, as though a game had just been won. She turned her back to them suddenly to run.

In the far corner, Father Francis was busy erecting a new cross for the enclosure, a grave marker for Sister Philomena, the last living member of the faction upon whose support he had once relied. She had survived the plague only to slip on the stairs and break her hip five years later. Though she languished painfully for months with ample time to reconsider the choices of her youth, she never came to regret that it was her power over Gaerdegen's purse that allowed the priest to build his wall.

Francis worked on his knees, scooping dirt with hard, knotted hands, then climbed to his feet and stood a wooden cross snugly in the dark, moist earth. He worked with his back to the nuns but jerked around to face them when voices stretched across the yard, turning in time to see a dozen nuns jump to their feet and the girl, to his horror, racing toward him. The abbess called after her—a nun's voice, high-pitched and frightened: "Maureen, Maureen." But in a moment she stood before him, staring up with small eyes though Mother John's call to her rang sternly: "Maureen!"

Father Francis stepped behind his cross, backing away, and looked down on the child with dread. Orange-haired and green-eyed, as though the girl from the bakehouse had returned to haunt him. Yet watching her grow these past years he had noticed in her face and manner not just a shadow of the young beauty whose destruction he had abetted but another presence from the awful night in the sharpening shed. He felt the press of a foot on the back of his neck whenever he heard her laugh and knew with a certainty he usually lacked that she was the daughter of the man who had taken half his sight.

"Maureen!" the nun shouted again. Even her name offended him. It was a daily reminder of both the day he failed to intervene for an innocent and the night his authority was flouted. It was a guarantee, he thought, that Death would again conquer the convent walls, just as they had those years before, on the Feast of Saint Mary Magdalene.

Mother John watched from across the yard but did not approach, not even as Maureen fell to her knees in front of the priest. Francis's face grew pinched and red when the girl spoke. He stared bitterly at the abbess then seized the child by the arm, tugging her to her feet and dragging her behind him, back toward the nuns.

The sisters gasped at the severity of his actions and cowered as he drew near. He strode bolstered by the hatred he felt for this girl and the part he was fated to play in her life. When she stumbled, he hoisted her from the ground, gripping her by the wrist at arm's length like a rat by its tail. He stopped at the gray stone fountain and fixed his eye hard on Mother John, throwing the girl to the ground between them. Maureen let out a whimper, but the nuns just stared. What could they do?

Francis pointed a crooked finger to the girl at his feet. "Am I to baptize this sinful thing?"

The abbess's eyes began to tear; she knew what the girl must have said. Sister James moved toward the child but was frightened away by the priest's next words. "Am I to christen the child that brought Death upon us? She should have been burned with the sickbeds, and now you'd have her baptized?"

Maureen looked up from the ground. She too was in tears, not from being handled so roughly but because she did not understand his words. Death was a baby bird that fell from its nest; how had she brought it in?

Above her Mother John was speaking. "Is it not your responsibility, Father, to see that the sacraments are provided to the sisters of our Order?" She had not asked for the girl to be baptized, but her authority had been challenged, and she would not be bullied. An angry tone invaded her voice. "Our young sister Maureen is need of baptism, and you will provide it, as is your commission. Else your superiors may hear of it, and of other offenses."

Father Francis nodded slowly, taking measure of the abbess. Though he did not believe the nun would dare speak out against him, this was not worth the risk. With the distance of years, he had come to recognize that the excesses building the wall had led him to would not be viewed favorably in the episcopal palace. He could not imagine any punishment worse than his life sentence at Gaerdegen but did not doubt the bishop's ability to invent one.

Between the mother and the father, the child climbed to her feet. Maureen was not quite standing when the priest lunged forward and grabbed her again, twisting his fingers in the roots of her hair.

"Very well," he said, speaking under his breath as he yanked her with him to the fountain and pressed her face against the smooth carved stone. The nuns watched, unmoving and helpless, as the priest lifted a hand full of water from the fountain and poured it over Maureen's orange crown of hair then traced two lines across her forehead with a rough finger.

"In the name of the Father and of the Son and of the Holy Spirit," he says, "I baptize you." His tone was officious as befitting this solemn rite of the church; his gestures carefully loveless, pressing on the girl's soft skin as if carving oak. Maureen squirmed at his touch, but the priest held firm, his left hand pinning her against the font even as his right made her holy.

"From this day on," he said, "you are sealed by the blood of our Savior. You will share his life and share his cross and by his grace share in eternal life. From this day on your hope and your salvation shall be in the name of the Lord, and so you shall be known by your name in Christ."

The priest paused and looked to the abbess. How presumptuous, he thought, to have dared take in this child when he had forbidden it; how presumptuous to give her a name when the Church reserved the power of naming to men like himself. Mother John was also in tears, to see this girl so helpless in his control. He looked away from the nun back to the girl, still squirming, her face growing crying red, and lifted another handful from the fountain, this time laying it flat on her little head.

"I baptize you *Magdalene*," he said, raising his voice for all the nuns to hear. "So that we will never forget the day of your birth, the day that allowed Death within our walls."

Father Francis snapped his hands away, and the girl fell limply to the ground. Then he turned and went slowly across the yard to resume his work straightening and strengthening the cross.

The nuns rushed to the girl's side to help her to her feet. Her cheek wore an imprint of flowers where it had pressed hardest against the fountain. But she pulled away and ran to the piles of cloth that had been dropped and forgotten to find the same tattered veil Mother John had taken.

"Now?" she asked.

Her sisters stared in horror, at the priest, at the girl they would come to call Sister Magdalene. She was smiling bravely and held the veil wrapped tightly around her head, hiding her hair, her ears, cloth across her cheeks like the wings of a dove. The veil dropped loosely over her shoulders and covered the small of her back, reaching down to her curveless hips. A white curtain falling on her youth.

# Chapter 33

OUTSIDE THE BAKEHOUSE, the wind had diminished. The snow that had been flying so wildly settled to the ground, joining the drifts that had already gathered, leaving the sky clear and dark.

In the distance, Magdalene could see a lonely black triangle, a nun's flowing veil, moving closer over the field of white between the bakehouse and the church. She knew it must be Mother, for no other sister would venture out on such a night. Magdalene smiled at the sight of the older nun but was saddened by the storm's sudden absence. She closed the door to warm the room for the abbess, then returned to her baking, bending down to pick up the things that had fallen.

Mother John huffed in relief at the warmth when she entered. Her cheeks were red, bitten by the cold. She shook snow from her habit, then raised her arms half toward the ceiling to do the same for her sleeves, which slid to her elbows and revealed milky wrists. She rubbed her hands slowly, smoothing fingers over fingers, fingers over palms, then moved them in the air before her chest, raising an eyebrow of inflection and concern as she signed: *Missed Vespers?*

Magdalene bristled at the silence, squeezing bread dough through her fingers.

"Forgive me, Mother," she said, eyes fixed on the fine flour dust on the tabletop. "Tonight our need for bread seemed more pressing than my presence in the church. Sister Lazarus injured her hand and is unable to bake the evening loaves. And if the storm should continue, we may be snowbound for days and kept from the oven. We can't have the sisters grow hungry."

Mother John nodded her head, not quite in agreement.

"We'll grow worse than that if our prayers should cease. What other hope have we in this world?"

The abbess smiled only to see the young nun's face sour and turn quickly away, as if frightened or sickened by the words.

"What is it, Sister? Have you forgotten the purpose of our life?" she asked, and her voice hung uncomfortably in the air.

Magdalene closed her eyes and listened to the storm. The wind seemed to have regathered its strength and now gave a long shrill cry, shaking the shutters and knocking the door in its frame, finding the fire, making the flames leap. Shadows played on the floor and walls; they climbed across the tabletop and darkened the nuns' white habits.

The abbess turned back to signal she still awaited an answer. Magdalene opened her eyes when the wind's call faded, then looked down to her work, took cold dough in her hands and rolled it slowly, saying nothing. How could she forget the purpose of their life, she wondered, when she had worn this veil as long as she could remember, when this was the only life she had known?

"It seems the storm has given us a reprieve," Magdalene said. "The bishop and his clerk must have been delayed by the snow. Who knows when the roads will again grant passage."

"They will come when they come," John said.

Magdalene studied the older woman's face. The light from the fire reflected in her eyes. There and then gone, there and gone.

"And will you know why they have come, when they do?"

"I know why today."

Beyond the safety of the bakehouse's stone walls, the wind roared so loudly that Magdalene could not envision a living soul within it. She wondered if the bishop and Brother Daniel sat somewhere trapped in their carriage, its wheels caught in an icy rut or drift, or perhaps turned on its side by a particularly violent gust. Would the carriage driver sit with them, sorry to be stuck but glad to be out of the snow? And what of their horses? Would they stay close out of habit or break free to save themselves?

"I don't grieve their failure to arrive," Magdalene said. "But I had hoped the visit might bring some resolution to our concerns."

"Resolution belongs only to God," the abbess replied.

"Mother, I must tell you. There may come a time when I am unable to help you. You will have to find a place to hide the scrolls where they will not be found."

"Oh, yes," John said.

If she intended to continue, the words drifted away—thought, perhaps, but unspoken. Magdalene waited until it seemed clear the older nun would say no more on the subject. She wondered when she might broach it again, and if, when she did so, Mother John would believe they were speaking of the matter for the first time.

The abbess came forward, cautiously, habit sweeping along the stones of the floor. She stopped at the baking table and stood close by Magdalene's side, watching her work. Her thin fingers squeezed and released the dough, moving it forward and back through the flour. She gripped it like a thigh, like pushing and pulling fingers through muscle to loosen its tension or restore its strength. Magdalene seemed to lose herself in the kneading. She only watched the table before her, breathing slowly, occasionally closing her eyes.

Mother John went to the oven and began replenishing it, pushing fuel inside with a long paddle. She raised her hands into the bakehouse air and held them just below her chin, like a child catching snowflakes in her palms, then let a long sigh pass her lips and spoke wistfully, her voice soft with a sad kind of joy.

"Can you feel it?" she asked.

Magdalene, though, was in another place. Her hands were there, within the bakehouse, mixing, then rolling butter-white dough, but she was without, in the roar of the storm, with the snow and ice and the swirling wind. She heard its force pound the door again, then the walls, and felt the cold draft lap gently against her cheeks and chin. Her heart raced at the sharpness of its cries, and she felt the sweat beneath her habit, which clung wetly to her back and upper arms. She rolled the dough feverishly under her palms and dreamed of a wind that could roll stones away, that would tear down the convent and find her inside.

"Sister, tell me, can you feel it?" Mother John asked again.

"Feel, Mother?"

"The love of God," she said. "It burns like a fire, and we are right at this moment consumed in its flames."

*I've lost her*, Magdalene thought.

But then she followed Mother's gaze into the mouth of the bread oven. Tubes of parchment stood at the edges of the fire chamber, each smoking like a chimney as they neared the moment of combustion. Their tips glowed orange in a ring around the plump loaves at the center.

"Now we share her wisdom with the sky," Mother John said as the first roll of parchment burst into flames. Flakes of ash rose with the heat of the air, wafting through the chimney toward the frigid night above, as if to alert the wind to the presence of the two women inside.

Orange light shone, then faded from the oven, rising then falling like fast, quivering breaths. It blinked on the powder-white walls and cast Mother John's long shadow across the tabletop. Then the room was washed in light as the remaining rolls of parchment became pages of flame.

"Mother, you can't!" Magdalene said.

"I can. I did. And when we eat these loaves, Ursula's words will become part of us as never before." Her eyes gleamed in a flash of firelight.

And then there was darkness. The storm's low growl had climbed to a scream and pushed through to the oven, coursing down the chimney shaft, snuffing the fire. Wind pierced the room as the door swung open and the gust set the shutters flapping like wings. It knocked both Magdalene and Mother John to their knees, sweeping the tabletop clear. The air filled with flour and salt that whipped with the snow and stung the nuns' eyes.

All over the convent it was the same: despite their defenses, the blizzard came crashing through. It battered the gatehouse and cracked the cloister's wooden shields, while the priest's shack crumpled beneath a covering of white. Even the church roof, with its trunk-sized beams, caved in under the weight of the snow and the pounding gale, letting flurries again fall on the altar and the cross.

Snow and ice filled the bakehouse, and the two nuns struggled to their feet, black veils flying about their faces, white habits blown taut against their stomachs and thighs. They reached out in the darkness and found waiting hands, and pulled each other close in a frightened embrace.

"Christ, come quickly," Mother John whispered, but the wind blew still, drowning her prayers, filling the night with a low then high call.

Magdalene's eyes widened at the sound. She listened as if its moaning and keening were meant only for her.

"*Maureen*," she heard in the wind. "*Maureen. Maureen.*"

The name seemed all there was.

Magdalene pulled away from the abbess and went toward the door. She tore her veil away and let it drop, then stood tall and orange-haired and answered the call, speaking through tears.

"I'm coming," she said.

And was gone.

# PART 8

# COMPLINE

# Chapter 34

In the years to come, they would say they could feel her touch in the movements of the wind. They would claim the voice they had heard so often in the choir returned to sing in the courtyard and in the open cloister, that she brought soothing words when the air was hot, warming tones to break a wintry chill. They would insist that she joined them in their chanting Hours and made certain their prayers were heard.

Many stories would be told. But now there was only the hard fact of absence.

Mother John prayed softly until the storm subsided, then struggled to her feet, alone in the bakehouse. The room was quiet and lit by moon glow pouring through the open window and door.

John shook the flakes from her habit and then passed through the doorway to a muffled white world, where at last there was no wind.

Nor were there footprints. Around her the snow rose waist deep, chest deep in the drifts, and the bakehouse was an island in an unbroken sea. Not a mark, not a step, in any direction. Perhaps the girl had run but did not get far. Perhaps she had fallen and lay buried minutes away or inches from the door. Perhaps she was screaming beneath four feet of silence.

The abbess climbed into the snowbank and made her way slowly toward the church, which loomed in the distance. Between the bakehouse and the cloister, the chaplain's workshop was a mound of snow. Its chimney had collapsed along with three of its walls. Broken roof beams jutted from the snowfield like fangs.

She paid them no mind, pulled forward by the distant sound of her sisters. Inside, she knew, the nuns of Gaerdegen were gathered in the safety of the washroom's cavernous walls. She could hear their hymns through stacked stone. As she drew closer, the rocks themselves seemed to sing.

Only when she stood among the others did she pause to take stock of herself, to see what they must see. Her white habit was gray and battered, stiffened and weighed down with ice. Her black veil wrapped wet and tight against her face, no longer flowing.

But no matter. The sisters rejoiced at the sight. Novices huddled close and pressed their eyes shut, praying rapidly, *Salve Regina, mother of mercy*. Older nuns crossed themselves quickly then grasped cold hands.

A moment later they halted their prayers to ask the obvious question.

"And Sister Magdalene?" Sister Bartholomew asked. "She is with you?"

Seventeen faces, veiled and hopeful, crowded around.

"No," John replied. "She is gone."

Bartholomew let out a sob and fell into the abbess's arms. "I am sorry, Mother John!" she moaned. "I did it. I told Magdalene I wished she would disappear in the wind, and now it has come to pass!"

"You did nothing, child," John said. "Did you make the wind? Did you make the snow or the cold? What good is our faith if it does not allow us to know that God is not just the sunshine but also the storm?"

The abbess turned from her sisters before words like why could be spoken. Directing her step to the church, she knew they would follow.

The nuns fell silent, looking to each other and to the slate floor worn smooth by so many sisters called to meet their savior, then closing their eyes because only this was true: she was gone, and everything was broken.

A moment later, the call of a church bell filled the night.

Because the nuns of Gaerdegen never found her, and because no less an authority than their abbess had verified that the storm had called her by a name that only God and few living souls still remembered, there were some who said she had been snatched by a divine hand reaching down to set the earth aright.

Others claimed the missing nun had not left at all but had simply put on daylight as her habit, dark night as her veil, and could still be viewed in certain plays of light upon the mountains. The region had been crowded with cairn spirits and mother goddesses since before the arrival of Christ, and so the spectral presence known variously as Magda and Marin and Our Lady of the Storm found a welcome reception.

In time, tales of the nun whom the storm had called by name came to outshine even the pious legends of Ursula of Gaerdegen. Their fates in fact became interchangeable to many. As it was later said, "There were too many holy women in those days to know who trained the birds and who flew like one." Or, as local aphorists like to note when carefully guarded secrets became so widely known that their original significance was lost, "Both Sister Magdalene and the Book of Ursula were rewritten by the wind." Though the meaning of this expression was inscrutable beyond the borders of the surrounding forest villages, those steeped in the lore of the abbey would nod and agree it was true.

One story never told of the storm and the nun it took began with a priest carrying a cross over a snow-covered yard to the abbey barn.

While the nuns lingered in prayer after Vespers in the convent church, Father Francis dragged the two carved planks of hornbeam behind him. He carried them stacked together, their carved sides facing, one end laid flat on his shoulder, the other trailing on the ground like a rudder cutting through the snowy sea, digging a trench in his wake.

He had left his workshop just as the roof began to fall. As he trudged forward, he did not look back, even as he heard his home for the last twenty years buckling in on itself. As far as Francis was concerned, he had accomplished all he might in that tiny shack and wanted only to finish the cross he was hefting as Christ once did down the Via Dolorosa.

The abbey barn was barely visible ahead of him, but Francis had walked this way so often to tend to the ox and his wood cart that he knew he simply had to start in the right direction and push on for a hundred steps.

Brother Daniel, however, had never walked between the buildings of the abbey. In fact, before that moment he had not dared to go deeper into Gaerdegen than the visitors' room, where he and Sister Magdalene had spoken and sparred and, as he had realized at some point while traveling with the bishop for the purpose of investigating the abbey's heretical teachings, fallen in love.

He had left the episcopal entourage at first light that day, traveling by horseback as the snow began to fall. Even under the partial protection of the wooded paths that made up most of his journey, his cloak soon froze to his side in stiff sheets. By midday any sign of road or track had disappeared. By evening he had only the sound of the convent bell to follow as unbroken whiteness shrouded the way ahead and behind.

When he finally reached the gatehouse, its door had been knocked in by the force of the storm. He might have remained there in relative safety, but once within the abbey enclosure he believed it would not be too difficult to locate the one he had come to find.

Only out in the snow field did he realize his mistake. The gale and stinging flakes kept his eyes downcast, and he could scarcely see beyond each forward step. It was all he could do to watch one foot then another rise and fall through the drifts. He could make out none of Gaerdegen's buildings, not the convent church though it loomed directly above him, not the refectory or chapterhouse. He knew they must be close, though in which direction he could not tell. When his footing began to fail, in desperation he began to call for her, using the name that she had told him, the secret they shared.

"Maureen!" he shouted, fighting the wind. "Maureen!"

He had nearly given up from exhaustion, feeling the cold and wet seep into his clothing, when suddenly she was there with him.

Magdalene enveloped him in the flowing sleeves of her habit. She pulled him close to her, and he put his hands on her head, smoothing hair that for too long had been exposed to neither another's touch nor the open sky.

"You are here," she said.

"And nearly buried."

"But where is the bishop?"

"A day behind at least, if he survives the journey."

"We'll not survive ourselves unless we get back inside."

With her eyes cast down to shield them from the wind, she noticed a line traced in the snow, stretching from where they stood until it disappeared amid the blowing ice.

"Come," she said, and together they struggled through the crusted drifts of snow, following the line that seemed to have been drawn in its surface for their benefit, leading them to safety.

They did not see the abbey barn until they were upon it, then put their hands on its wooden walls and groped along until they found a way in.

Inside, the priest looked up in fright. He was standing beside his oxcart, serving now as a workbench, the two planks of wood set before him. His hammer raised above his head, he had been intent on connecting with a nail when the barn door swung upon.

"Father, forgive me," Magdalene said.

"Must we do this again?" Father Francis replied.

"No, I—we, are only in need of shelter. We will not trouble you."

As if the storm was not trouble already, Francis thought. As if Gaerdegen was not trouble already. As if this girl through her life and what it had meant to his own these past twenty years was not trouble already. He stared at her a moment and then with alarm at the man beside her, the first man other than himself to have come this far within the abbey enclosure since the forest girl's father—this nun's grandfather—had died in the abbess's cottage during the plague. Even the bishop during his visits had never ventured beyond the abbey church.

"This is the one you were waiting for?" he asked. "The one who would never arrive?"

Magdalene blushed and stammered; her companion stepped forward with a bow.

"Daniel Budge," he said. "I was until recently the bishop's clerk."

"Budge?"

Francis started at the name and stared at the man facing him. Yes, there was no doubting it: He could see Helena's strong brow, the slant of her nose, the curve of her ear. It was as if he had carved a statue of his younger self while thinking of the woman he had longed for since he was barely more than a boy. He fell back a step and took in the two of them together; this full-grown man and full-grown woman, two children of his sin—one of commission, one of omission. Under very different circumstances, he realized, he had baptized them both.

"Is that so?" Francis said. "I have known some bishop's clerks in my time."

"I hope we have been a help to you."

Francis laughed, then took another long look at his guests in the abbey barn. Daniel did not flinch at his ruined face, while the priest openly studied him, glancing up then down. The young man's hands appeared far softer than his own, but their shape was familiar, as was the turn of his shoulders under his cloak, the line of his neck where it met his jaw. As a craftsman, Francis had never imagined his greatest work might not be made of wood, that any act of creation he performed might not merely seem to live but truly to do so.

He had long since gotten used to having his vision cut by half. His mind adapted to the truncated field of view; he had come to feel it made little difference. Yet, seeing these children grown, it was clear to him his partial blindness had never been merely physical. Here before him was evidence that all had not been lost in the plague. Some part of who he once was, who he might have been, remained. Though his vision still was reduced, he felt now he could see the world in all its fullness—its roots, its trunk, its branches, and all that might be made of them.

Francis stood up straighter than he had in years, as if size and strength had begun to return to his body from whatever source had depleted it.

"A help?" Francis said. "Yes, boy, that is precisely what you have been. Where would I be without the bishop's clerks? Where would we all be?"

The priest muttered to himself as he wandered back toward the oxcart where he had been working. The ox stood beside it, sleeping amid the sounds of the storm.

Only now could Daniel explain to Magdalene how he had come to be there. Until the day before, he told her, he had been resigned to seeing the bishop's mission through to its unfortunate end. A heresy tribunal, many in the episcopal court urged him, would be very good for his career, particularly if he could bring about the conviction of such a high-ranking woman as the abbess of Gaerdegen. But then as their carriage rolled through the gathering storm that night, he had thought he heard the name she once was called spoken on the wind.

"My imagination, to be sure," he said, "but how else does God speak? The sound reminded me of my hope to remake the world. I told the bishop I could no longer assist in his investigation of Mother John. When we reached the village to the south, I took a horse from the carriage team and came to beg your abbess to burn the book before its teachings put her in danger."

"It is done," Magdalene said. "Cast into the bakehouse fire this very night."

"The bishop will be frustrated to find nothing that will condemn her," Daniel said, "and will look for a way to save face. If heresy has been hidden, he will attempt to root out its protectors. Should he hear from your sisters that the Book of Ursula was recently destroyed, he is certain to deem me responsible."

"No," Father Francis shouted from the far side of the barn. "I am the man responsible," he said. "I am responsible for it all."

"But, Father," Magdalene said.

"When the bishop asks, I will say the Book of Ursula never existed," the priest continued. "I have been here since the plague and have never seen it, so can say truthfully that as far as I have seen, it is naught but a rumor among novices, which is no more reliable than a twittering of birds. But still it would be better if you are not here when he arrives. Better if no one knows you were here at all."

The priest beckoned them to his side, where they saw the oxcart had been upturned, two wide planks of carved hornbeam laying before it.

"Help me," he said, directing them to hold up one plank and then the next as he fixed them to the bottom of the wheels, which he had locked in place with iron spikes. The three then together lifted the old cart and set it down on its new skids.

"It won't get you far, but perhaps far enough."

Since they had entered, the noise of the gale and creaking of the barn had gradually diminished, and when they opened the oxcart door, they saw the storm had stopped completely, at least for the moment.

"Thank you, Father," they both said, and though he had been addressed by this word more times than he could remember, it had never before felt more true.

He hitched the ox to its cart and led it to the wide postern in the abbey wall, where the wooden gate had been knocked loose of its hinges.

"Why help us?" Magdalene asked. "Surely if you aided the bishop in proving heresy at Gaerdegen, he might allow you to leave."

"I once knew your mother," Francis said to Daniel. "And yours as well," he said to Magdalene. "It is too late to ask their forgiveness but perhaps not yours."

He slapped the ox's backside and then watched them slide away, coasting over the snowdrifts on the cross he had hoped would be his redemption.

# Chapter 35

WHO COULD HAVE looked upon the snowfall surrounding the Abbey of Gaerdegen that night and doubted it was a deluge like Noah had known, though frozen, and without warning or time to build an ark? Yet somehow, even so, a small vessel floated along the surface, first under the cover of the trees whose arcing branches preserved a smooth tunnel beneath, then into the heights above the abbey, toward the mountain passes.

As Magdalene and Daniel ascended, the sight of doves flying in the clearing sky seemed to mark their destination. Soon they found the cave where the old woman still lived. A blazing fire vented through a natural chimney above. Bird droppings painted the walls with intricate designs that resembled messages from a bygone civilization.

Though Daniel had prepared himself to become an inquisitor of her works, and though Magdalene had grown up on her stories, neither had set eyes upon her, of course. She wore the same dark veil and white habit of the Order she had joined at the start of the century, when she was a young widow with money enough to dream of knowing God. When Magdalene looked closely, she believed she could see that new nun in the ancient anchoress's eyes.

Ursula continued to keep the rule of silence and offered little by way of greeting. She simply ladled tankards of warm brew from a steaming cauldron, wrapped her guests in sheepskins, and together they stared into the firelight.

In time they would tell her who they were and how they came to be there, but in truth it seemed she already knew whatever they might explain, and perhaps far more besides. After twenty years of living alone in her cave high above the abbey, it was said by the people of the forest, who would give the holy woman gifts to sustain her, that she knew the future the way others knew memory.

She knew they would leave that place after a few days' rest to gather their strength, when the mountain passes might clear enough to allow their oxcart through. She knew that on the far side of the next valley north, they would start their lives anew. Daniel would find distant Budge cousins from whom to learn the family craft; Magdalene would teach their children to sing in Latin like their mother. Ursula knew that their grandchildren would laugh at the carved wooden planks on the bottom of the oxcart, which by then would form a mantelpiece surrounding the hearth of their home. The children would guess at the significance of the icons in the carefully carved scenes—the trees, the church, the wall—getting them all wrong but two near the center.

"Is this your father?" they would ask their grandfather as they pointed at the carved priest holding a knife. "Is this your mother?" they would ask their grandmother of the carved girl staring through a gate.

"No, no," Magdalene and Daniel would answer as honestly as they were able, because they did not know how this could be so. But Ursula did.

As her visitors drifted off to exhausted sleep that first night, Ursula climbed out from her anchorhold and gazed down in the direction of the convent. She could not see it from her vantage, and even if she could, all she would have seen was a boundless field of empty white, as if the church, the bakehouse, and even the wall had been erased by the Advent wind.

Returning to the comfort of her cave, Ursula mixed pigment and water in a small bowl, stirring until the effort yielded ink as thick as blood. She then dipped a dove feather in the liquid and scratched its nib across clean parchment. Was it not miraculous, she considered as she wrote, that her words could be anywhere, anytime, even when she was nowhere at all? *Laborare est orare*, she remembered, to work is to pray, and this act of turning thoughts into lines and curls was to her the truest expression of each.

When she was finished, she rolled the page into a thin tube secured with a vine, tied one end to a small stone, and entrusted it to the safety of her best dove's tiny claws. Then she lifted the bird before her face, kissed its head, and let it go into the night air, disappearing as she heard a bell tolling in the distance.

*Come.*

*Come.*

Eighteen nuns gathered in the ruins of the convent church. Nearly half of the roof had fallen and lay in pieces on the snow-strewn floor, and with its collapse, piled snow had poured into the nave. The choir stalls were nearly buried, and, at the head of the church, drifts sloped on all sides of the altar, which seemed a great white mountain rising from the floor.

The sisters entered solemnly and bowed low to the body of the Lord and prayed silently, *Pater noster qui es in caelis sanctificetur nomen tuum* . . . until Mother John recited a blessing for the Hour:

"Yet you, O Lord, are in the midst of us, and your holy name is called upon us. Leave us not, O Lord our God."

Then all answered, "Thanks be to God," and began to sing once more in the cold of the church: the words that ended their every day; the words they hoped would end their lives. The abbess sang slowly, with her sisters in reply:

"Into your hands, O Lord, I commend my spirit. Let us sleep, O God. Let us rest in your peace."

Three psalms, two hymns, and then an underwater quiet. The last Hour ended and the nuns made their way through the cloister, to sleep, if they could, and wait for morning.

Several sunrises later, after Father Francis had begun to make repairs to the abbey buildings that remained standing, after the nuns had given up hope of finding their lost sister, though they did not lose faith that she was somehow with them still, Mother John found a scroll jutting from the snow in the cloister garth like a hand reaching to heaven from the frozen earth.

"Remember, my sisters," she read, "from my little hole in the side of a mountain, there is nothing I cannot see . . ."

*Down the slope of the valley, the abbey we built together rests in moonglow. The snow has passed on and all that we loved is layered under a thick shroud of white. A shroud, yes, but is the world itself dead?*

*What is the point of your hours, doves of my heart, if it is not always true that we are dying, and yet always also true that this is never the last word? Always and forever the beginning of the new rolls back a stone from the tomb of the old. Impossible day emerges from impregnable night. New life climbs from a womb that is doomed. And so, too, the nuns of Gaerdegen must gather again to sing and pray. Her voice has gone, but there are others in waiting, and there will yet be more still.*

*Do not fear that the judgment of men will find you when the wall of ice that has grown up around your prayers surrenders to the spring. Every season brings its own liturgy, its own trials, its own transformation. Whenever the bishop should come, he can only be changed by your songs.*

*Once you found a light shining in the darkness in the midst of a plague. Search now for a blessing even in the wreckage this storm has left behind. Look all around you, my sisters. On this day you are given an empty expanse in every direction. What will you write on this new blank page of creation?*

# Acknowledgments

THIS BOOK BEGAN twenty-five years ago as a short story about a nun who fell in love with the wind. In the quarter century since, it grew in fits and starts while I published ten other books and periodically found myself thinking about a fourteenth century convent and the sisters who lived there as if recalling details from a faintly remembered dream. In developing its early iterations, I benefited from the suggestions and encouragement of several teachers at the University of Massachusetts-Amherst, including Julius Lester, Lucien Miller, and Elizabeth Petroff. For many rich and challenging conversations about the story as it began to take form more than two decades later, I am most grateful to my agent Kathleen Anderson.

While a work wholly of the imagination, *The Maiden of All Our Desires* has been informed by a number of essential nonfiction books, including Eileen Power's *Medieval People*, Barbara Tuchman's *A Distant Mirror*, John Kelly's *The Great*

*Mortality*, and the classic photographic history *The Monastic World: 1000–1300* by Christopher Brooke and Wim Swaan. Over the long course of writing I also consulted more primary sources than can be recalled or named here, among them *Revelations of Divine Love* by Julian of Norwich, *Imitation of Christ* by Thomas à Kempis, the *Monologion* by Anselm of Canterbury, the anonymous work of fourteenth century mysticism, *The Cloud of Unknowing*, the letters of Abelard and Heloise, the twelfth-century drinking song *Confession of Golias*, and the plague chronicle of Agnolo di Tura.

As has been the case with all my books, I owe the greatest debt of gratitude to my family. No matter how long I may spend cloistered in my writing shed, I have yet to imagine any love stronger than the one that draws me home.